A LITTLE BIT

OF

ANARCHY

A NOVEL

by
Rodger Christopherson

1

Other books by the author:
Out of the Fire Mist
Beverly Hills Women
Monkey in a Tree
After the President Disappeared
Illusions
Three weeks Until Tomorrow
Health and the Real Cause of Illness - non fiction
Beyond Heaven and Hell - The Greater Reality - non fiction
Origins & Meaning - How Science and Religion have failed humanity - non fiction
Circles in the Sand - Poetry

intercept777@centurylink.net

DISCLAIMER

It was a different world back then, long before 9/11and the menace of terrorism from abroad. Back then the threat came from within and eco-warriors were appearing on the scene, determined to give the counrty a wake-up call because the environment was being destroyed and the planet, itself, was in jeopardy because of over indulgence and wastefulness. But how to get the average citizen to listen when they didn't want to hear it or give up anything to help improve the situation, that was the question. Perhaps the only way to accomplish that would be to deprive them all of something vital to their intemperate life styles. Something like a free flowing source of cheap electricity, for example. And a few other things. That was the goal the characters in this book set for themselves, back then, when things were very different.

ONE

Somehow, using dynamite seemed like such a crude way of doing things. But, what else was there? That was the question he hoped Mike would be able to answer.

The two tall, lean, long legged men strolled slowly along the gracefully curved, twenty five foot wide upper crest of the huge dam. Mike, of perpetual good humor, a few years the younger, out from the east by invitation to see his more serious minded friend Kohl. Kohl, who seemed to have gone off on a wild tangent with his life by bringing him up here. Kohl who purposely led the way, pointing out various key aspects of this marvel of twentieth century engineering located out in the middle of a bone dry, searingly hot, no-man's land.

It was a colossus of a structure, all right, composed in part of five million cubic yards of concrete. Ten million tons, by weight, of aggregate and cement poured into place over thousands of miles of steel reinforcement to create a seven hundred and ten foot high, obnoxious obstacle that had begun impeding the flow of the Colorado River back in nineteen hundred and sixty three. Glen Canyon Dam, the damned thing.

Mike stopped and leaned out over the downstream curve that

fell away to the briskly flowing river far below and shook his head in semi-veneration. The water, free at last from the grandiose holding pond above, was doing its best to rush hurriedly away from its former bondage, laughing and playing again in the sunlight as it went. He stared at it awhile and, in staring, could almost feel the joy it must have felt when at last its work was done inside the turbines and it was spewed out some four hundred feet below where it had entered through the penstock up on the backside of the dam.

Kohl, in turn, watched Mike watch the river. Good, he thought, I think he feels it too. Mike then went to the upstream side and examined it also, trying to imagine what it might look like if he were in a diving suit, working his way down the steep wall beneath the surface ripples of the water.

"What's the bottom side thickness?" Mike asked, his almost perfect teeth flashing through the black bush of a Gonzales mustache. Too bad about that one discolored victim of a root canal in front, though. Still, it never seemed to slow the ladies down so maybe that explained why he had never bothered to have it fixed during all the years that Kohl had known him.

"About three hundred feet," Kohl said.

"It's an exercise in futility," Mike replied. "Let's go back up the hill and have a beer."

"Not yet. You haven't seen the rest of it."

They took the elevator downward the equivalent of a forty one story building in reverse. At the bottom they exited into a wide concrete corridor, letting the door shut behind them. Kohl stopped and stood quietly, waiting so that Mike might get some further feel for the immensity of it, then moved on down the square sided tunnel to the end. Here they took a left turn and followed it to the double doors that led out onto the open walkway which crossed over to the generating station and peered through the glass wall into the six hundred foot long room. According to the indicator lights on the display panel, seven of the eight gigantic, water driven, power producing monsters were presently in operation, pumping out an approximate total of a million kilowatts of electricity, enough to run every microwave, wash machine and television set in the whole country all turned on at the same time.

Kohl punched the button on the visitors video display and waited so Mike could listen to the pre taped message that accompanied the simplified explanation. When it ended, they continued out onto the exterior deck overlooking the much diminished river below. They examined the bank of ninety ton transformers and followed the inch and a half diameter conductors upward eight hundred feet to the steel towers on the cliffs above, then looked over the edge of the deck from its position still fifty feet above the water.

Mike took his time. There was plenty of time, to be sure. This dam wasn't going anywhere. Not yet anyway. Not for a long, long time under normal circumstances. He scanned everything in sight, studied it, made mental notes as he went, trying to let as much as possible register in his mind. The slick, shear rock faces of the canyon, the visitors center far above, the eleven hundred foot long highway bridge high overhead and just downstream. The two mile long, vehicular service tunnel opening on the bottom east side of the canyon with its adits, or windows, in the cliffside showing its rate of climb, the eight foot diameter emergency valves imbedded in the abutment at the base of the dam across the river and whatever else he could see from where they stood. Concrete, stone and steel everywhere.

Kohl, meanwhile, scrutinized the immensity of the dam for what was his third time in the last month. Big, ugly son-of-a-bitchin thing, he said to himself. Was it alive? Had they breathed life into it when they had built it? Did it have a secret, stubborn heart of its own, thumping away somewhere inside all that concrete, pumping some strange seminal fluid through all those miles of steel mesh and bars? Could he find that heart and pierce it, run it through and knock the life out of it? Or was the dam simply that which it appeared to be? Just an inert, synthesized mass of man made might, a giant sink stopper of a stupid plug backing up the now fetid water? Alive or dead, it was hard to tell.

Back inside the main structure Mike stopped at a service tunnel running back through the concrete towards the rear of the dam. He pointed to the damp spot on the wall.

"What's the water pressure at this point?" he asked Kohl, wishing there weren't so many no smoking signs stuck up everywhere. Being down here so far below the surface of the water that had been backed up for a hundred and eighty miles was beginning to make him nervous.

"Two hundred and fifty pounds per square inch, give or take," Kohl said matter of factly.

Mike whistled softly. "How far does this run back?"

"I'm not sure."

Mike stared down the passageway. "Wish we had a key," he said and rattled the padlock on the wire gate. "But this might be a major possibility," he continued as he stared down the narrow passageway. "If there is one."

"One of the strong possibilities, I'd say," Kohl said.

Mike smiled. "So maybe it is possible," he said. "Damned near impossible, but possible. But not possible in the sense that you want it to be, I don't think."

"Who's to say," Kohl replied. "What I really need is a set of construction plans."

"You could always write the Bureau of Reclamation, since they built it in the first place."

"Maybe they could even supply the dynamite. And an air drill and some divers so we can attack it from both sides."

"What's this, we, shit?"

"I thought you might want to light the fuse when the time came."

"I sincerely hope I'm in South America."

"You're no fun at all anymore, Mike."

They walked back to the elevator, hit the call button, waited, got on, went back to the top and out into the sunshine again. Yes, it did have a heart of its own, Kohl decided from up above, but it was not malevolent. No, poor thing, it too was as innocent as the river, this artificially inseminated product of a drafting board conceived from the mental masturbations of politicians and bureaucrats. Not only did he feel it to be innocent, but also quite willing to be sacrificed for a higher good. In fact, now that he thought of it, the dam almost seemed to be pleading with them to be done away with in the name of freedom, and more importantly, of justice.

Mike took out his camera and began taking pictures. "If

nothing else," he said. "Maybe you could get some explosive through the penstock strainers and down the spillways. At least it would screw up the generators."

"And reduce the number of tourists stumbling around."

"That, too. The public doesn't need to look at all this technological shit. They don't understand it anyway."

"But they're impressed, even though they don't know exactly what it is that has impressed them."

"And pleased, I suppose, by what bureaucracy was able to accomplish before it began spending all the taxpayers money on weaponry and war, Savings and Loan bailouts and riot control."

"Well, I don't know. You have to admit there was a lot of ego boosting entertainment value in the last war for all the patriotic couch potatoes."

"And you expect people who enjoy seeing innocent people killed by remote control to give a damn about the wilderness?"

"No," Kohl said.

"What then?"

"Doesn't really matter. I care, and hopefully you care, or I can get you to care. Some of us care and that's all that counts. To hell with the rest of them. We aren't doing it for them."

"That's a small point in your favor, thank god. They don't deserve it, whatever it is you hope to accomplish."

"Certainly not just a temporary disruption of service. That's not good enough," Kohl said. "Got to take enough of the son-of-a-bitch out to make it completely unfeasible to reconstruct. If I can't think of a way for my characters to demolish it entirely, I at least have to believe someone could punch a hole in it or weaken it sufficiently so that the river will take out the rest."

"I see," Mike said in acknowledgment

They began walking back toward the hillside tunnel that led to the second elevator back to the visitor's center still hundreds of feet above.

"Anything else strike your fancy?" Kohl asked, stopping near the entrance. He removed his Stetson in the process and wiped his brow as he studied Mike's face.

"Maybe you could capture old Saddam and tie him up down inside the dam. One phone call to the White House and the Air Force would blow it up for you," Mike said, smoothing his thick, wavy black hair.

"Not bad, but not what I was referring to."

"What did I miss?" he asked.

"The weep holes. What about the weep holes?"

"What's a weep hole?"

"Those holes bored into the rock face along the sides there to let out the seepage," Kohl pointed out. "If they weren't there the pressure would eventually build up and split off more rock strata. Loosen enough of that and guess what?"

Mike hung over the edge once more and surveyed the shear stone face of the canyon wall immediately below the dam. "The layering looks vertical to me. Is it?" he said, referring to the structure of the sandstone.

"Yes."

Kohl wasn't a geologist so he couldn't explain exactly what ancient mishap had caused the earth to tilt up on its side in this particular region of the world but it was still a fact. The one time prehistoric sea bottom, previously deposited in layers and long since compressed into red sandstone, was now tipped up on its side to form vertical slices that had to be held together with steel anchor bolts embedded over seventy five feet into the sides of the cliffs to keep them from spalling off.

"Do you suppose those holes go as deep as the anchor bolts they put in elsewhere?"

"Probably," Kohl said.

Mike thought about the ends of the dam's smooth arc jammed into all the layered imperfections of the canyon walls by the mighty millions of tons of pressure from the backed up river. Wasn't that interesting, he thought as he evaluated the possibilities. The way Mike's mind worked had always amazed Kohl and had made it a pleasure to have been able to work with him at one time on more formally accepted tasks.

A different set of priorities had been in existence back then, though, in that long ago when they were engaged in the surreptitious design of missile guidance systems for the US government. Or so it had appeared. To be sure, Khrushchev was not Gorbachev and the Soviet Union had still been intact. The threat, therefore, was different, had been different, wasn't it? Looking back, it was hard to tell. One couldn't believe the

8

administration, the politicians or the media in those days either. But, fortunately for both him and Mike, they were soon out of the double dealing aerospace weapons business and on to better things, even though their careers had split along different lines.

For Mike, it was an involvement in a series of highly scientific, super sensitive earth resources satellites and then the vice presidency of a small earth technology company doing some real, state-of-the-art, things for commercial application.

Kohl, meantime, had stepped into the sophisticated world of electro-optical systems, computerized special effects equipment for the motion picture industry, diagnostics for the medical field, anything and everything that combined a number of different technologies. Chief engineer, vice president, operations manager, president, chief engineer again. But then, one day, the world of business had also stopped making any sense to him and he had once again set out on yet another path. Mike, on the other hand, was still engaged in that line of endeavor, something which Kohl felt strongly compelled to rescue him from.

By the time that series of memories had passed Kohl's mind, Mike had arrived at his conclusion. Half a dozen sticks of high explosive in half a dozen or so weep holes and...

"It's still totally ridiculous," Mike said however, in response to the thought, shaking his head and waving his arms a bit. "Totally ridiculous."

"What?"

"What demented do-gooder would ever be insane enough to skinny down that rockface on a piece of rope and stuff dynamite into those holes in full view of the staff? Not me, not you, nor anyone I ever met, read about or ever heard of. It would be a suicide mission."

"Probably, but don't take it so seriously. It's just a story."

"I'd almost forgotten," Mike said, as Kohl put his arm on his shoulder in a gesture of good faith. "But sometimes, when you talk about it, I begin to think you've gone over the edge."

"Just trying to make it realistic."

They were outside now, heading up onto the walkway of Glen Canyon Bridge. A quarter of the way out towards the middle they stopped and stared back at the dam far below. The backed up, brilliant blue waters of Lake Powell shimmered in the sun and spread out behind the concrete curve into the surrounding, inundated, forlorn desert, a harsh land of barren beauty that appeared to extend forever in all directions.

"Well, you have to admit there's not a hell of a lot out there," Mike said, waving at the landscape.

"Only to the novice my friend. Only to the uninformed, misinformed, unseeing, uncaring novice," Kohl stated.

"Meaning who? Me?"

"When you can stay a little longer sometime, I'll take you out there and show you just how many creatures really live there."

"Well, it's not Colorado, or Maryland, or Minnesota, that's for sure, so it's kinda lacking in foliage and the color green, from my point of view. Just a personal preference, you understand. But if there really is life out there, that's something else again."

"There's more than that out there, also. Buried beneath all that water are some of the most beautiful and most unusual canyons in the world. There are Indian ruins, petroglyphs and pictographs all which are a part of our ancient history. They also destroyed a tremendous amount of natural habitat for all the wild birds and animals of the region and thus helped destroy the creatures in the process. And for what? By the time our grandchildren are as old as we are the damned thing will be inoperable because it will all be filled up with silt and absolutely useless. Now does that make any sense?"

"I see your point," Mike said.

They stood quietly, side by side, as they leaned on the railing and stared out at the vast expanse of the surrounding Utah desert. After a while Mike sighed. It was a lot to think about. "Ready for that beer?" he asked.

"Sure," said Kohl, "but first we have to say a small prayer."

"I seldom pray," Mike said. "What's the occasion?"

"The dam was not designed to sustain a large earthquake."

"You're kidding," Mike said with a look of extreme surprise.

"The area is considered to be quite benign in the seismological sense."

"I see," Mike said and nodded in appreciation of the possible oversight. "As long as we're here, what the hell. Can't hurt."

"Good. But first we have to be in the center of the bridge."

"What difference does it make?"

"Cause that's where Seldom Seen did it."

"I've seldom seen anybody do their praying from a bridge. What are you talking about? "

"The character in the book."

"What character in what book?"

"In Ed Abbey's book, Seldom Seen Smith. That's where I got the idea to begin with. Great stuff, but Abbey died before he got around to writing the final story where his characters actually destroyed the thing. So I thought I would continue the cause. Come on. Pray first. I'll tell you more about it later," Kohl said, and motioned.

"Shit," Mike said and followed Kohl to the middle. Reverently they stood there in the heat and the bleaching sun. Dark and slightly shaggy haired Mike in his designer jeans and one hundred dollar tennies, and even shaggier Kohl in his faded denims and old boots holding his battered Stetson over his heart.

Two minutes later they returned to the parking area, climbed into Kohl's old truck and drove up the hill towards Page, Arizona, following behind a new and shiny, never been off the road, four wheel drive, imported, Japanese made pickup which displayed the words, America- Love IT OR LEAVE IT, on the bumper sticker attached to the tailgate. The long, black hair of the Native American driver flowed in the still hot breeze of the receding day as his three hundred watt speakers, turned up to full, excruciating volume, contaminated the serenity of the surrounding area with the over amplified sounds of heavy metal. His half white, half drunk female companion half hung out the passenger side window beating her hand on the shiny door in time with the noise. Mike chuckled and asked what was so important about Edward Abbey's books.

Kohl told him how Abbey was considered to be the Thoreau of the American Southwest, how his earlier books were probably the focal point and the stimulus for many of the original environmental groups, how...well, it took the rest of the ride into town and three beers each to get to the end of it.

TWO

Kohl shut off the shower, reached for his oversized towel and dried himself briskly. He then pawed through his hair in an attempt to straighten it, dressed and locked up the architecturally unique house he happened to be residing in for the time being. It was an oversized structure with two foot thick stone walls, double paned windows, huge beamed ceilings and a living room that was equally as big as the entire house he had last lived in. The fireplace, which took up most of the eastern wall of that big room, was in the form of a huge Aztec face. The eyes doubled as heat vents, the large blunt nose was there for effect while the mouth was a huge, jagged opening that contained a grate large enough to put a five foot log on. Built by a business tycoon who had the misfortune of dying just before he was ready to move in, Kohl had found the place through a property management firm and had been there nearly six months.

He shut the door quietly so as not to surprise the covey of quail that often hung around the yard until mid morning. They were there as usual, chattering and gossiping away as they foraged for seeds among the irregular stones. Another amenity of the property, the gutsy roadrunner who would sometimes sit on the courtyard wall not more than five feet away to watch him drink his morning coffee, was out in the drive looking for bugs and rasped at Kohl as he went by, making his way towards the paint deficient old Blazer parked in the driveway.

The place also came with a pack of wild coyotes who often woke him up late at night with their frenetic yelps and howls down in the wash below the house. And, before hunting season began, there was also a large herd of antelope which grazed in the native grass alongside the long driveway.

Most impressive of all, however, was the view, something considered to be quite spectacular by those few who had been up to visit the house on the ridge. Not that Kohl was a snob. He wasn't. He loved people, some of them at least, some of the time, some more than others. When they came he always sat with them out on the patio in front of the house where one could see the entire range of red rocked cliffs that ringed the more than twenty mile expanse of the Verde Valley to the north. The panorama extended from Sycamore Canyon above Clarkdale, clear on around to Cathedral Rock in the Village of Oak Creek, then flattened out and continued southward to become the Mogollon Rim. Then, back to the north, beyond that, high lighting the scene were the snow covered tops of the San Francisco peaks some fifty or sixty miles away as was Williams Mountain at an even greater distance to the west. But if one looked closer, it was not paradise.

Three miles up the mountain was Jerome, a ramshackle, falling down the hill remnant of an old mining town that once boasted fifteen thousand people. The town itself wasn't so bad. It was what it had stood for, along with all the ugly scars that still remained in the earth where the land had been ripped away in the hungry search for copper and gold. Additionally, there were the immense piles of tailings that had been lifted out of the bowels of the mountain and dumped down the slopes. Still being dumped down the slopes, as a matter of fact, by the mining magnates out to make a buck and to hell with the environment. No, Jerome was not a pretty site to Kohl, but a smarting, eyesore instead.

Then there was that revolting cement plant embedded in the hills to the west, three quarters of a mile away. Another monster tearing away at the native earth, making horrific noises in the middle of the night that sometimes jarred him awake. And often, just before dawn, if you happened to be up that early, you would find it spewing vast clouds of fine, abrasive dust into the air. Fortunately for Kohl, however, he didn't have to breath the stuff. The prevailing air flow tended to be down hill and around to the north towards Clarkdale and the west side of Cottonwood, flooding the lower reaches of the valley floor instead.

He had a friend who lived down that way who was constantly wiping a fine gray film off the furniture, the TV, the bedroom window sills, everywhere. Must be good for the lungs. And now the place was trying to get a permit to burn old tires for fuel in the kilns, instead of, or along with, coal. Obviously, sooting and cementing the lungs of the local population shut wasn't enough. Now they wanted to vulcanize them too.

And then there were the hundred plus, million ton slag piles down by the river that had been disgorged from the smelters those many years ago, judiciously placed so that the runoff from the rains would carry any chemical residue left in them directly into the Verde River where it could be shared by all. Trace elements, mostly. Arsenic, lead, chromium, that kind of thing.

And what was that strange place adjacent to the slag pile? The one with the high topped fence crowned with coiled rolls of heavy barbed wire and an armed guard at the gate, a part of the abandoned old smelter with the windows all knocked out. Why does a place like that need that kind of protection? Perhaps the local rumors were true. It was part of a federal, hazardous waste dumping ground. Who knows? Whatever it was, it didn't look like it needed around the clock security. But what did the good, complacent, over accommodating folks in the Clarkdale area say about all this? Live and let live, even if it might kill you in the process. Don't make waves, that's what. Especially about the cement plant. It provided jobs. What else was important?

Regardless of what flaws the place might be accused of having, however, living there had certainly beat trying to make out the forms of Century City high rise buildings against the sky through the brown poison that hung in the air over west Los Angeles and his former abode on the perimeter of Beverly Hills. Now that was really disgusting. And as for the people, well, there had been some good times, but that too, had its limits.

He had played that rather flawed game when he was living there, too, black tie affairs and all. He had been to the best of them, tasted the imported black caviar, shaken hands with the movie stars, danced with the platinum haired goddess and indulged in other self important fantasy. Always elegant in his tux, he could bring himself to mingle well when the occasion demanded it, but, when all was said and done and as far as he was concerned, jeans and boots were a much more appropriate mode of dress for a truth seeking man. Thank god for fresh air, fresh faces, open spaces and a place he was able to feel alive in.

Kohl climbed into the truck, started the engine and rolled down the hill, heading east. Half an hour later he walked into the Coffee Pot restaurant in Sedona and asked for a seat on the patio. Just as he rounded the corner under the shaded deck, Buck Hudson looked up from the morning paper, caught Kohl's eye and waved him over. "Damn, Buck. I thought you were still in Palm Springs," Kohl said and sat down opposite him.

Buck tossed the paper into the empty chair and wrinkled his

grizzled face into a grin. "Got in last night."

"So how did it go?"

"I hate the goddamned place."

"Really?"

"There's too damned many Californians in California anymore. And the quality of people has deteriorated considerably."

"Which is why we live in Arizona."

"Until a few more Californians find out about it. Then we'll have to move again."

Pam, the waitress, came by in her monogrammed T-shirt and bluejeans, said good morning to Kohl, poured him some coffee, topped off Buck's cup and asked Kohl if he wanted to order.

"Sausage and eggs medium, hash browns, wheat toast."

"Juice?"

"No."

"How about you, Buck?"

"Same thing," he said, indicating what Kohl had ordered.

Pam smiled at Kohl, scribbled on her pad and left.

"So why go there?" Kohl asked, leaning back in his chair.

"You mean Palm Springs?"

"That's where you went wasn't it?" Kohl said, looking into Buck's dark, bleary eyes.

"Clients, my friend. Clients."

"You mean that widow who comes out from New York for the winter still lets you thump on her skin?" Kohl asked. Kohl loved to taunt Buck, probably because he was one of the few people who could get away with it. Where others saw a gruff, bad tempered old bear, Kohl saw a well hidden warmth, a crafty, native intelligence and a loyalty to living that had been ingrained in him like the rings in a tree trunk. A burly, mean son-of-a-bitch, however, if you ever made the mistake of trying to intimidate him, especially with big city sophistry.

"Massage, Kohl. Therapeutic massage, remember?" Buck said and faked a seriousness.

Kohl looked at the prodigious bump on Buck's face some people referred to as his nose. It looked pretty good today. Buck was sometimes known to try and light it by mistake when he was drunk and his cigar went out. It always reminded Kohl of another time when Buck and he had gone for steak after the bars had closed and Buck's slab of steer had slid off his plate when he made a move on it. Using good sense, Buck had simply pushed the plate away and carved the meat up directly on the table top. Kohl smiled. "And for this she gives you money?" he asked.

"In advance. And if I rub her fluffy a little afterward, she gives me a bonus."

"I'll bet."

"Some fluffy."

"Yeah? That's the reason you went?"

"Had to stop and see Jackie."

"Oh yes, Jackie. I thought she threw you out?" Kohl said, as he visualized the older, but voluptuous queen of big breasted women. A little overweight but none of it on her waistline. What the hell she ever saw in this hoodlum Kohl never knew.

"We finally came to an understanding," Buck said. "I don't break her new boyfriend's neck as long as she shares her bed with me when I'm in town and she doesn't tell me whose back to rub when I'm there as long as I don't try and sneak anyone into her house while she's at work."

"What could be more fair?" Kohl laughed. When would this boy ever settle down, he wondered. Master of many trades, he was, but follower of none. Carpenter, house painter, mechanic, masseur, part time sculptor, motorcycle freak, maverick, multi-sided madman and more. Wherever there was a dollar to be made that didn't have a lot of conditions attached to it, that's where he went. Had to hang loose and stay flexible, Buck always said. Nothing wrong with that, Kohl had agreed.

"So what about you?" Buck wanted to know. "What else are you doing besides sitting on the hill watching the sun come up?"

"Is that all the credit I get? What about my full moon bonfires and poetry readings?"

"I suppose, Kohl. You always were kind of an esoteric shit."

"Such flattery, Buck. That's not like you at all."

"So what are you up to? Are you going to tell me or not?"

"Researching another book, I guess you could say."

"That's more like it. What's it about?"

Kohl tried to explain what he was working on.

"You don't look like the monkey wrench type to me."

"No, probably not, but the idea is certainly fascinating. But I

16

can see where it could be dangerous, however, if you began to take it too seriously."

"It has been for a few, that's for sure."

"Anybody you know?"

"Nah, I just read the paper once in a while."

"You sure about that?"

"Of course. Besides, I'd rather talk about women."

"Okay. There was this woman who wrote some great books I read a few years ago. I liked them so much I even fantasized about being in love with her, if you know what I mean. I even wrote her a letter once. Surprisingly enough, she answered it and invited me to have tea with her if I ever got that far north but she died in a car accident before I got the chance. Took some of the magic out of my life, I think."

"How could you be in love with someone you never met?"

"Maybe it was the way her mind worked. But there was also something about the picture on the back of the book cover. You know how those things are."

"Unfortunately, I can appreciate that. What did she write?"

"She was a great, none degreed graduate of the world, a home grown psychologist of sorts who did some deep stuff about life and relationships."

"Too heavy for me."

"You never know, Buck. You might learn something."

"Nah," Buck said, instead. "Tell me about your book. Are you really going to blow up the dam?"

"If I can do it justice. Unfortunately, I haven't come up with any strong characters as yet and I don't know much about explosives, sabots or how to derail a bulldozer. I do have some idea as to what the weak points in the dam are, however, since I took Mike up there and had him look at it with me."

"Mike? You mean that hippie buddy of yours from back east that was out here last fall?"

"Don't look so skeptical. He's not a hippy anymore."

"Another coward, turncoat abdicator."

"Not Mike. Now he's living on a boat."

"So?"

"So he bought this iron hulled vessel in Holland and sailed it across the Atlantic to Annapolis. He's living on it with this cops ex wife from California that introduced him to smoking pot."

"I apologize, I think. But he's still one of those technical, gee whiz guys like you were, right? Nine to five and all that shit?"

"Gee whiz, yes, but nine to five, never. Not Mike. He has always come and gone pretty much on his own terms."

"That good, huh?"

"Always was anyway, in spite of his role changing."

"What's that mean?"

"When I met him he was just a kid fresh out of college. The first thing he did after he was on the payroll was to buy this humongous Harley which he then took time off from work to ride all through Mexico on. He hit the back roads and isolated villages and lived with the natives in their huts. Then he came back, worked a few more months and married the most beautiful girl I have ever seen. The tragedy was, however, that he couldn't get along with her. So, after a bit he packed it up and went to Colorado. This time it was a jeep, bow and arrow, guns, living in the woods half the time. Then he turned hippie."

"Remind me to invite him over for a beer and a smoke next time he's in town."

"We'll see."

"In the meantime get yourself a copy of TM-31-210 and FM-5-25." Buck instructed him.

"Which are?"

"Military tech manual and field manual. The field manual will tell you how to form, place and detonate charges. Even shows you exactly how to demolish any one of a number of different kinds of bridges. The tech manual gives all the recipes for home brewed explosives made from readily available materials and other handy bits of information for the novice such as pipe bombs and improvised guns."

"Where did you learn about those?"

"I think I helped write the goddamned things. Had them pretty well memorized at one time anyway."

"I didn't know."

"I don't like to talk about it."

The waitress brought their food and refilled the coffee. Buck vacuumed up his meal in about thirty seconds, then went back to his paper while Kohl finished his. When Kohl was done, Buck put his paper back down and spoke. "If you're going to write a book just remember, there's nothing like first hand experience."

"I know. I'm writing it myself, like I always do."

"That's not what I mean."

"I should blow up the dam first, then write about it?"

Buck shrugged. Why not, was the expression on his face.

"Not me, man," Kohl said. "My weapon is my pencil, rather, my computer. Ink on paper, ideas, imaginings, illusions, pungent, provocative projections of what might be. And what might be is good enough for me."

"Bullshit. No realism."

"Christ, Buck."

"At least go and chop down some billboards like Ed Abbey did, maybe saw the legs off some power line towers, find a small earthen dam and pick a hole in it, or something. Anything. Start small, but do get your hands a little dirty first," Buck said, staring disdainfully at Kohl.

Kohl was silent, his only response to take a sip of his coffee and look away. Buck continued. "If something doesn't fall on you and break your neck and you decide you like the work," he said, "you can go on to bigger things. Doesn't pay a hell of a lot but it's interesting. Might even help keep you from going blind squinting at your computer monitor."

Kohl raised his eyes. This time he stared at Buck. "Maybe you could give me some lessons sometime," he said, probing.

Buck's gaze never wavered. "Maybe," he said.

"Well, anyway," Kohl said. "I have this friend who thinks old Abbey is still alive. Has this feeling she's going to run into him out there wandering about the back roads of Utah."

"Hmmm," said Buck.

THREE

Kohl had gone uptown, stopped and opened his empty post office box, relocked it and headed up the street on foot. The town was full of tourists. Nearly four blocks later he hadn't met a soul he knew. He decided he was lonely. It was nothing new, the feeling gnawed at him quietly, just a minor thirst he had felt half the time recently. But was he the only one, he wondered Didn't other people ever get lonely or was it just something they wouldn't admit. Did they consider it to be a sign of failure perhaps, not to be mentioned, or a personality defect best kept out of sight, away from other people's notice? Damn. One thing was for sure, anyway. It didn't pay to let it show. No sir, he thought as he walked down the street. Keep smiling, Kohl. Stop thinking about it. She'll come along one of these days, I hope, I hope, I hope. In the meantime you have a book to write. Yeah, right. And what the hell was he trying to do that for?

It was a self appointed task at best. No one had called up and ordered it, there was no check in the mail, either. It was nothing more than pure blind, ridiculous speculation, another stack of paper to waste postage on trying to find an agent crazy enough to realize its potential. Besides, he already had enough letters of rejection to wallpaper half the house from some of his previous efforts, ceilings included. Why wasn't he just independently wealthy, instead? Then he could run off to Tahiti and spend his days sitting on a topless beach.

He turned into the ice cream shop, bought a double dip chocolate yogurt in a waffle cone and proceeded down the street trying to think, but, it seemed impossible. He couldn't even stay on the sidewalk. There were boisterous, bumbling, bumping into everything tourists everywhere. Fickle, foolish, foolhardy fools who spent hours, and sometimes days, driving to Sedona from California, or Iowa, or Texas, or flew in from New York, or Europe, or wherever, to this place of once wild and impossible beauty that begged for understanding and appreciation only to spend their days wandering in and out of all the look alike, under inspired, over priced gift shops, and that did not make any sense at all.

Why had he bothered to come downtown anyway? Oh yes, he wanted to talk to that cute little clerk he had met last week. But, as it turned out, it was her day off and he didn't even know her last name. Life is cruel. Time to do something sensible, Kohl, like go for a hike. He turned around to go back to his truck and bumped into someone else much too wide to permit him to pass. He stepped off the curb and kept on going. He found his vehicle, drove to Pass Road, turned right, wandered through the houses and took a dirt road he had never been down before. He followed it to the end, parked in the trees, grabbed his canteen and day pack and headed off through the woods without a specific destination in mind.

There was a jackrabbit behind the bush, however, birds in the trees, deer tracks in the sand and that alone was reason enough to be there. Half an hour later he heard voices off to the right higher up. He found his way through the trees and brush to a clearing where he saw two male hikers coming down over the sandstone in the distance so he crossed the wash and headed for higher ground to get away from them. Skirting the base of the cliffs he came at last to a trail. The sun was hot out here in the open and he was beginning to sweat. He drank heavily from his canteen, capped it and just once decided to follow the trail for a while. He was only out for the exercise anyway.

Gaining more altitude, he could begin to see portions of the town lying in the valley behind him. Ahead and higher still there was a large alcove in the face of the rock. No, it looked like an arch. It was an arch, free standing, separated from the cliffside by a crevice. There were women's voices up top. Now that was more like it. He went under the arch, climbed up one level higher, worked his way along the internal ledge to the far end, climbed up through the crack between the rocks and found himself on top of a mesa looking at three females. The chunky one was talking to the one with the gunny sergeant's voice he had been listening to for some time. The third one was reading a book. That might be a good sign.

He ignored the other two and picked a path closest to the loner. She wore shorts, a halter and sandals. The shorts looked short, the halter full. "Hi," he said when he was close enough. Was that a small tattoo peeking out just over the rise of her left breast?

She looked up, blinked and returned the greeting. He stared ahead. "Can you see the rest of the town from around over there," he asked.

"I don't know. We didn't go that far."

"Hmm, well, guess I'll go see. Want to walk along?" he said, trying to remain casual.

She looked at her friends. They were still talking. "Sure," she said, rising, discreetly adjusting her halter to hide the tattoo.

Petite little thing, he observed as he smiled at her. She smiled back and they proceeded. He wanted her to lead so he could check out her legs but she, however, preferred him to go first. So, as much as possible, he tried to walk side by side with her. Where are you from? Phoenix. And you? Sedona. Really? Yes, etc, etc. They chatted and walked, soon came to the straight down, southern edge of the mesa, stopped and looked out and over and chatted some more. He slipped off his pack, broke out a plastic container, offered her some of his own special brand of trail mix that consisted of chocolate, peanuts and raisins.

Then the conversation dead ended. They began to walk back. "Just here for the day?" he asked.

"No, for the weekend. We're attending a seminar tomorrow and Sunday."

"What kind?"

"Ascension."

"Ascension? You mean like Christ was supposed to have?"

"Did."

Well, no point in arguing that one, he decided. "Who's teaching it?" he asked.

"It's being channeled by Mentira. Do you know her?"

"I doubt it. Who's she channeling," he ask, half kidding.

"Arc Angel Michael. He's an ascended master."

"Really? What's an ascended master?"

"A spiritual being so highly developed that they can take their body with them. That way when they choose to come back to earth they don't have to go through the whole process of being born again. They can come as an adult and begin to help people."

"Is this what you hope to become?"

"That's what I'm working on," she said in dead earnest.

"Well, instead of channeling these guys, why doesn't this Mentira just ask them to reappear and help teach the seminar directly," he said. "Now that would really be impressive."

She gave him a cold stare. "Well, what do you believe in?" she asked. "Nothing, I suppose?"

"Not true," he said.

"What then? What do you believe in?"

He thought a moment. "Well, I'm not really sure. Maybe dynamite." he said. "Yes, I think I'm beginning to believe in dynamite. We'll see." End of conversation. No wonder he was alone, no wonder he felt lonely. There was no one out there anymore, in there, that is, behind the eyes, wherever it was people were supposed to be. Shit. Maybe it was time to get that job, put some routine back in his life, be around people on a regular basis, stop being such a dissenter and get re involved in the normal world again, he told himself. First he shivered and then began to sweat. Cold, terror produced sweat. Forgive me, oh Jose on high in the sky for even contemplating such thoughts even for such a brief instant, he murmured. It was time to get out of there, time to find a surplus store and pick up those manuals Buck was telling him about and then it was time to go home and light up the screen on that word crunching computer. There were no ascended masters in there to muck things up.

FOUR

Jennie Trent had been in Sedona for nearly two years now. She loved the place with a passion that was only exceeded by the sincerity of her being and the statement she made by just being alive. But not the people. No, they were as mixed a bag as you would find anywhere, tolerable at times, some of them even lovable, but in the majority, to be avoided as much as possible. No, it wasn't them, there was nothing special there. Instead, she loved the place for what had been carved out of the rocks, the mysteries of the canyons, the sense of ancient cultures that still lingered suggestively in the ruins, the pictographs, petroglyphs and the terrain. Things still alive in the songs of birds, in the cellular memories of the tall pines and the gnarled old juniper, in the lonesome howl of the coyote, the silent countenance of the sculptured sandstone and in the very soil upon which she so often respectfully trod in her own solitary explorations.

And in the winter the place even transcended itself and turned ethereal when the dark clouds blustered and hid the tops of the peaks as they sprinkled white amongst the trees and over the rocks, then paled and retreated into the rifts between the hills. True spiritual magic, a time of deep, uncommon communion for her. She had left a husband, a yuppie-world career, a closet full of sequined gowns and seventy five pairs of over priced high heeled shoes behind just to be there and had accepted a part time job at the small animal clinic at a fifth of her previous earnings for the privilege. It was perfect. Three days a week devoted to income gathering, four to her own pursuits. A house shared with two others was an acceptable compromise. There were so many things she didn't need anymore in her greater abundance.

Friends still came from San Diego to visit occasionally and tried to persuade her of her folly but soon retreated to the safety of their own value system and came less and less frequently. She was thankful. They were so boring with their strange ways, wanting only to shop or to dine out at the more expense resorts. And so unreachable, except in superficial ways. That was the frustrating part. She tried to get them to ride in her little car, just to Red Rock Crossing or up Schnebley Hill even, but all they did was complain about the heat or the red dust that got on their shoes. It was impossible. No wonder the world was in trouble. But what to do about it? How did you help people like that, she asked herself often. There had to be a way.

Then one day she quit her job at the clinic and obtained one with a jeep tour company as a guide and driver. Better. Here were people who had come to town and at least wanted a cursory look at the natural surroundings bad enough to pay money for it and ride in the back of a dusty, open vehicle. And once aboard, they were all her's for an hour or two. She talked of the geology, the wildlife, the plant life, the unseen delicate balance, the mysterious disappearance of the Sinagua and the Anasazi, the necessity of preservation, the need of protection, the far reaching effects of volcanic eruption in the Philippines, the ever burning oil well fires in Kuwait. Pollution, waste, lack of concern, projections about the fate of the world, all was done as gently and discretely as possible, but done nevertheless. On rare occasion she would even see the clear light of understanding in someone's eyes and they would respond. It was always a refreshing moment of joy, but still, it too seemed so inadequate.

There were no men in her life either, the brutes. Drinking canned beer, shouting at the television set all weekend as if all their noise and bluster could somehow affect the outcome of a game being played between a bunch of tobacco chewing assholes who had nothing better to do than chase a little white ball around a field. And when that wasn't there to keep them occupied, they were churlish, childish, course, crude, self centered and shallow, requiring regular encounters with contemporary males for back slapping, bullshit and bolstering up in order to keep on functioning even at some minimal level where they spent more money on car polish than they did on their wives or girlfriends.

Not that they were all bad. She had met two or three who had been exceptions to the rule but never under circumstances which could have led to anything permanent. Fortunately, however, she had a few female friends with both brain hemispheres still functioning that helped take up the slack until such time, if ever, another good man should come along.

One of her girlfriends was Linda. "Hi Linda," she said as she walked out onto the shaded deck at the Hideout where they had agreed to have lunch that day and sat down at the small table opposite the short, dark haired girl dressed in a long, full beaded denim dress. "Sorry I'm late. God, what a morning."

"Run out of gas on the Broken Arrow trail?"

"Wish I had. It might have been easier."

"More eccentric tourists, huh?"

"Tedious, would be a better description."

"At least your job is outdoors. That must give you some sense of freedom."

"Beats slinging hash, as they say," Linda continued. "But, as I say, slinging hash beats being a big city executive secretary any day. Commuting twenty five miles to work, trapped on the fortieth floor of an air conditioned concrete coffin all day long, waiting for the big one to come along and shake it down. Spending your nights watching old movies with Oliver. That's not exactly the way to spend the best ten years of your life."

Linda's brown eyes reflected a passing trace of bitterness while she spoke. She was nonetheless, cute. She had also been to Ethiopia. Alone, with backpack, the year she had left Oliver, making her way across the country on a sparse budget, on up through Egypt, across to Greece and back home. Very commendable, especially for five foot two.

"Do you still hear from him?"

"I will always hear from Oliver as long as he thinks I'm still eligible to inherit the family fortune."

"Or until you remarry."

"He doesn't believe I will ever do that."

"Why not?"

"Thinks he can never be replaced," Linda smiled dryly.

"Poor Oliver. What's his problem?" Jennie asked. For some reason they had never gotten around to talking about the details of her former marriage.

"I was a virgin when I met him. How was I supposed to know that sex could be fun? Never would have found out if his old college buddy hadn't looked him up one day," Linda said in a somewhat more pleased tone.

Jennie smiled, then turned sad. Memories. Hope and desire unfulfilled. Well, at least Linda was from a rich family, or claimed to be. But if so, why did she live so frugally, Jennie wondered. Why not find out. "Is your family wealthy?" she asked, straight out.

"My mother and my aunt are. You've met my aunt."

"I did?"

"Sue Alexander. From Denver. She comes every summer."

"She's your aunt? I thought she was your older sister."

"She is more like a sister. She's probably also worth twice what my mother is, thanks to my father, poor man. It was all inherited money anyway but he lost a good share of his part in a bad business deal before he died."

"Then why did you live in that place you did all last spring? Wouldn't your mother help?"

"I never told her. I wanted to see if I could make it on my own, which I managed to do." Damned right she had. She knew how to tough it out. It was one of the best experiences she had ever had. But, at the same time, one she had vowed she would never repeat. "Let mother have her Bel Aire mansion. I'm doing just fine where I am. Never been happier in my life," she said, half in truth and half in lie.

"You didn't tell Sue either?"

"Only later. She just laughed and told me I was being silly. But it doesn't matter, everything still turned out well."

"So things are good with Paul?" Jennie asked as she pictured Paul, the latest man in Linda's life, not too sure about Linda's taste in men.

Linda was about to reply when she felt a hand settle on her shoulder. She turned and looked up at the smiling dark blue of

26

Kohl's eyes and the four day old stubble on his face.

"Kohl," she said, rising. "How are you?" She gave him a big hug, then thought to introduce him. "Kohl, this is Jennie."

Kohl was already quite aware of Jennie and had been from the first moment he entered. He was even more pleased to find her sitting with someone he knew. Now he indulged himself close hand. The haphazard, soft swirl of blond curls casually piled on top of her head, delicately freckled nose, high cheekbones, steady blue eyes, white, translucent teeth, firm but feminine chin. No makeup required for this face.

"Hi Jennie," he said and extended his strong hand.

She took it briefly as she examined him. Might not be bad looking except for all that hair on his face. What was wrong with him? Too cheap to buy a razor or too lazy to use it? The same question had also occurred to Linda.

"What's this? she asked, and rubbed Kohl's cheek teasingly, thinking how badly he had spoiled a good face she was rather fond of.

"I'm embarrassed to tell you," Kohl said apologetically.

Linda looked at Jennie. "She'll understand," she said, hopefully. "Tell us."

"Well, it's been weeks since I've had a bona fide night out with a woman. Been bathing and shaving regularly but couldn't seem to get any of the local girls to even look at me. So, I decided to let my hair and whiskers grow, bought me a new black Stetson and some black T-shirts like the hometown barroom cowboys. Thought it might help if I gave the girls what they're used too."

Is this guy serious? Jennie wondered. If he is, I'm leaving.

"Did it work?" Linda questioned, still standing, looking at up the ex-lover who towered over her.

"Somebody smiled at me today."

"So why are you embarrassed?"

"It's the first time in all the time I've been in this town that, other than for you, I've ever met anyone I'd really want to impress," he said and shrugged as he glanced at Jennie.

Oh shit, Jennie said silently. He's making a move on me. Now I'm really leaving.

"Nice to have met you, a...Kohl," she said, starting to rise, "but I really need to get back to work."

"No you don't, Jennie," Linda told her. "Sit down and let's order. Want to join us, Kohl?"

Kohl looked at Jennie but Jennie refused to look back, determined to ignore him into going away.

"No," Kohl said. "No, I was just passing by, thought I saw your car out front."

"My car's not out front. Paul dropped me off."

"Oh. Yeah, well, I have to take care of some other things up the street anyway. So...I'll see you later."

"God, Jennie," Linda said after he was gone. "What's wrong with you?"

"I wasn't impressed," she said.

"With Kohl?" Incredulous, how could this be? "You didn't give him a chance."

"What for?"

"He's one of the nicest men I ever met."

"He didn't look very nice. He also has a strange sense of humor."

"I really don't think he was joking."

"You don't?" Jennie asked, somewhat surprised.

"How come you go to bed with a book every night?" Linda dug into her. "Cause there are no good men around, you say. Well, maybe he has the same problem, except maybe he's gotten to the point where he's willing to compromise. You know what most of the men in this town are like. Give him credit for having some imagination."

Jennie thought about it for a moment. "So what kind of a person is he?" she asked, trying to soothe Linda a bit.

"Intelligent, sensitive, decent, honorable."

"Him?"

"Yes, and damned good in the boudoir."

"You've slept with him?"

"Before I met Paul."

"How come you dumped him if he's so damned wonderful?"

"I didn't. He was just visiting at the time, before he decided to move here. I hadn't seen nor heard from him for three months and then Paul came along."

"Oh, I see," Jennie said and looked in the direction where Kohl had exited.

"I'm sorry. I guess I shouldn't have told you I slept with him. Maybe that wasn't fair."

"Why not?"

"Because I think you two were made for each other and if either one of you would have come out of hiding long enough, I would have introduced you months ago."

Jennie was silent. She picked up the menu. "Let's order," she said. "I'm hungry."

It was three forty five in the afternoon a full week later and Jennie's day to handle the complimentary, promotional passes the company gave away every week. No problem for the driver. The pay was the same and the tips could often be just as good.

"How many?" she asked the dispatcher. "I see four."

"Five. There's one who said he would wait in the jeep."

Jennie gathered up the four and headed them towards the street where her vehicle was parked. Sitting far in the back of the extended machine when she got there was a man in a dark hat, head on his chest as though he were napping.

"This is it," she told the others. "Best to get in on that side. Fasten your seat belt so we don't have a problem with the local police and we'll be on our way," she instructed them as she watched the man in the back.

He stirred, removed his hat and smiled at her. "Hello," he said and nodded in his clean shaven, trimmed hair, pressed shirt and new jeans, way.

She stared. "Kohl?"

"Thought you might have forgotten."

"No," she said, unable to take her eyes off him.

"Well," he asked, after soaking up as much of her gaze as seemed proper, "where are you taking us today?"

Jennie straightened her own western hat, dusted off her seat, climbed in and, after a brief stammer, automatically began her well practiced elucidation. Kohl gave her his full, red blooded, aching hearted attention. Dammit girl, you sure do justice to a pair of boots, tight fitting jeans, deerskin jacket and cowgirl hat.

But while the others talked and asked questions, he remained silent. Hope I haven't embarrassed her by being here, he said to himself at last. God, I don't want to embarrass you, pretty girl. Hope you don't dislike me too much. Hope you can tolerate me long enough for me to show you my good side. I think I have one. I hope to Christ I do. If I don't I intend to find one, you can bet your beautiful little behind on that. And if I can't, well then, I'm going to wade out into that pool above the crossing with my boots full of rocks where it's known to be well over my head.

They rode past Thunder Mountain, up Long's Canyon, dipped into Boynton, went past Doe Mountain, up Red Canyon and back out and drove to Loy Butte, stopping often along the way while Jennie pointed out all the rock people, elaborated on the geology, talked of the earlier inhabitants of the region and favored them all with Juniper berries, pinyon nuts, prickly pear fruit, mesquite pods and half a dozen other edible things indigenous to the landscape that even Kohl wasn't aware of.

Three hours later they were back in town parked at the curb. Kohl made sure he was last in line to thank her. He did so politely and handed her a rolled up bill. She smiled, much less warily than before. Maybe not even warily at all, he thought.

"Long day for you," he stated sympathetically.

"Yes," she said, agreeing for the most part.

"Not too long, I hope."

"No," she responded bravely enough.

"You must be hungry. Could I...could we...?"

"What did you have in mind?" It was a cautious question, but not too cautious.

"Something quiet where we can talk. How about that little Italian place on the west end?"

"Sounds okay. I'll meet you there. Say, half an hour?"

She was sounding amenable enough. "Do you have to go check in first? I'd be happy to wait. We can ride together," he said, pushing it a little further.

"I'll meet you there."

"Are you sure it's okay?"

"I'll meet you there." she said because, yes dammit, she wanted to. Give me a chance.

"I really enjoyed the tour," he told her as she sat studying the plastic laminated menu from across the small table replete with linen and a fresh flower.

"Is that why you over tipped me?" she asked, looking up at him. She really felt he did.

"I didn't. Did I?" Now he wasn't sure. Maybe he had.

"You did," she said and looked at him a bit critically.

"Well, I'm sorry. I didn't know what was proper since it was a free ride."

"You're sure?" she asked, mellowing, smiling at him.

"Yes. Why?"

"I almost didn't stop by because I thought you were trying to impress me."

"If I thought I had to impress you I wouldn't have asked you to have dinner with me," he said looking directly at her, his eyes unwavering. Nothing emotional in the look, just the truth.

"What would you have done instead?"

"Gone home, whipped up an egg and tomato sandwich on a cinnamon, raisin bagel, had a beer and gone to bed."

She laughed. "I'm glad. You had me worried for a while," she said, her eyes dilating even more as she spoke.

That's a good sign, Kohl told himself. I believe she likes me. They returned to their menus, sipped their coffee and ordered. Then they exchanged background information while they waited to be served and told each other the how and why of what had brought them to Sedona. "Do you consider yourself to be an environmentalist?" Kohl then asked her.

"Do you?"

"I don't like labels."

"Nor I. But I love nature. At times I think I would die for it."

"You feel that strongly?" Kohl wondered. He didn't know if he'd die for nature but he might give up his life for this fair maiden, if it ever came to that.

"I'm not sure I'd want to bring it to the test but I think so."

Kohl gracefully encouraged her to continue talking as they ate, helping her to explore the many sides of her feelings about the many sides of herself. But it was difficult, divinely difficult. He listened carefully, yet every time she tossed her head or brushed back her mischievous curls or turned the profound blue-green of her eyes to his he felt weak, lost his chain of thought and had to

31

remind himself to start breathing again.

"I don't understand why I have been talking so much," she finally said with much concern as they finished their food some considerable amount of time later.

"My pleasure," he said happily.

"But I don't even know you," Jennie said, sounding regretful, as though she had exposed herself far too much to this man whom she was still somewhat convinced she shouldn't feel quite so comfortable with."

"It's only our first date," he commented.

"It's not a date," she pointed out, making sure that got straightened out right away.

"I'm glad of that," he said, sounding relieved and serious. "I hate to date."

"Really? Why?" she asked. Wasn't this the guy who had let his whiskers grow just so he could meet more women?

"Silly games. I hate games. If you like each other you go out, have a good time, enjoy each other's company." He insisted, studying her face again for the fifteenth time that evening.

"Isn't that dating?" she wanted to know, fully aware of how he was looking at her.

"No. Dating is different. Dating is usually a deceitful, deceptive, frivolous and foolish ritual."

"Such strong words. What's so deceitful about it?" she asked, somewhat defensively.

"It's a masked costume dance where the rules change from day to day and from player to player and the real people seldom fail to emerge until they've danced themselves into a corner somewhere down stream. Then, when the masks come off, everyone feels deceived. That makes it frivolous and foolish."

"So, it's too complicated for you," she said, half teasing.

"I'm just an ordinary, every day, down home kind of a guy," he said and shrugged nonchalantly.

"Just a simple little country boy who used to live in Beverly Hills," she chided.

"Who told you that?" he asked, leaning back in his chair.

"Linda," she said, watching his face as he said it.

"What else did she tell you?" Nothing, he hoped.

"Nothing," she lied. "She just mentioned that you came here

32

from California about a year ago."

"I see," he said, not totally convinced. Still, even if she knew about his previous encounter with Linda, he certainly wasn't going to apologize for some minor historical fact.

A quiet lull settled over them.

Finally Jennie asked, "Do you know what time it is?"

"Five watches in my dresser drawer and not a one has any live batteries in it," he said, showing her his empty wrist.

"Now I'm really impressed," she said, smiling at him again with her devilish smile.

"Maybe that's why I stopped dating. I wouldn't know what time to go and pick anyone up."

"Well, it must be late and I have to get home," she said, serious again. "But let me say this, Mr? What's your last name?"

"Logan."

"Mr. Logan. You've convinced me that dating probably isn't any fun but if sometime you think you might like to, aaa..."

"Go out? Gee, I'd have to look at my calendar," he said and grinned at her. "Could you call me at my office tomorrow? If I'm not there, leave word with my secretary."

"Forget it."

"Jennie, Jennie."

"What?"

"You're adorable. And delightful and delectable and probably very delicious and of all the people in the whole world you're the one person I'd most like to go out with. Hell, I'd even ask you for a date. If I had to, of course. Say, tomorrow night and Friday night and all day Saturday and Sunday and..."

Jennie fought back a blush over the delicious part of his comment but managed to respond. "I have to work on Saturday and Sunday. However, the evenings are free."

"Done."

"One final condition though."

"Name it."

"Next time it's your turn."

"For what?"

"To do the talking."

"You'll be sorry."

FIVE

Jennie climbed down out of Kohl's truck and looked through the simmering, shimmering, rising waves of heat emanating from the oven hot road to where the baked asphalt merged with the sky in a dancing mirage, then she turned and stared out across the dry, desolate landscape of hot sand, scorched stones and randomly scattered, blistered scraggles of brown brush and cooked cactus, all near death from lack of moisture.

"You told me we were going for a hike," she said in a piqued voice to Kohl, who had by now come around to her side of the panting vehicle. "What in hell are we doing out here?"

"I love it when you swear," he said and kissed her nose.

"You haven't answered my question," she said and pulled away from him.

"Research," he replied casually.

"Research? In this heat? Are you mad?" she asked, looking at him as if he were.

"That's what I had in mind," he said and adjusted his hat to shade more of his face.

"Forget it," she said with a pout.

"Be a sport, please?"

"I'm not a sport so don't sport me, or I'll hitchhike home."

"Sorry. What if I pour water all over your T-shirt instead?"

"Ha!" she replied and backed away.

"Let me help you out of it then," he volunteered and made a playful move for her.

"So that's why you brought me out here," she said and crossed her arms in front of her.

"I will if you will."

"I'll hitchhike home," she threatened him again and stood her ground, holding him at bay, continuing the game they had started almost a month ago. Why had she let it go on so long? Heaven knew she would have liked nothing better than to have stripped for this man. How had she gotten herself into such a corner? How did she go about telling him he didn't have to go on being such a gentleman any longer? Maybe if they went someplace else out of this unbearable heat.

Kohl slipped on his day pack and slung a canteen over each

shoulder He locked up the truck and looked at the sun. "Should start cooling off pretty soon," he said, determined that they were going to go no matter what.

"Kohl? Do we have to?" she pleaded.

"It's not so bad. Look over there. See that dip in the landscape?" he said and pointed.

"It all looks the same to me," she replied, shaking her head.

"Well, it drops off into a small valley. It's too deep to see from here but there are actually some trees down in there and a small, spring fed stream. Just a mile or two. Three at the most."

Jennie moaned. "Some research project."

"The valley's secondary. The real reason is over there." Kohl gestured to the north. He was standing beside her now, letting their arms touch.

"Where? All I see is lots and lots of nothing," she said, staying close by his side, squinting in the brightness.

"Those steel towers with the big wires on them."

"What's so special about them?"

"They cross the valley floor up a ways carrying power from the Navajo generating plant in Page. They're part of the grid system that supplies most of the southwest with electricity."

"What about them?"

"We came to check them out."

"Why don't you just ask the power company what you want to know? They must have maps or something, and books full of numbers, how many light bulbs they can turn on, all that kind of stuff," she replied and looked up at him, wishing he would kiss her again. "Can we go home now?"

"It's not what I need to know. Come on," he said, determined to go through with whatever had motivated him to bring her here. "I'll explain it to you when we get there."

Jennie shrugged, said no more and like a brave trooper set out with him at her side. They proceeded through the broiling heat at a slow but steady pace, stopping just long enough and often enough to have drained one small canteen by the time they arrived at the eastern edge of the unnaturally wide rift in the otherwise relatively flat terrain.

"Oh," she said, surprised at the amount of green spread out below them. They paused briefly as she took it in. Then she spotted a clump of tall cottonwoods signaling to them with shiny green leaves that rustled in what must have been a slight breeze down below. "Are we going that way?" she asked hopefully. What was wrong with a little shade anyway, if they had to be out in this god awful place?

He pointed out a possible path and followed her down through the thickening presence of vegetation. They stopped first under a low, dusty green Juniper surrounded by a thicket of red barked manzanita. A good twenty degrees differential in the shade, maybe more. Jennie sighed and sat down. But ten minutes was all Kohl would allow. "We'll take a longer break under the cottonwoods," he promised her and held out his hand.

She let him pull her up. He put his arm around her and offered her another drink from the big canteen. She hoisted it up, took a swallow from the heavy container and managed to spill some of the lukewarm liquid down her front, causing her nipples to firm. Kohl took it from her, screwed the cap back on and stared at her, seeing what seemed to be permission coming from her eyes. He reached for her, kissed her, let his hands move up, cupped her, found the hard protrusions, kissed her silky neck, started to work his way up her back to the clasp on her bra. She kissed him back and leaned away from him. "Didn't you say it would be cooler down there?" she asked huskily.

He fought for composure, finally nodded. Was she making him a promise of more to come or stalling him again, he wondered. He let her go. They started off anew.

"See the tower on the top of the east side?" he said at last, pointing through the trees after they had arrived and rested in the shade. Business first. Dammit, but this woman was driving him crazy. Christ he wanted her.

"Yes," she said, no longer sure she was seriously interested after the interlude back under the Juniper tree.

"One there, and because of the angle the line intersects the valley, there are three down here below and then another up top on the western side way down that way. Five in all. If one could get all five to tip over at once they would probably pull down two or three more, maybe destroy three or four miles of power line."

She gave him a strange look? "Is that why we came here?"

He nodded.

"I hope you're not serious," she replied, seeming perplexed.

He shrugged.

"This isn't fair Kohl."

"What isn't?" he asked somewhat worried because there was a sharp, somewhat helpless tone in her voice.

"Why didn't you tell me you were an eco-warrior nut case? Are you part of Earth First, or what?" Now she was upset. She had that look in her eye.

"It's for my book. Remember, I told you I was writing a book. Honest. I swear to you. I'm just writing a book."

She started to relax a little. "I asked you what it was about a couple of times. Why didn't you tell me then?"

"Maybe I wasn't sure I was serious about finishing it."

"What? Writing the book, or knocking down power lines?"

"I'm not the hero type."

"But isn't that just as bad?"

"What, being a coward?"

"No, writing such a story. Won't it encourage others?"

"Maybe that's the idea. Somebody needs to do it."

"I suppose you want to blow up 'The Dam,' too," she said accusingly.

"How did you know?"

"I've read the same books."

"But you don't approve?"

"It's destructive."

"That's the whole idea."

"How can you say that?"

"The dam is destructive, so is that power line."

"How?" she asked skeptically, studying him.

He took her hands, held them. "The dam destroyed the river and the canyon," he said quietly. "If you read all the books then you know what was there before and you also know how destructive the rising and falling levels of water in the reservoir are to the wildlife. You know that easy access to the water by boat brings more pollution. You know that thousands of acre feet of water are lost each year to evaporation and you know that eventually the damned thing will all fill up with silt and become totally useless anyway."

He continued. "But what no one wants to admit and everyone

minimizes is the fact that we have tampered with nature in a very big way and we can only guess how badly the ecology of the southwest and the entire balance of nature has been upset. In fact, it may even have been pushed beyond recovery. And in the end the dam will have become one of the biggest monuments to stupidity that man has ever created. Of course that's a few generations in the future, so what the hell. Who cares, right?"

"Okay, that I can agree with, but how is a power line destructive? It's a totally passive thing sitting there minding its own business."

"It's not the lines themselves, it's what's hooked onto both ends of them. In one case a dam that's destroying the ecology and in another a coal fired generating plant which is far, far worse. In this country approximately seventy percent of the electrical power comes from fuel burning generating stations. Coal. Burning fossil fuel robs the earth of its resources and pollutes the atmosphere and contributes to the Greenhouse Effect. One coal fired plant alone can put up to three or four thousand tons of ash, sulfur dioxide and oxides of nitrogen into the air in one day. Not in a week or a month or a year, but in one day. There is also poisonous mercury coming out the smoke stacks as well as traces of radioactivity. One coal fired plant does that. That's what it's putting into the atmosphere."

"And how many coal fired plants are there in this country?"

"I don't know the latest count. Hundreds probably. And increasing."

"Well, doesn't matter. One's obviously too many."

"What it's doing to the earth is equally bad," Kohl said. And although he didn't know all the national figures, he did have a good idea what was going on in the southwest. "Immense strip mines such as the one at Black Mesa, literally stolen from the Indians with the help of the federal government, that rip away the surface to get at the coal and lay the earth bare where the formerly deep, toxic elements of the soil are brought to the top and left so the rain will carry them into the daily water supply of the Indians. As much as ten million tons of coal per year for just one plant because the damned things are so inefficient."

"Then there's the water that they need for washing, cooling and transporting the coal through pipelines. A couple of thousand gallons per minute being pumped from the deep water table under the mesa and hundred of thousands of acre feet of water per year being diverted from the Colorado and its tributaries, contaminated and wasted and that's only a small part of the story. That's on one end of the power line. Somewhere in between is the institution of the power company itself, which adds extra charges to the consumers bill to pay for advertising to promote the use of more electricity rather than less so the whole problem can be compounded. Just like the coal companies, dollars are more important than lives."

Jennie was overwhelmed. All she could do was listen.

"And, on the other end are all the users, the ones really responsible," Kohl went on.

She thought about it. "Well, I always did think all those lights in Las Vegas were ridiculous."

"Ridiculous? Jennie, they're obscene. The most flagrant waste of natural resources possible, as are all the over air conditioned, over heated, over illuminated buildings, non essential appliances and services, self indulgent shit like spas and swimming pools, manufacturing of products that don't last and which we don't need anyway. It goes on and on from there and it's a long, long list and getting worse. Do you realize that since nineteen fifty the amount of energy consumed per person in this country has increased sixteen times. For what? Is the quality of life any better?"

"Hardly It's probably sixteen times worse, and still deteriorating," she admitted.

"Exactly, and I'm sorry," Kohl said. "I didn't mean to give you such a lecture. But I do get a little hot about it sometimes."

She came closer, put her arms around his waist as he cuddled her, "It's all right. We all need to hear about it."

"Probably," Kohl said, and was silent as he looked at the glint on the power line wires, more red than silver now that the sun was approaching the horizon.

"Well, maybe it will all resolve itself one of these days," Jennie said with a trace of gloom in her voice.

"Not without some help, I don't think," Kohl said.

"Maybe some of that other stuff is true."

"What stuff?"

"You know. The Purification, that kind of stuff."

"Where did you learn about that?" he asked, looking at her.

"I have a couple of Hopi friends," she replied.

"Interesting term they have there, isn't it? Appropriate, too. Exactly what the world needs."

"Purification?"

"Yeah, long overdue, perhaps."

"It's also in the Mayan prophecy."

"And in the Talmud Jmmanuel, the Lady of Fatima, Nostradamus and a half dozen other places."

"And in the collective subconscious of so many these days, if you'll pardon the use of a Jungian term," she said.

Bright girl, Kohl thought. Where had she learned all these things? "Give me a kiss," he said to her, feeling even more pleased with what he saw.

She tipped her face up. He found her lips, gave her a brief, friendly kiss. They hugged each other quietly for a moment. "You're right, of course," he told her. "Half the population seems to have this nagging half awareness that something isn't quite right with the world anymore and an unexplainable feeling of impending, drastic change."

"But you know what most psychiatrists say?"

"No."

"Visions of world destruction are often the prelude to an acute schizophrenic episode," she said, kidding him a bit.

"So I'm comfortably schizophrenic," Kohl stated with a smile, not caring if it was true.

"And R.D. Lange said that schizophrenics are people who possess superior wisdom but are living in an insane society," Jennie continued, tossing out more things for the fun of it.

"Bless him. And superior wisdom or not, I sure as hell think the world has gone bonkers."

"The same world that will throw stones at you if you write such a book," she pointed out. "And you know it."

"Stones I can handle. Shotgun slugs might be something else," Kohl affirmed.

"But you're serious about the book?" she asked, because she wasn't yet totally sure of his real intentions.

He stopped talking for a moment, nuzzled her hair and kissed her on the ear. "As serious as I am about you," he said, pulling her even closer.

"How serious is that?" she wanted to know with eyes turned up to his face and lips slightly parted, heartbeat beginning to rise.

In answer to her question he kissed her in the dying light of the sun and crushed her to him under the cool cottonwood tree that rustled softly in approval. She wrapped her arms around his neck as they collapsed onto the small blanket he had judiciously taken from the pack earlier and spread on the ground.

He kissed her mouth and her eyes and her nose and her ears and her neck and pulled her top up over the full, firm softness of her unrestrained breasts and kissed her rising brown nipples and caressed her and lifted his own shirt and pressed his bare chest against her and held her and rocked her in his arms and kissed her face and her neck all over again until she thought she would surely die. "Kohl," she said very softly, panting a bit between the kisses she returned to his face and neck.

"What Jennie?"

"I'm ready now. Please make love to me."

"You're sure?"

"I'm sure."

"I can wait some more if you think it best."

"I think it would be best if you helped me out of my jeans," she said and reached for her belt buckle.

Soon stripped, hot and demanding, souls on fire, it was the stuff and substance of lightning bolts, the promise of heaven, the magic of eternity. "I'm sorry I made you wait so long," she said much later as she gently stroked his face when they lay resting.

"I would have waited a year."

"That long?" she said, playing with the hairs on his chest.

He kissed her on the nipple. "Well, maybe not," he admitted.

"How long then?"

"Another week, perhaps."

"Then what?"

"Rape."

"Mmmm," she said and ran her fingers down his tummy.

"I love you Jennie," he replied and kissed her mouth.

"And I love you," she said and kissed him back.

"And you are delicious."

"Oh, am I now?"

"Quadrupally."

More kisses.

"Remember when we had dinner together and you said that?"
"About how I thought you would be delicious?"
"Yes, you embarrassed me but I guess I knew I wanted you even then."
"I know."
"How do you know that?"
"Because you squirmed when I said it."
"I did not," she said with denial.
"You did."

They woke on the living room floor of Kohl's house. The sun, already thirty degrees up into the morning sky, streamed in through the open door, flooding them with light and warmth as the old grandfather clock in the corner chimed deeply ten times in a row. Jennie sighed and smiled as Kohl kissed her on the cheek. Her arms went up around his neck. She smiled blissfully back at him. "It's been the nicest twenty hours of my life."

"Yes. An almost perfect day."

"What do you mean, almost perfect?"

"A day is twenty four hours long. Four more to go. And unless you insist on breakfast..."

"Who's thinking about food?" she asked.

"Not me," he said.

The sunlight glistened on the heavy perspiration of their bodies as suggestive shadows again danced on the floor behind them, the female figure astride the male. She paused in her actions for a moment and said, "Kohl, I think we should try it."

"Try what?"

"I think we should blow up the dam."

"Dear lady, what are you talking about?"

"The dam, dammit. You know what dam. Or if not that then maybe the power lines, or something."

SIX
He picked up the phone on the third ring.

"Hey, Kohl, did I wake you?" said Mike's familiar voice.

"No. I was out giving the road runner some breakfast."

"Road runner?"

"The one who pecks on the window and wakes me up."

"How long did you say you've been living alone?"

"Quite a while now."

"Obviously."

"But I'm thinking of changing all that."

"Good, Kohl. Glad to hear it."

"Thanks, Mike. Anyway, what's up?"

"Remember that ten meter long CO_2 laser back in Anaheim that could burn a hole through a fire brick in half a minute?"

"Of course."

"That technology must have come a long ways since then."

"Probably has. Maybe I should use the idea in my book."

"Wonder what it would cost to build one?"

"Its all hypothetical, remember?"

"I know, but think of it! You could be half a mile away and topple tall chimneys with it, burn holes through steel posts, etch your way through a dam." Mike said with enthusiasm.

"It would be one hell-of-a-thing to play around with, no doubt about that."

"Anyway, listen. I'll be out that way on Friday," Mike informed him. "Thought I might stop by."

"I already have a date," Kohl kidded him.

"Doesn't she have any friends?"

"I don't know Kohl," Mike said as he studied Sue Alexander from across the restaurant where they had all agreed to meet. Sue was seated with Jennie at a far table waiting for the two men. An already opened bottle of champagne sat in the ice bucket.

"About what?"

"She's not my type at all."

"You haven't even met her yet,"

"I can see, dammit. Look at her. Snooty, aristocratic bitch, flaunting her Cartier and her Chanel. It'll never work."

"Come on Mike, your eyes aren't that good," Kohl said.

The hostess appeared from off the floor. "Do you have reservations?" she asked, looking at the way they were dressed and wondered what corner she might seat them in.

"Yes," Kohl said, and tried to tell her who they were with but Mike kept on talking.

"Okay, the watch I'm not sure about but the dress is definitely Chanel. I ought to know, I paid for one once," he said.

"Enough, Mike. They're drinking all that champagne by themselves." Kohl said as the hostess continued to stare at them. Back by the kitchen door for these two, she had decided.

"We're with those two women," Kohl told the hostess.

Couldn't be, she said to herself.

"Be nice now," Kohl warned Mike and without waiting for the hostess to take the lead, he moved to the distant table with Mike close behind.

"You could have at least told me to wear a tie," Mike complained to his backside.

Mike stood staring at Sue. What a jerk he had been, he decided. She looked great. He started to smile, his grin growing in magnitude by the second.

"My god Kohl. How come you know so many beautiful women," he asked, looking from Sue to Jennie and then back at Sue. "It's not fair," he continued as he tried to capture the entirety of something that hadn't been so clearly visible from fifty feet away in the dim light of the town's best eating establishment. He put out his hand as Sue returned the gesture, then said hello to Jennie again for the second time that day. Then they sat down, men opposite women.

"Don't worry," Kohl said to Sue. "He talks big but he's harmless," he told Sue. "One of those intellectuals, if you know what I mean. Theorizes a lot."

"I like intelligent men," Sue said, and gave Mike a silent appraisal. If he was, she would decide for herself.

Guess he should have told Mike to wear a tie, Kohl decided and asked Sue how long she was going to be in town.

The dinner went well enough but the conversation seemed scattered throughout and by the time it was over Kohl thought, well, so much for that. Maybe he and Mike could stop for a beer on the way home. Outside, however, Sue suggested that Jennie go with Kohl because she wanted to talk with Mike some more and

44

she would bring him home later.

"Come on, Mike. Try and pull yourself back down to earth," Kohl said with approaching frustration. It was already ten thirty the next morning.

"I can't help it Kohl. I like that woman. I mean, I really like that woman," Mike said exuberantly as he paced around Kohl's court yard, far too excited to risk sitting down. Baggy eyed, weak kneed and sleep deprived, he had been there for half an hour now, running on and on about Sue.

"Well, I sure screwed that one up," Kohl finally replied.

"What?"

"I should never have put you two together."

"You're kidding."

"Never."

"Why not?"

"You're the guy who spent three days convincing me we should try to build a monster laser and now that I'm ready, there goes the only person I know in the whole world who has the kind of money it would take to do it."

"Where is she going?"

"Who knows. You spent the whole night with her."

"What's wrong with that? It's perfect,"

"No it's not, Mike. If she gives us money just because you had enough stamina to keep her up all night, then it becomes a con game. I won't do it." Kohl rose from the lawn chair he was sitting in. Mike appeared somewhat annoyed by the comment but remained silent. "Come in the house," Kohl said at last, trying to be nice. Let me fix you something to eat. What would you like? About ten eggs over medium, pound of ham, eight slices of toast, hash browns, gallon of orange juice, what else?"

"Skip the juice," Mike stated gruffly. "Dammit," he started to say something but stifled it and let Kohl lead him inside. Keep cool, he told himself. Eat first, then talk. Inside he sat down and watched Kohl do ten things at once. Eggs in the pan, bread in the toaster, meat in the microwave, coffee in his cup. "Yuk," Mike said, afraid to swallow.

"Sorry, last of the pot. Here, let me dilute it a little." Kohl took the cup away from him, topped it off with hot water from the faucet and gave it back.

"Better, but still poisonous," Mike said, his face even more vitriolic than the coffee.

"Drink it, you need it," Kohl commanded him as he continued with his task.

Slam, bang, bump, thump, slap, slop. Barely edible, according to Mike's appraisal, but he ate it anyway.

"Never said I knew how to cook," Kohl told him as he watched the way Mike sorted through his plate. When it was finally gone he said, "Sorry Mike. Didn't mean to be so churlish. I didn't get much sleep last night either."

"That Jennie sure is a beautiful girl," Mike agreed, feeling all of ten percent better.

"No, I mean it. I'm happy for you both. How often does something like that happen? It's wonderful."

"You should know."

"Yeah, I do. Took longer than one night though. For her that is, not me, so I know how you feel. And that's far more important than any old infrared, c w, narrow banded, photon emitting super zapper any day, wouldn't you say?"

"I would, but I don't think you believe it."

"Okay, all kidding aside. I do mean it. Maybe we can think of something else. I know a guy back in Illinois who might be interested. If he's still alive."

"But we don't have to think of something else. Not yet."

"What do you mean?"

"Sue want's us all to get together tomorrow and discuss it."

"You asked her? Wasn't that a little premature?"

"Hell no. Be up front, be honest, you always tell me, so I was. Told her straight out the kind of money we needed," Mike said wiping the back of his hand across his mustache.

"When did you find time to do that?" Kohl asked, having regained his sense of humor.

"Some of us can do more than one thing at a time," Mike chided him back. "We had a nice long discussion, as a matter of fact, someplace around three a.m..

"And she didn't throw you off the porch when you told her the magnitude of money it would take?"

"No, she just..." Mike stopped as something brought a private little grin to his face. He got up and carried his empty plate to the sink and sat it down.

"Did you tell her exactly what we had in mind?"

"Only that we wanted to build a state-of-the-art device that could be used for constructive purposes."

"That's all?"

"Of course. She wanted to know who the principals would be so I told her, you and me, and possibly Buck."

"Buck?"

"Well, sure. You talked about him enough and he seemed like the likely candidate for such a project. As the man-in-the-field, so to speak, putting it to good use."

"This is getting out of hand," Kohl said, wondering if maybe it wasn't time to take that trip to Australia he had been planning for the last three years.

The color had returned to Mike's face as Kohl's began to pale.

"Don't panic," Mike told him. "Sit down, drink some of your own coffee. Everything's under control. Seems she knows Buck, or, knows of him quite well. Apparently he's a friend of her niece, what's her name, Linda? The one you used to shack up with once in a while."

"I slept on the couch."

"Have it your own way."

"Okay. Linda's an interesting lady. That's how I first met Buck."

"Well, anyhow. Sue sounded like she's on your side, Kohl. Our side, this side, whatever side we're on. I got the impression she'd like to see that dam go almost as badly as Jennie would."

"Really? How about that."

"So is it all right if I get some sleep?" Mike wanted to know.

"Hell yes," Kohl said, looking sideways at Mike, "and I owe you another apology."

"Probably do, but for what?"

"For doubting you. Christ, I could have at least taken you downtown for something decent to eat."

Kohl was in the booth with Sue, Mike and a Mr. Julius Trulock. Thus far, it was difficult to tell where Sue's mind was at as her gaze shifted back and forth amongst the three men while she

47

played with her desert and contributed to the small talk. Mike visually feasted on Sue as sallow faced, shallow faced Trulock, bookkeeping virtuoso that he was supposed to be, merely mumbled at the proper moments. Well, so much for that, Kohl said to himself after Sue made her first serious comments. He looked at Trulock clearly out of place in his starched shirt and pin striped tie. And look at him trying hard not to smile. Was that what had happened? Had they had been subverted by this conservative looking snook who had driven up from the big city of Phoenix when their backs were turned?

Mike took a moment to suppress his own disappointment, then replied, "It's all right Sue, maybe it's just as..."

"Not about funding your new venture, just how we go about handling it," Sue clarified as she found Mike's hand and placed hers over it, making it clear that her accountant was not privy to her full confidence. Trulock's face quickly returned to normal.

Kohl sighed. "No problem Sue," he said. "Whatever is best for you," he said. "We would expect you to do that anyway." He wasn't patronizing her, just stating his true feelings.

"Of course. That's why I wanted us all to meet so it's clear for everyone," she said, as though it were more for Trulock's benefit than for theirs. "So," she continued. "After thinking about it some more, I decided it might be best to give you as free a hand as possible. Better for everyone, I think."

"Well, yes, but...," Mike said, pleased but not pleased.

"Yeah," Kohl said. "Maybe we should discuss it."

"I appreciate your concern but it doesn't matter if I don't know exactly where all the money goes," she said very clearly as Trulock did his best to hide his disapproval. "Or even how much exactly, if it comes to that."

"But you need some accountability. We want to give you that," Mike stated more strongly.

"I think they have a good point, Miss Alexander," Trulock advised. "And after all, that is what you have me on your payroll for. Accountability."

"No, not in this case. All I care about here is that whatever is spent is done in a way that allows me to write some of it off when you do my taxes," Sue said, patting Mike's hand one more time before taking hers back and summarily pushing her half finished piece of blueberry pie away.

"Which means accountability, as this gentleman said," Kohl pointed out, hoping he hadn't put the wrong emphasis on the word gentleman.

"But, like we said, we also have no idea how much it's going to cost yet or what kind of a spending rate," Mike stated truthfully.

"We'll have accounting then, without accountability," Sue said with finality.

"It seems unwise," Trulock stated. But then after seeing the look on her face, he gave her a weak smile and added patronizingly, "but, it is your money, so..."

"Which I now choose to share with these two renegades. So I want you to set up a draw account for the two of them. Two hundred thousand." It was not a request, it was an order.

Even though Trulock almost swallowed his tongue, as did Kohl at the figure she mentioned, still he had to give him credit. The man had sense enough to straighten his tie instead of opening his mouth any further, even though he coughed a little before doing so. To make things even worse, Sue also stated. "If you run out before year end, let me know." It was at this moment that Trulock chose to start studying the cracks in the ceiling.

"God Sue. Are you sure? That's a lot of money," Mike said in an astonished voice.

"Yes, I am. I'd rather see it wind up in your pocket than the US Treasury any day," she assured them with a broad smile. "Talk about mismanagement and lack of accountability. Nothing you could ever do would equal that."

Well, how could anyone disagree with that, Kohl acknowledged. He looked at Mike looking at Sue, knowing that Mike truly wouldn't have cared if Sue was flat broke. And, in all fairness to him, it might have been a lot easier if she were. Regardless of the facts, however, their's was a destiny destined to happen under any set of conditions.

At this point Trulock excused himself to go to the men's room whereupon Sue then took both Kohl's and Mike's hands in her own and the three of them spent the next few moments grinning at each other. "Don't worry about Julius," Sue said. "He can be a stuffy asshole, but he's good at what he does."

"I'm sure he is," Kohl acknowledged, trying to minimize the uncomfortable feeling the man had left him with.

"But, if you have a problem with him, let me know."

"Are you sure you're happy with this arrangement?" Mike questioned one last time, still not believing their good fortune.

"Why? Do you think you seduced me into doing something I might not otherwise have been inclined to do?" she asked, teasing him with her eyes.

"I would hope not. It was much too good for that," Mike said, meaning every word of it as he stared back at her.

"Well, don't worry. I'm neither young enough or old enough to be that foolish, no matter what my personal feelings might be towards you," Sue assured him with a squeeze of his hand and a smile, then reached out and smoothed his thick, bristly mustache.

Mike was quiet. He could think of nothing other than how good she looked and when he had last seen her smile like that.

"You do seem to have a rather unconventional attitude towards money," Kohl interjected offhandedly in his own off handed way.

Sue seemed surprised at the remark. "No," she said, shaking her head. "I don't think so."

"You don't?"

"You're just as unconventional as I am."

"Impossible. I don't have enough money to be unconventional with."

"My point exactly. But when you have it, you spend it. And freely. So don't pick on me because I'm trying to do the same thing," she replied without irritation.

"But you seem to have so much. Maybe you should be more protective of it."

"God Kohl. I think you're serious."

"Yeah, well, maybe a little. Of course."

"I appreciate the concern but, thanks to my dear old daddy, I have more money than I can easily spend in two more lifetimes," Sue said, underscoring her position. "And if there is anything that's more ridiculous than having too much, it's trying to hang onto it. Especially when there are so many other good uses one can put it to besides accumulating interest."

"Well," Kohl stated in reconsideration. "In that case we'll do our best to help change that. Right Mike?"

"Damned right, hell yes," Mike said, finally getting into the swing of it. He turned and looked at Sue. "Why don't you send that stuffy old bean counter of yours back to his office and we'll take you up the street and buy you a drink," he replied. "Out of our own pockets, of course."

"Done. Just one last favor though..." Sue said, putting her hands back on top of theirs as she looked from one to the other with her deep, dark eyes.

"Of course," Mike and Kohl said simultaneously.

"When this...thing...whatever it is, is completed, I want you to give me a first hand demonstration."

"First hand?" Kohl said.

"First hand. You must promise me that."

"I don't know," Mike said. "Maybe that's not a good idea."

"He's right," Kohl said in agreement. "It's not a good idea."

"Honey, believe us. It's not," Mike reemphasized.

"I already know that. That's not the point."

"You'd never be able to plead innocent."

"I don't want to be innocent. I want to be involved. Please," she pleaded.

The two men looked at each other then back at Sue. "Well," they said, but were unable to come up with something more.

"It's agreed then," Sue stated, making sure each of them acknowledged her look.

"Okay," Kohl relinquished at last. "Provided it works. But we also haven't decided exactly what to try it out on either. Maybe you'll change your opinion."

"Pick something close to home."

As she said it, Mike's face began to light up.

"What are you grinning about, lover boy?" Kohl asked.

"I think I have something in mind. Yes, I know just the thing," Mike said and smiled mischievously back, his eyes twinkling like Arcturus on a cold and clear December night.

SEVEN

Linda sat on the plush carpet of Sue's large living room, her back against the oversized couch, and sipped her coke, wondering how to approach the matter that was beginning to concern her. Sue waited. Finally Linda was able to get to it. It was about Kohl and

Mike and the money.

What about it, Sue wanted to know, and how do you know?

"Well..." Linda stumbled around some more. "Buck seems to be spending a lot of time in their company in that building they rented out there on the edge of town," she said. And that can't be good because she's known Buck for quite a while and she's heard some of the stories about him.

"What stories?" Sue asked. She wasn't upset, not yet anyway, knowing that if Linda was concerned, it was probably not for selfish reasons.

Well, actually there weren't any really verifiable stories, as there shouldn't be, because Buck was very, very careful about whom he shared his adventures with.

What then? Sue wanted to know. How do you know I'm giving them money in the first place? And how do you know it's a lot of money?

"It wouldn't be fair to tell you," Linda replied.

"It wouldn't be fair not to tell me," Sue pointed out. "I can't believe it was Kohl or Mike, was it?"

"Well...No."

"Who then?" Sue demanded. This had gone far enough.

Linda told her.

"Trulock! That son-of-a-bitch! How dare he!" Sue was on her feet by now. There was fire in her eyes.

"One hundred and forty thousand is a lot of money in five months, Sue. It would seem like my concern is normal. After all, I am family," Linda explained. "Who else would he tell?" she asked, rising to face Sue.

"Me. No one but me."

"Maybe he doesn't feel that he can."

"Maybe he just thinks Mike is using me. That's it, isn't it? And what do you think, Linda?"

"I don't know Sue. I hope he's not," Linda said, looking at Sue as straight as she could.

Sue returned her gaze. "Doesn't matter if he is, I really don't care, although I sincerely believe it's not the case," she said.

"I admit he doesn't seem like the type but how do you know?" Linda tossed out.

"I guess that's one of the disadvantages of being rich. You can never be sure, when money is involved. Besides, what choice do I have? I'm in love with him," Sue said and smiled. It was not a pleading, helpless smile, however, but a very happy one instead, coming from someone who seemed to know exactly what she was doing.

"Okay," Linda said. " I'm sorry I brought it up."

"I'm glad you did," she said and went to the kitchen to use the phone. Linda followed. Sue's business manager came on the line. Go find Trulock, he was instructed. Don't call him first, go directly to his office, unannounced. Pick up all copies of my accounting records, tax statements and anything else he may have. Tell him whatever you have to, to make sure he doesn't hold anything back. Don't let him make copies of anything. Clear? Then as soon as you have it all, tell him to call me."

"What are you going to do?" Linda asked in a worried voice.

"Fire the bastard," Sue stated vehemently.

"Why?" Linda asked, a bit shocked, not quite sure that was the fair thing to do.

"Confidentiality is confidentiality. He violated that."

"But only to me."

"How do we know? If what I'm doing bothered him enough to tell you, who knows what he might do next. I should have known better."

"Why do you say that?"

"He was always making snide little innuendos about easy come, easy go, and, if you have to work for your money, you appreciate it more. God, I was his biggest account."

Trulock berated his wife all through dinner. The vegetables were half cooked, the meat was over done, the coffee too strong. Biting her lip, she suffered through it, determined not to cry, wishing that after all these years he would learn to talk about things instead of taking them out on her, the under-reacting, over-reacting, unpredictable putz. Finally she got him feed and out of the kitchen where they usually dined during the week.

He retreated to the den and turned on the news but hardly noticed the events of the day. Damn that rich Alexander bitch, how dare she dismiss him like that, he repeated over and over to himself, obsessed. He got up, went to the wet bar and poured himself a scotch and water, minus the water. It didn't help. He fixed another then went back to his chair. Something peculiar was going on, that's for damned sure, he told himself. It just wasn't normal to let someone spend that much of your money on some wild, untalked about project, lover boy or no lover boy. He kept the internal dialog going, not seeing the jealousy that crept into his ramblings. It wasn't fair to treat him like that, either. All he had done was talk to her niece about money going out the door for who knows what. And did she appreciate it? Hell no. And as for that niece, she was the one really to blame. She should have kept her big mouth shut, damn her. He changed the TV channel, grumbled some more and changed it again. It was too peculiar all right. Wonder what the IRS would say about it if they took a good look, he asked himself as he thought about the reward they were supposed to offer for uncovering cheats.

EIGHT

Ollie Williams left the maintenance room and clomped outside into the waning light of the quarter moon to see why the number two conveyor belt had stopped. No hurry, it wasn't an unusual occurrence. Nor was it serious, as long as the drive motor hadn't shorted out. But, there was no smell of electrical insulation in the quiet air so he stopped to light his pipe and stepped around the corner of the concrete silo to relieve himself well out of sight of the office. It was very symbolic act. He hated working here. He hated the life destroying night shift, the ear shattering noise, the lung destroying dust, the dignity destroying necessity of having to work so hard just to make a living. Too much work, too much bullshit, too little pay and no respect gained from the old lady sitting at home, getting fatter with the years, and harsher and uglier. Piss on it. Piss on it all, he thought, and did.

And then, just as he began zipping up his pants he heard something hit the ground a little further around behind the tower in the dark. He turned on his flashlight and went in that direction only to be quite astounded by what he saw. The concrete was glowing. Not only was it glowing but, it was flowing. A small stream of molten material was oozing from a growing horizontal slot in the wall of the tower about head high. He examined the extent of the slot further with his light. Jesus, it ran nearly half way around the structure. Worse yet, there was another, earlier slot that had been carved out about six feet higher up which angled downward to join the bottom one like someone might do to notch a tree for felling in the forest.

Good god, what was going on? Fascinated, his gaze locked onto the puddling concrete and growing opening. He stared, unable to move from where he stood. What was causing it? There was no sound, no light except for the glow of the hot material bubbling out of the lengthening opening, no external object sawing away, no vibration, nothing. Then he heard a groan. The groan of the weakened edifice, increasing in volume as portions of it began to crumble. Holy fucking hell, it was beginning to collapse. Finally his feet came to their senses and he began to run. Faster, faster. Come on dammit, the son-of-a-bitch is going over. He ran as he had never run before, not even in High School football. Nor was he running to the shouts of his classmates either but to the frightening tune of crumbling concrete, twisting metal, popping rivets, snapping cables and falling structure, instead. Hell, even old Goliath himself wouldn't have stuck around.

Two minutes later he tried to move his legs. He couldn't. He had stumbled and fallen and now he was half buried in fine gray powder that was in his shoes and up his pants legs and up his nose and in his eyes, his ears and his hair. He coughed, spit, swore, shook his head and tugged at his legs, working one free, then the other. He stood up and attempted to brush the gray dust off his clothes, trying to keep his eyes closed in the process. Impossible. He stopped brushing and started working his way outward into the shallower area of the powder pile that was still settling. Eventually he fumbled his way into the side of the maintenance building a hundred feet away, felt his way along the wall until he found the water tap, turned it on and stuck his head under it to wash out his eyes.

Moments later, soaking wet, he surveyed the damage in the full illumination of the yard lights which someone had by now turned on. He heard voices. "What the hell happened?" someone was shouting. "What the hell happened," everyone was shouting. What indeed, Ollie wondered. And how would he ever explain what he thought he had seen to anyone? He'd loose his job for sure. One thing was certain though. If they didn't think he was a complete nut case it would be a long time before he had to worry about that malfunctioning conveyor. It was crushed, twisted and buried under two hundred tons of debris and cement powder from the seventy five foot tall, reinforced concrete silo.

Kohl was in the process of filling up everyone's Bloody Mary glass the following morning as the Sheriff's vehicle started up his long, winding driveway. When he pulled up behind the house the occupant of the vehicle noted that there were three vehicles in the parking area. A fourteen year old Blazer, a ten year old pickup, a little Mazda Miata and a brand new Mercedes convertible. There was no garage or other buildings, only the house. When the officer knocked loudly on the front door, Kohl shouted, "Around here," from the patio.

When the sun tanned, gun laden, khaki uniformed man in his tightly tapered shirt came around the corner of the house he was greeted by six people who stared at him in mock surprise. "Just in time," Kohl said good naturedly.

The man scowled and looked them over. Kohl, Mike, Jennie, Sue, Buck and Linda. He finally stopped his swiveling head and stared at sinister looking, black bearded Buck sitting there in his black Harley shirt, black pants and black boots who stared unflinchingly back. "Who's house is this?" the stern eyed deputy wanted to know.

"Not mine," Buck said as his eyes clearly added the word, asshole, to his words.

"Belongs to someone in Georgia, I believe," Kohl said.

"What are you all doing here if it's not your house?"

Ha! He thinks he's got us, Buck said to himself.

"I'm sorry but I didn't get your name," Kohl said politely.

"Deputy Richard Ashworth. Want to see some ID?"

"Not for me," Kohl said. "You Mike?"

"Nah," Mike said and shook his head.

"Buck?"

Buck waved his hand indicating no.

"I rent the place through a real estate company," Kohl explained to the man. "Absentee landlord. I'm sure they could tell you where to reach him.".

"You live here then?" he asked Kohl in jutting jawed fashion.

"Yeah," Kohl said, a touch of hardness showing in his eyes.

"Alone?"

"Most of the time. Why?"

"Were you at home last night? Were any of your ah...friends here?" he asked, still eyeballing Buck. Who the hell would want him for a friend? he wondered, examining Buck from a cop's point of view.

"I was at her house in Sedona," Kohl said, looking at Jennie. Jennie smiled coyly and took the opportunity to lean back in her chair, putting a heavy strain on the front of her over stuffed T-shirt. The deputy flushed at that and wished he had enough sense to wear his sunglasses so he might cop a few more looks without being so obvious.

"And I was in Sedona," Mike said with a twinkle in his eyes that seldom left them anymore.

"With me," Sue stated as she rose, went to the table and bent over, thrusting her marvelous buns outward in the deputies direction as she poured herself another drink. Turning around again, she added, "All night!"

As soon as he had recovered sufficiently the man spoke again. "I'm not interested in all that," he lied, wondering how he might somehow learn the identities of all these beautifully stacked females. "Just wanted to know if the person who lived here was home last night." he continued, hoping the opportunity might arise.

"What time did you leave and what time did you get back?" he finally asked Kohl, unable to think of anything else.

"Why? What's wrong?" Kohl wanted to know.

"Something rather unusual happened at the concrete plant last night. Just wondered if you had seen anything. But of course if you weren't here I guess you couldn't have seen anything, could you?" He smiled, now trying hard to appear pleasant, turning the brightest part of it towards Linda who seemed more like his type.

Instead, they pretended to barely notice and all of them turned to look at the complex in the distance across the highway. "Seems to be a lot of activity there for a Sunday morning," Kohl said. "What going on?"

"Sabotage," the officer replied with conviction.

"Sabotage?" Kohl said and gave him a puzzled look, then turned back to the scene across the road. "Looks different somehow," he commented. He went inside, brought out his binoculars and began to scan the complex. "Hmmm," he said in an impressive way and handed them to Mike. "Looks like one of those towers or silos, or whatever they are, fell over."

"Was anyone hurt?" Jennie asked.

"Nothing serious. The night maintenance man inhaled a little cement powder is all."

"That's a relief," Jennie said with a sigh as the officer turned to give her a curious look.

"What happened?" Kohl quickly interjected.

The man turned his attention back to Kohl's demanding voice. "Someone apparently burned through the side of the silo and caused it to collapse," he said as he looked at Buck, the knid of guy who looked suspicious no matter where he might find himself.

"Burned through it?" Kohl said, incredulously. "They look like they're made of concrete. You can't burn through concrete." I should get the academy award for this one, Kohl told himself.

"I know it sounds strange," the deputy said. Hell, it was strange and he was downright puzzled. He also felt like a fool trying to explain such a thing. So what was he trying to explain it for? He didn't have to, but these women had him rattled. Calm yourself, he cautioned. He was here to ask questions, not to answer them. They were supposed to be doing that. "Seen anything unusual around here at all in the last few days?" he asked sternly enough, once again.

"Like what?" Kohl wanted to know.

"I don't know. Anything unusual, I guess."

"Well, I saw this character with his Planet of the Apes monkey mask on trying to ride his bike up the hill yesterday before I left," Kohl said. "Second time this week."

"That's just Willie, our local drug burnout."

"Well, Willie then. That's about it. And the usual tourist traffic up and down the hill."

"You say someone burned a hole throw the concrete tower?" Mike asked the man with grand skepticism, putting him back on the defensive. "Where bouts? Around on the other side?"

All three of the women were looking at him again, waiting.

What else could he do but respond? "Yes," he said, "on the other side. But we're really not sure it was burned through. That's just what the night maintenance man said it looked like happened. They're still digging through the debris to try and find out."

"Ridiculous," Mike said. "That's it? Nothing else?"

"I don't think so but I don't know if it's proper to talk about it yet either, while we're investigating."

"Why not? I live here too, dammit," Kohl said. "And in a concrete house. What if someone tries to burn it down?"

"I'll try and keep you informed," the officer said, looking at Linda's breast's out of the corner of his eye. Then another question occurred to him. "Any of you work there?" he asked. What was it these girls did for a living, he wondered. And how could that one with the short shorts and the marvelous tits ever have admitted to having spent the night with that grease ball bum in the motorcycle shirt? Jesus, shit. Maybe he didn't like her as much as he thought he did.

They all shook their heads in complete innocence. It was the truth. Nothing like the truth.

"Any of you ever work there in the past?"

No, no, no. "Why, do think maybe someone had a grudge against the place?" Sue asked, beaming at him sweetly.

"Don't know. Just asking," he said politely enough.

"I bet it was one of them UFO's," Buck put in. "They can do things like that."

"Or maybe one of those telemetry disks you saw a while back, Kohl," Linda said.

The deputy perked up. "What telemetry disks?" the he wanted to know. "What's a telemetry disk?"

"One night I saw this bright ball of light come down over the house here and skim on over the ridge and down towards the river. It was about two feet in diameter, glowing white and traveling about ten miles an hour. I saw it again a couple of weeks later on the back road into old town Cottonwood. I'm told they're remotely controlled telemetry disks."

"Controlled by who?"

Kohl pointed upward to the sky.

"Let's be serious," the deputy said as he adjusted his gun belt in subconscious emphasis. "This is serious business."

"I'm being serious," Kohl assured him, only to receive an even more dubious look.

"I tried to warn him once before about spending so much time up here alone, but he wouldn't listen," Mike said.

"It's not that," Buck added. "It's just that cheap local beer he's been drinking lately. We'll try and upgrade his taste a little in the future, officer."

The man frowned, squinted and looked them all over again. No sense of humor whatsoever, Buck told himself.

"Can I fix you a drink before you leave?" Kohl asked.

The deputy nodded in the negative, adjusted his Smokey the Bear hat and said, "Well, if you think of anything else, be sure and call us."

"I will be sure and do that," Kohl said as nicely as he was able.

"Salute," they all said in unison as the black and white sedan rolled down the driveway and out the gate. All except Linda.

"What was that all about?" Linda asked, suddenly letting her suspicions rise. Did it have anything to do with all that money Sue had given to Kohl and Mike? She hoped not, also a little jealous of the fact that she hadn't gotten any of it.

"Well, I'm disappointed," Buck said, diverting Linda's question. "He didn't ask me where I was. Too bad you already have a boyfriend, Linda. I would have loved to tell him I was with you."

"All night?"

"Damn right. Even half the night. Or just an hour or so."

"Well, dream on. Maybe some day, big guy," she replied, trying to think of something to get back to her own concerns. But what to say. Maybe Kohl and Mike were where they had said they were all night. That wouldn't surprise her, but still. She felt that she was being shut out of Sue's life a little lately. Why was that?

"Do you think he will be back?" she asked, trying to see if any of them might be concerned.

"Him? Definitely. He'll find an excuse if he thinks you girls are here," Mike said and looked Linda in the eye.

Jennie laughed. "Did you see him blush?" she asked. "His face was redder than my Bloody Mary."

"He seemed to have taken an instant liking to Buck, I noticed,"

Sue commented and flashed Buck a fond look.

"Love at first sight."

"Wasn't it though."

"Well, what do you think happened over there?" Linda asked, directing the question to Kohl, determined to push a little further.

"I have no idea. Sounds pretty bizzare to me. Maybe the maintainence man had too much to drink. Maybe that concrete silo just collapsed from old age or something. What do you think, Mike?"

"I guess we could take a ride up the mountain behind it for a better look. If you're interested."

"Not really. Whatever it was, it couldn't have been very disruptive. All those big cement carriers are still coming and going."

Well, okay, Linda finally decided and got up. "Guess I'd better be going too. Paul is taking me out to dinner tonight."

"Lucky man," Buck said, meaning it sincerely. Linda was definitely on his list. He'd love to get his grizly bear paws on her, all right.

"Thanks. Who knows. Maybe someday you'll get lucky too. Well, see you all later."

"Thanks for coming," Koll said. "We'll walk you to your car."

They all rose and went around the house to the graveled parking area where Linda got in the Miata and drove off.

"Okay," Sue and Jenny both said. "Now that Linda's gone, tell us how you did it."

So far all they knew for sure was that Kohl and Mike had spent hours and hours and days and days working in their rented workspace doing something. It hadn't been that they wanted to withhold anything from the two women, they justed wanted to wait and explain it all once they had done something successful and surprise them with it. And so, now that they had proven the feasability of their approach to things to themselves, it was time to share it with the two people who had helped bring it into existence. Jenny by encouraging Kohl to do something other than just write a book and Sue for trusting them with so much of her money.

"Our machine, the van, was parked here last night with the back pointing off towards the hillside over there," Kohl said. "That's where Buck was with the night scope watching the tower."

"In the dark all alone. Just me, the night vision scope and my mechanized mirror," Buck said. What he hadn't told them was that he also had his music. Whenever Buck was doing something creative, such as blowing up a power line, destroying bulldozers or generally creating havoc, he always took his old Sony Walker along, plugging himself into something classically appropriate for the occasion. Quite often it was Shostakovich, Madam Butterfly, Carmen or some other equally sensitive and powerful work. This time, however, it had been the subdued strains of Beethoven, more in keeping with his removed position from the center of action, he felt. His obsession with music, in sharp contrast to the rest of his life, was his own little quirk, his own secret.

"But how?" Jenny asked. "What did you use that can melt through concrete?"

"An invisible, ultra high powered laser," Kohl elaborated. "Let's just call it an energy beam for now," he said, and went on. "We also had a motorized, remotely controlled, very expensive gold plated mirror over there on the hill to bounce it off of so that we could move it slowly back and forth, causing the beam to scan over the surface of the silo, burning a slot through it."

"That's really possible? Wow. But if it's invisible, how do you know where to point it?"

"It has a small visible laser with a tiny, red beam boresighted to it that we turn on to see where we're aimed. Once we got it spotted on the center of the mirror and buck got the mirror pointed at the right point on the target, we turned on the big laser. Then the battery powered mirror moved the beam back and forth across the target and carved a few neat notches in the concrete. At this point the silo conveniently collapsed in the prescribed direction, wiping out the conveyor system and taking a good portion of the kiln drying tubes with it. Buck then picked up the mirror system and the battery pack and came home. As simple as that."

"Simple hell," Buck said, flexing his shoulders. "You weren't out there stumbling around in the dark through a nest of rattlesnakes with fifty pounds of gear on your back."

"You volunteered."

"Next time I want the executive position."

"What's that?" Linda asked.

"The guy who gets to sit in the van and throw the switch."

"We'll draw straws," Mike said.

"Agreed," Kohl confirmed.

They all stood in a line and surveyed their handy work some more. "Marvelous," Buck said after a while. "I never would have believed it was possible."

"Isn't technology wonderful," Jennie said brightly as she put her arm around Kohl.

"Not perfect though," Buck clarified. "We damned near wiped out the maintenance man. Good thing the dumb fuck stopped to take a piss where he did," Buck said, having watched the man through the night vision scope.

"Yeah," Kohl said, wiping his brow. "Too damned close."

"We're going to have to refine our approach a bit, I guess," Mike said. "Call in a bomb threat or something so they evacuate before we get started."

"Maybe we just don't do it anymore," Kohl suggested.

"You're kidding?" Buck said in extreme disbelief.

"I'm not," Kohl said seriously.

"Kohl!" Jennie said, turning to him.

"What?"

"You promised, remember?"

"What?"

"In there on your living room floor...that morning?"

Kohl was silent for a while, thinking. He turned and put his arms around her, drawing her close. "I'll never forget that morning," he said.

"And I won't let you forget your promise."

"Well, we'll see," he said.

It was a somber moment for them all. Finally Sue asked another question. "Do you think they'll be able to figure it out?"

"I'm sure they will."

"Then what?"

"That's why we used the remote mirror. It will make it look like whoever did it was up on the hilltop over there. To add to that deception Buck sort of borrowed a mini pickup truck yesterday, then drove around up there and backed up to the edge. Left some good prints."

"Is that where you were when I was making lunch?" Jennie said looking at Kohl's truck and glad they hadn't used it instead. "What did you do with it?"

"It's back on the used car lot where Buck found it. So...they'll figure it out but they won't believe it."

"Why not?"

"Because no one would believe you could fit an apparatus like that into a mobile unit as small as a pickup or even that van we bought, simply because it can't be done. I don't think."

"Then what?"

"First they'll try and blame it on the terrorists."

"Except that it doesn't come off as a typical terrorist act."

"That's the problem."

"And after that? Let's hope they don't start looking closer to home."

"Well, one step at a time," Mike said.

"But what about the company you started? What about Sue?" Jenny asked, now a bit concerned, once the reality of it became apparent. "Can't they trace something?"

"It's doubtful. I think we created a very tangled web for anyone to try and unravel," Mike said. He was standing behind Sue now, with his arms around her waist.

"But..."

"But it's all right," Sue said to her. "It's all right. In fact, it's even better than all right. I've never had so much fun in my life."

"She's a big girl," Buck stated candidly. "So are you."

Jenny pondered the thought. What had started out as a highly romantic fantasy was now turning into something serious. Is that what she really wanted? Oh my.

"Well," Sue said after a minute. "We had best be getting back." With that she freed herself from Mike's arms and turned around to look up at him. "See you tonight?" she asked.

He kissed her warmly and said, "Uh huh," in a very affirmative manner.

Kohl, however, didn't have to ask Jenny. She had already told Kohl she was staying there with him so Sue climbed into her very expensive and very bright red car alone. She hit the starter, put down the top, backed around and took off down the hill, her long mane of dark hair flowing in the breeze, leaving a waving foursome behind.

"I still think it was too easy, dammit," Buck said in an irritated voice as he scratched his ten day old beard and sucked at his beer. For some reason Buck's beard always looked ten days old. Never shorter, never longer, always course, curly and crude. How he managed that Kohl never quite understood, but those were the facts. Buck had switched back to beer while the others were still working on the half empty bowl of Bloody Marys. "Too damned easy," Buck emphasized again.

"It was supposed to be," Mike informed him. "That's the whole idea."

"Bullshit."

"Bullshit, bullshit. No blasting caps to worry about going off inside your back pack if you stumble. No dynamite exploding, telling the world for forty miles around what you've been up to, knocking you down in the process, rupturing your eardrums, throwing rocks and shit at you. Are you crazy?"

"Hell no. It's just too damned easy, that's all."

"Dammit Buck. You have to admit that it sure reduces the chances of getting caught, too, when you can be half a mile away from the target."

"Yeah, but. There's something you number crunching, screwdriver wielding, big city boys don't understand at all. That's half the fun of it."

"What is?" Jennie asked, a bit perplexed, now that were back inside Kohl's big house.

"Letting them know what you've done, then outsmarting the assholes and sneaking away in the night."

"Leaving pieces of wire, footprints, fingerprints, scraps of explosive and who knows what else behind," Kohl elaborated.

"Since you haven't tried it, don't knock it. Besides, using the laser is the kinda thing that leaves a signature behind that's pretty unique too, wouldn't you say? That alone could be even more dangerous than dynamite."

"Yes. But, unless they catch us in the act, they have no evidence that we were the ones who did it. Or even that the laser did it, if it came right down to it since any other ordinary, high powered, long wavelength, little old laser would do the same thing."

"If another such beast even existed, which it don't as far as you know. And what if they find the van, then what? Then you're screwed, that's what."

"The van is nicely registered to a fellow who showed up in the obituary last spring. The warehouse is rented in the name of another deceased individual. And as for the van, it's immaculate. Ask Mike. We went over it inch by inch. No fingerprints, no lint, no nothing. And we're going to keep it that way."

The "Van", as they called it was a long bodied, windowless vehicle of the type commonly used by service and trades people. It was a, not too old, not too new, not too shiny, somewhat faded white in color, production line product with four wheel drive, combination off road tires, and roof lights. Nothing obviously extraordinary in and of itself as viewed from the exterior. Nothing to attract undo attention at first glance. Second glance however, might be something else. Modified suspension, skid plates, dual range gear box, overdrive, eight thousand pound winches out of sight underneath front and back bumpers. These were but some of the options, the most deceiving of which lay nested under the stock and slightly dented profile of the factory hood. Securely bolted in place was a rebored, restroked, recammed and reworked eight cylinder block of cast iron with solid lifters, polished ports, tuned headers, fuel injection and ever other bit of finesse and finality that could be funneled into one of Detroit's finest reciprocators.

This gas guzzling, super torque producing monster was in turn connected to a over sturdy, heavy duty four speed automatic gear shifter with beefed up bands and crisp action kit installed. It also had a power takeoff that could be engaged by the operator to drive the specially designed ten kilowatt generator needed by the laser mounted inside what appeared to be an oversized tool box behind the front seats. Sitting there idling, awaiting a word from its master, this dream machine purred as quiet and smooth as a well feed house cat sitting on a warm lap but once in gear, watch out. Pound the accelerator pedal to the floor and the beast roared like an angry bull elephant and grabbed the dirt like a thousand pound African lion going after a gazelle with all claws extended.

Amazingly, even with over sized tires, low ratio differentials and a thousand pounds of dead weight in the back, the thing could still lay down fifty yards of smoking, stinking rubber on the cold asphalt starting from a dead stop.

Inside, the cab was further equipped with compass, radar detector, CB radio, FM Weather Bureau receiver, earth satellite position system and a police emergency band scanners and radios. It also had such convenient niceties as a remotely controlled rear license plate device that could flip any one of three different plates quickly into view as well as switches to shut off the tail lights and the stop lights if desired. To aid in further deception it contained a rack of magnetized, stick-on signs for the doors that proclaimed everything from Plumber to Carpet Cleaners to Telephone Company service vehicle. Other valuable addendum's to the pile were, Road Closed, Detour and Bridge Out signs as gleaned from Abbey readings, as well as Private Property, No Trespassing and other declarative postings. And, as an additional piece of trickery and emergency precaution, it also had a small paint sprayer with ready to apply, fast drying paint in such assorted colors as black, Forest Service green and military olive drab, should they ever get themselves into something really difficult.

But as wonderful as it was or would have been to any fancier of fun, none of it was for show or for play. It had a singular, totally functional purpose. To be able to carry the big laser to within performance range of potential targets and to get it out again and safely home. The laser itself, masterpiece of modern engineering that it was, was cradled inside a steel framed, shock mounted support structure located inside of what could be, or might have been an old storage tank of the kind that one might use to pump out septic tanks, with fake hose attached and all.

Unaware and unconcerned about her distasteful looking exterior, the device's many feet of fully transparent optical grade, gas filled, fuzed quartz tubing still winked and blinked and hummed and glowed happily when powered up as its highly excited molecular contents alternated between an elevated energy state and one of lower value that resulted in an, invisible to the human eye, coherent stream of emerging photons in sufficient and continuous quantity to sear the paint off the bottom side of a passing airliner two miles over head. This prodigious bundle of energy, all contained within a mere two inch diameter beam, was piped up an optical periscope which emerged from the roof vent and could be steered through three hundred sixty degrees in the horizontal and plus or minus thirty five in the vertical. When all was said and done, there was very little that could escape her threat if she was of a mind to make it.

All in all, this extraordinary accomplishment cost the benevolent and farsighted Sue Alexander some two hundred and fifty three thousand dollars in labor and materials. But Sue, bless her, lovely lady that she, only smiled at the bill and bought champagne because the project, in turn, deprived the federal government of nearly half that amount in taxes. Her only regret was the relative emptiness of her king sized bed during the machine's incubation period due to the seemingly unending, months long, multitude of hours that Mike had devoted to the project along with Kohl and, to a large extent, Buck. A regret often shared equally by Jennie and by Jackie since Buck hadn't made the trip to Palm Springs in over six months.

"Well," said Buck accusingly to Kohl. "What's the point of keeping the van flawless and fingerprint free if we're not going after anything else with it? Was this cement plant episode just something to impress the ladies with?"

"I'm impressed, I certainly am," Jennie said. "And you are too, Buck. Admit it, you shit."

"Well...goddammit. I think we..."

"Hold it, hold it. First things first," Mike said, reaching into his pocket and withdrawing a pack of airline tickets. He handed two to Kohl and two to Buck.

"What the hell is this?" Buck asked as he looked at the destination on the first ticket.

"You're off to Hawaii."

"I can't carry dynamite on a commercial airliner. Besides, what's in Hawaii that's worth destroying?"

"Not dynamite, Buck. Jackie."

"Jackie? Why Jackie?"

"Play time."

"No comprende."

"Two weeks. Just you and Jackie and the beach. Want it?"

"Sue's picking up the tab?"

"We set a little aside from the original fund. Kohl and Jennie are off to the Bahamas, Sue and I, the Mediterranean. Anything else we have to discuss can wait till we get back. Okay?"

Buck examined his tickets for the second time, finally finding Jackie's name on one of them. "But what if Jackie won't go? Can I take Linda instead?"

"Jackie will meet you in L.A., day after tomorrow."

"No shit?"

"No shit."

"Son-of-a-bitch."

"My sentiments exactly," Kohl said, looking at Jennie. "Can I lust you on the beach?" he asked her.

"I'd lust you anywhere," Jennie told him in a subdued voice, giving him a small kiss, then stood with her arm around him in a preoccupied way that seemed to have overtaken her.

Later, after Mike and Buck had departed and they were sitting on the patio watching the sunset, Kohl spoke. "Why so quiet?"

Jennie shrugged and refused to look at him.

"Don't you want take this trip?"

She made another gesture that said, I don't know.

Kohl pulled his chair closer. "What's wrong? Tell me please."

She looked at him. Her face seemed sad, as if she were about to cry. "I'm afraid," she said.

"Afraid? Afraid of what?"

"Myself. You. All of it."

"All of what?"

"All of it. Falling in love. It's been so wonderful Kohl, but I feel my old self drifting away, changing, merging with you."

"What's so wrong about that?"

"My identity. I feel as though I'm no longer a separate human being. My existence is getting all scrambled up with yours, more and more. Sometimes it frightens me," she said and rose from her chair and walked away.

Kohl followed and stood by her side. "That's strange," he said. "I've never felt so whole in my life."

She leaned against him. "But I love you Kohl. Too much, I think. And that frightens me."

He waited.

"What if something should happen?"

"What could happen?"

"I don't know. What if you get caught? The thought of that is terrifying."

"So, what do you want to do? We can put an end to the whole thing right now."

"You'd do that for me, even though I was the one who encouraged you and Mike?"

"Absolutely. Is that what you want?"

"I don't know. But if we ended our relationship now an something serious did happen, I could still survive, I think. If we go on much longer I could never live without you."

"You're strong, Jennie. I'd want you to survive, just as you'd want me to."

"I couldn't," she said so quietly her words were almost lost, and started to cry.

He pulled her up, held her close and let the tears come. Later he kissed them away, took her inside, made her a cup of tea and sat beside her.

"So," he asked, "why are we worrying about such silly things just yet. We have a trip to the Bahamas. We'll pretend we just met, go as friends, keep it casual, sun, swim, walk on the beach..."

She brightened, smiled a little, set down her cup, moved closer to him, looked into his eyes. "Casual, you say? What about the lust part?"

"I think we have a room with twin beds."

"Twin beds? Are you kidding?"

"No. That way we have to sleep really close together."

"Who wants to sleep. But why two of them?

"One for nights and one for days."

"Yeah," she said as she put his arms around him.

NINE

Inspector Digand Pry bent down and tried to brush the fine grained, powdery gray dust from his pants cuffs and his shoes. It was impossible. Professor Witley, however, seemed not to notice the mess on his own pants and shoes from wading through the debris below the fallen silo at the cement plant. Shorter, round bellied, baggy clothed, he brushed back his long, shaggy hair instead and adjusted his round, thin, wire framed spectacles, then smoothed out his thick, salt and pepper mustache. Good grief, Pry thought, the guy's got a fixation. He thinks he's Mr. Einstein. Still, in spite of his peculiarities, he seemed pretty astute. There had been no doubt in the professor's mind about the instrument of destruction, either. Carbon dioxide laser, that much was certain. Pry didn't understand the professor's explanation of how the thing worked but it didn't matter, it was obviously the culprit, as had been previously suspected. But, so what? The big question still remained. Who? And why? Unfortunately a whole damned week had already gone by since the crime. Precious time that had been lost because that demented cowboy of a Sheriff had refused to admit he was dead ended before finally turning to the FBI for assistance.

No matter, Pry always got his man, or men, or women as the case might be. And he would get this one too, one way or the other, by gosh. He stroked his badly receding hairline and asked the professor the next question. "Who would have possession of such a device," he wanted to know. "Besides the military."

"My dear fellow. I sincerely doubt if anyone else could."

"That's impossible," Pry said and led the professor away from the damage site out to the parking lot where he had left his car. "The military wouldn't do such a thing."

"Who else, then, my dear Mr. Pry?"

"Don't know. Anything's possible. I learned that somewhere or other. No doubt about that."

"But it takes a great deal of time, money and expertise to build such a device," the professor made clear. "Maybe someone stole it from the government."

Pry merely shook his head in denial. No such luck. He had already checked.

"A foreign power, perhaps?" Witley proposed, and reached inside his suit jacket for his long stemmed pipe. It still had half a load of tobacco in it which he packed down with his forefinger and re-lit with his ten year old Ronson.

"Doubtful," Pry said. Even the Mexicans weren't that desperate or would be that foolish. No, it had to be something else. If he could just figure out the why, then he would know who to begin looking for. And whoever it was, they were clever all right. They had pushed the state of the art in laser development a big step or two. Maybe more than that because, if the professor knew what he was talking about, it was quite impossible to fit a system with the kind of power output that had been demonstrated into anything less than a full sized semi truck, let alone the compact whatever that seemed to be have been used. The power source alone would have taken up half the vehicle. Additionally, the laser itself was also far too delicate to be hauled down a wash board gravel road in the middle of the night. So what was the answer? Two vehicles? A helicopter? Maybe that alien spacecraft Deputy Ashworth kept joking about.

He disengaged himself from Professor Witley and got on the radio with Bradley, his newly assigned partner from the Phoenix office to find out if anyone had noticed anything unusual on the rim road behind the cement plant late that night a week ago. Nothing yet, he was told. Now what? Keep asking questions, he told Bradley. I'll do the same.

Sues ex accountant,Trulock, picked up the small pile of newspapers that had accumulated in the utility room of his Phoenix home and carried them into the living room where he put them down on the fireplace hearth. Maybe if he built a nice cozy fire and got her a glass of wine, his wife might let him back into her bed again. It had been a long time since he had lost the Alexander account. Over four months in fact. Christ, he had apologized to his wife for his bad behavior a dozen times but so far it hadn't done much good. It was time to try something different. But if this didn't work, to hell with it. His secretary wasn't the best looking of women but this was getting ridiculous.

He unfolded the top issue and crumpled it up a sheet at a time, then started to do the same with the second one. As he opened it, however, a headline on the inside page caught his eye. What's this? he wondered and began reading about the mysterious destruction of a cement plant at Clarkdale. He read it a second time as memories of his early meetings with Kohl and Mike came back, along with the many unusual cash vouchers they were always turning in. And then there were the canceled checks made out to companies he had never heard of before, some of which didn't even seem to exist. He had checked on a couple of occasions. He looked at the article once again. No, it couldn't be. They were a couple of engineers or something all right but this was just too far fetched. Those two guys might have been smart enough to con the Alexander woman out of all that money but they weren't smart enough to pull off this. He started to crumple up the page but something stopped him. He tore out the article and placed it in his shirt pocket.

Mike was one who rarely dwelt in the past. No need. Life was a welcome and sought after challenge and he was full of adventure and curiosity, eagerly sampling what the world had to offer every step of the way, setting his own brisk pace for doing so. And here he was, once again involved in something that even his own vivid imagination couldn't have predicted a year ago. An even more powerful experience, thanks to Sue, the spice that sharpened his senses and enhanced his being.

Sue, on the other hand, had often felt stuck in the mucky mire of her own history. Her brutally arrogant, self righteous father and her weak and tearful mother had often left her in emotional disarray as a teenager and young adult with little place to turn in her moments of need. Something that had continually forced her inward to find her own self sufficiency. Thus it was that she had grown up to become what some would choose to label, a tough lady, as she matured. Not at all an invaluable trait, of course, except when it came to men. They, poor things, often felt intimidated. First, by what appeared to be her strength, and later, by her money, making her soon abandoned in favor of something more manageable for delicate egos.

And, as an additional complication, looking for the gentleness she had found so seriously lacking in her father, she had made a bad choice or two by mistaking weakness for tenderness. It included an ex husband. But she hadn't given up, thank god. And now, here was Mike, full of devilish delight, filling up all the voids, washing away the fears, releasing the woman within that had long been forced into restraint. Another flower beginning to bloom in the sun of love's brighter day where the word "more" became her most used word.

"More", she said when he kissed her, "more," when he teased her tenderly, "more," when he made love to her. Would there ever be enough, she sometimes wondered.

It was mutual. So too did Mike wonder if he would ever get enough of the wonder he found to be so wonderful in her. It was what he was feeling at that moment watching her sitting bronzed and golden on the edge of the dock in her bikini, moving her toes in the blue water of the Mediterranean, trying to attract the tiny tropical fish swimming nearby. She seemed so totally contented, yet there was one thing he had to know. "Any regrets?" he asked from where he sat by her side.

It seemed to puzzle her. She turned to him. "About what?"

"The money...the project...me."

"Mike, shame on you. You know how I feel."

"Yes, but technically you're a criminal now, thanks in part to me. What about that?"

"Not in part, thanks to you. Not at all, thanks to you. But of my own free will, remember."

"Well, maybe, but..."

"No buts and no regrets."

"But what if we continue?"

"Then I want to be involved. And not just as an observer."

"Sue," he said, very concerned.

She placed her fingers on his lips. "Shhh," she said gently. "I mean it. My life has taken on a whole new purpose, thanks to you and Kohl."

"Thanks to me and Kohl you may have gotten yourself into a lot of trouble," Mike reminded her.

She merely laughed at him. "It's so exciting. It's all so exciting. Loving you, thinking about the future and loving you some more, maybe someday even blowing up that damned dam, as Jennie calls it. Wouldn't that be something?"

Mike knew it would be something all right but he still didn't like the thought of her being so directly involved. No, he didn't like that at all. He wanted her safe and uninvolved as much as possible. Somehow he would have to change her mind if they continued on this path. He sat, not answering her, thinking about it. She took his head in her hands and turned his face back towards hers. "Kiss me," she told him and leaned closer. He kissed her lightly. "More," she said.

He kissed her again, longer this time. "More, she repeated sexily and squirmed even closer. What else could a man do with such a headstrong woman except to try and oblige her?

Four thousand miles away to the west Jennie and Kohl lay on the sand of a different shore soaking up the same sun. Thus far they had neither talked about the status of their present relationship nor about the future. Wisely, Kohl had avoided all such discussion and had simply dedicated himself to seeing that Jennie had a good time, which she appeared to be doing. So was he. He lay there on his side, head propped up on his arm, visually indulging himself while she seemed to be napping. As he lingered at her bustline, however, dressed as she was in a two piece suit whose upper half had been discarded, she turned from her back to her tummy, catching him in the act.

"Only one more day left," Jennie said with a regretful sigh after Kohl had adjusted his sun glasses and laid back down.

"Yeah," Kohl said in the same tone.

"Can't you and Mike also invent a time machine?"

"Where would you go if we did?"

"Nowhere."

"Then why the time machine?"

"Because, if it worked, it would seem that you should also be able to suspend time as well as go back and forth in it."

"You'd suspend it?"

"Yes, right here in this place. Keep things the same day after day. The sky and the sea, you and me, tranquility. No strife or worry, no insane world beating at us, no money to try and earn, no problems to solve."

"Dream on, fair damsel, and take my hand that I might be marooned here with you, should it come true."

"If only I had the power," she said and sat up. She wrapped her arms around her legs, put her chin on her knees and stared pensively out at the distance where sky and water merged. "Have you reached a decision?" she asked after a bit.

"About using the laser some more?"

"Not really. And to think I only started out to write a book. Just a simple little book. Abbey's sequel, damn him."

"Damn him?"

"Yes, dammit. He did his readers a terrible disservice by dying so soon, me included. I miss him, and all the books he was capable of writing had he lived a little longer. It's not fair. And now I can't do it either."

"But you could Kohl, and you can."

"What, document my step to step involvement in subterfuge and subversion? Not if we start up that van again."

"I suppose you're right."

"What a dilemma. It's also too late to try and convert that thing to some peaceful purpose, too. One look at it and we'd all be in the slammer."

"So, what do you want to do?"

"I'm content to quit while we are ahead," Kohl shrugged, reluctant to admit he had backed himself into such a corner.

"And if we don't?"

"Well, then I'd have to move out of that house."

"Why?"

"Too close to the scene of the original crime, too easy to keep an eye on, too easy to tell when we come and go. Too bad too. I'd really miss the view."

"It's a beautiful house. But mostly I'll miss that spot on the living room floor in front of the fireplace."

"Yes, that was very important," he agreed.

"What else?" she asked, knowing there was more to what he felt about where he lived.

Kohl explained how he was beginning to understand what Thoreau must have felt living at Waldon pond, getting a close look at the nature surrounding him. Something that he, Kohl, could only semi-relate to before. He told her again about watching the many varieties of ants all trying to carry away things three times bigger than themselves, the lizards who stopped to stare at him, bees who would land on his hand to see what he tasted like, field mice trying to sneak into the house when he left the screen door open, spiders who could reconstruct their webs over night, the bright blooming cactus, Road Runners squawking, Orioles in the ocotillo, the great white owl in the old mine shaft back on the hill. All of it. It would hurt to leave. Unfortunately, it seemed necessary if they were to continue.

"If only..." she said but didn't finish, knowing that such a dream was not to be had. The list of, if onlys, was much too long and mankind had gone too far astray to easily return to some point of balance and common sense where life might be peaceful and serene. Although there was still choice, the choice remaining, however, was either to just give up, with head deeply buried in dark, damp sand, or, to somehow make an effort to honor the truth as she saw it and to try and help bring about change. In the end therefore, being who she was and feeling what she did, there was no choice at all, only a path to follow.

Some many more time zones away in the mid-Pacific, Buck was having his own set of thoughts as he lay in bed next to Jackie on the top floor of the sparkling new and very expensive Kuwai Hahatuma Hotel. Jackie was quietly drifting off to sleep again after their, just completed, round of early morning instinctive compulsion that had always seemed to be the major focus of their relationship. Something which Jackie occasionally shed a tear or two over but Buck seldom noticed. Until they had come to Hawaii, that was. Now it had turned into what was mostly on his mind. He had hardly looked at another woman in all the time they had been there. Not even the tender young maidens lounging on the beach in their mini G-strings, and that had him bothered. Was he getting old, or what? And how come Jackie looked so damned good to him all of a sudden? Was it the fifteen pounds she had lost? No, it had to be more than that.

Suddenly he felt a strong tinge of sentiment wash over him and he began wishing he had treated her a little better sometimes back there in the past. He also had a vision of them living a little closer together. Ridiculous, he then told himself. His name was Buck and he didn't get all that hung up on one woman. That was pure folly. And besides, what about his reputation? Couldn't just let that slip away, now could he?

He forced himself to think of Linda, visualized getting his hands on her, helping her out of her clothes and onto her back. Yes, yes, yes. It helped for a moment but only a moment. The warmth of Jackie's smooth skin, much closer to home, soon pulled him back. They had shared some interesting adventures together, that was for damned sure. Remember that time when they were spiking trees up in Oregon and the helicopter spotted them? And what about having to spend a whole day lying together in that weed and water filled ditch over by Sequoia because they had lingered too long trying to sabotage every last bulldozer? Damn, she certainly would make a great ally in some of his upcoming adventures all right, provided Kohl and Mike had enough good sense to continue with what they had started, of course. The dumb shits. Didn't they see what they had at hand. They could revolutionize revolution and anarchy both.

The thought of not being able to take advantage of it made him feel nauseous. Then it dawned on him. Son-of-a-bitch. He'd steal the damned thing from them if they didn't continue, that's what. Hell, they'd be helpless to report it, that's for sure. Serve them right for wasting such an opportunity. Then he'd get Jackie to move to Arizona and they'd take care of all those things that needed taking care of, you could bet your butt on that.

Having finally arrived at that option as a possible solution to what seemed to have been bothering him the most, he smiled broadly, scratched his beard, scratched his belly, scratched his butt, got up, went to the bathroom, then snuck back in between the sheets, snuggling full length up to Jackie. She purred slightly in her dream and he was soon back to sleep. Two happy cats in their temporary, silk lined cradle, one always in heat, the other liking the scent now more than ever.

TEN

Tricky, tricky, tricky, far, far too complex, too, too complicated, much too much of a chance for a foul-up, intervening gremlins, the tricky trickster or plain old error, human frailty and fumbling failure. Not enough people for all the tasks either. Should have had at least a seven more for the job but only have six total and three are women, none of whom should have been there in the first place. And they were using dynamite, for God's sake, and that was something Kohl had an inherent distaste for right from the beginning. Maybe it was because he had no experience with it, didn't understand it and was therefore, afraid of it. But there seemed no other way, the job was too big and too complex and somehow he felt he could trust Buck to handle that part of it wisely. Besides, by now there were already one hundred and eight sticks in place, with but only eighteen or twenty left to go. Unfortunately, they would be much tougher to place, however.

There were lights on out there, everywhere.

There were also the phone lines that had to be cut, radios to knock out, police cars to immobilize, a highway to block at both approaches, the internal power plant to disable and, last but not least, the roofs of four immense concrete penstock towers to burn through and make collapse. Each and every thing in its turn, all in proper sequence for maximum effect and maximum disruption, the totality of which, when completed, left only a narrow window of time to be able to get the hell out of there in, to escape through, hopefully intact without leaving any body parts or damning evidence behind.

Timing, ever so critical, super critical. And there he stood in the darkness, waiting helplessly, a two week growth of itching, dark stubble on his face to help as a disguise in case he should be seen, along with a slouch hat, denims, boots and tool belt. Waiting, waiting as precious time ticked away while two goldbricking dip-heads stood outside on the deck by the breakers, talking not more than ten feet away.

They complained about their wives and their boss, slandered the fetching eyed change girl at the casino just up the road with dirty innuendos, bragged about their manhood and belittled the rest of humanity. Bullshit, bullshit, bullshit, on and on and on. Balls, Kohl said silently with all the mental energy he could summon. Shut the hell up, go away, go back to work, go take a shit, go somewhere else and talk. He still had oil to drain from three more giant electrical breakers. They didn't have to be empty either, half would do but that was over a hundred gallons apiece. And through a garden hose of all things. The fluid had to go into the river, couldn't help that, but not directly onto the deck. They would have been discovered hours ago if they had done that. Might even still be if these two dead heads were half conscious. One of them had even stood on the hose for a few minutes shutting off the flow. Good thing there was turbulence in the river where the spot lights shown on it here in the middle of the chilly January night along the Arizona-Nevada border.

It was a good thing too, that they had enough sense to shop for black hose instead of buying the standard, garden variety of household green when they purchased it. What a give away that would have been. Even these two would have caught on to that.

And now one of them was lighting up another cigarette.

Goddammit, Kohl muttered to himself. What was he doing here anyway? Why wasn't he home, sitting safely in front of his computer writing this story like he had originally intended to, walking through it on the keyboard without jeopardy instead of living it out like some mad, adrenaline soaked fool, lurking there in the damp, dark shadows of the night full of fear, anxiety and tension, senses strained to the breaking point?

Nice place, home. Nice contraptions, computers. Who needed all this "real life adventure" shit that Buck was so hung up on, anyway? Living it out on the machine had to be better. Then, if something broke, fell apart, got left behind, out of step, or overlooked it was a simple matter to backspace or cut and paste until you had it right. You could also withdraw at any moment, take a break without fear of discovery, have a cup of coffee, go take a leak, turn on the stereo, look out the window, take all the breaks you wanted. And then, when you had enough for one evening, you could light a fire in the fireplace, spread a blanket on the floor and sip sweet wine with Jennie. Unbutton buttons, feel fingers playing over soft skin, watch the shadows on the wall, fall asleep all warm, secure and entwined, wake to the sun of a new day and be able to start all over again.

Goddamned fool! Idiot! Bonehead! But it was too late now, wasn't it? Here he was five hundred and forty feet below the water level of Lake Mead held in place by the immensity of Hoover Dam. A furtive intruder he was, hiding behind a ten ton circuit breaker inside a high, wire mesh fence with a broken padlock hanging on the gate, forced to listen to an asinine, nerve frazzling, precious time wasting conversation while one hundred and thirty thousand volts of raw electrical energy quietly hummed and bussed through the bare and exposed conductor half as big around as his arm less than ten feet away overhead. Tamed and carefully controlled for the moment, but get a few feet closer and it had the full potential to turn him into a tiny, well done cinder crisp within microseconds, should he get tangled up in it. There was enough energy in that one little wire to light all the lights, power the appliances and run all the TV sets in fifty thousand typical, over indulgent, middle class American homes. Just this one wire, one phase of one power line.

There were seventeen hydro powered generators inside the dam in all, some paralleled together to yield nine major power lines leading off into the reaches of the southwest. Las Vegas, Phoenix, Anaheim, Burbank, Los Angeles and elsewhere. Nine power lines, three wires each, twenty seven total, with twenty seven separate circuit breakers here to protect them in case of emergency. And more batches of circuit breakers up on the hill alongside the road leading to Henderson, separated into two different substations. There were already more broken padlocks on the fences up there, and more oil saturating the ground. But only a direct, visual inspection would reveal that sabotage and no one ever went into the substations late on a chilly night unless there was a problem. From the viewpoint of the technicians working inside the generating station here deep inside the dam everything was still intact. Meters and gauges all read normal, sensing devices were all in the green. There was no power loss on the line, no remotely measurable difference in performance.

Billions and billions of electrons remained in silent, steady, rhythmic, sixty cycle motion, lighting homes hundreds of miles away, running refrigerators, pumping water, crisping the toast in the toaster. Even here at the source where Kohl crouched in the shadows where the one single, bare, brute of a wire hung dangerously and uncomfortably close to his own fragile body, it was still serene and misleadingly quiet. But not for much longer. Once they drained the arc suppressing oil from the breakers, blew up some of the towers down line and shorted that immense source of power to ground, guess what? The protective breakers would automatically begin to open as they were supposed to do, pulling the giant electrical contacts apart inside the bath of oil, attempting to break the flow of current in the line to safeguard the gargantuan, water driven generators inside the power house. Unfortunately, when they did the oil levels would be much too low, and, because of the tremendous voltages involved, the current would continue to flow, arcing across the gap with such intensity that it would fry all the insulation on the millions of dollars worth of generators inside the plant, rendering them totally useless and out of service for some extended period of time. Perhaps more than a year. Then, before completely melting the breaker contacts, the remaining fluid inside the vessel would become almost instantaneously superheated, creating a tremendous pressure that should in all likelihood throw shrapnel half way across the river when it ripped apart. It was no place to be when that moment arrived.

And in the meantime, while they were still down there secretly preparing the stage for such a grand display, and while there were still employees inside the dam, they had better hope to god that nothing happened somewhere else in the network. Hope that, for example, some hung over, lost all his money, small plane pilot taking off from Vegas didn't crash into a power line. Or that some strung out truck driver didn't leave the highway somewhere and knock down a tower. Or that a stray lightening bolt didn't hit the system anywhere within a hundred miles or so. Or, heaven forbid, that any one of their own hand built, one hundred and eight individual, radio controlled detonators didn't malfunction by failing to reject some unwanted signal from somewhere out there in the night. A CB radio perhaps, or a low flying aircraft, spurious noise, static, a marginal electronic component, whatever. There were at least a dozen distinct possibilities, any one of which would create a disaster if it were to go off ahead off schedule.

So what else could go wrong? Kohl asked himself for the hundredth time. Too damned many things, that's for damned sure, but better not think about that. Think about Jennie up there in the rocks behind the casino where he had left her two hours earlier after they had set all the charges on the tower lines scattered through the surrounding harsh, rocky, impossible countryside, picking only those towers that were well away from roads, paths, trails, buildings or houses to prevent any possibility of human injury.

Poor Jennie, all alone in the dark and the growing chill of the night, waiting for the final signal which was his to give. Sweet, sweet Jenny. How he wished that she, at least, were safely home where she belonged. She might be too, if the terrain had been more favorable and she hadn't insisted on being a part of it. They should have also built a remote relay station to handle that function, but hell, there had been just too damned much to do, too many details to be taken care of and they had to be here on this particular dark of the moon night. If they waited another month there would be larger night crews working, doing routine generator overhaul. The warmer weather would also mean more night traffic on the dam, too. Who knew what else.

But then it occurred to him that, if it weren't for Jennie, he wouldn't even be here. None of them would be. So much for promises made in the heat of the day on the living room floor. But he couldn't blame her. No one could. They were all adults, weren't they? Big people with freedom of choice. Any one, or all of them, could have changed their minds at any time, backed out and gone a different way. So, okay, forget that. But, what was it that seemed to be happening to Jennie herself, of late?

Had he sensed a change of attitude or was it just the growing anxiety she had felt along with everyone else as the final day approached? He wasn't sure. Had she done a trip on herself in the beginning, thinking about it, visualizing the excitement, seeing her involvement as valorous and glorious? And then, as the day of truth approached, did she begin to see the reality of it and begin to have other thoughts?

There certainly was no glamour here. There would be no glory, no public recognition, no outside reward, either. No, there was nothing but climbing over rocks in the dark carrying backpacks full of high explosives, stumbling around, skinning knees, sweating, swearing, worrying, waiting in the cold by herself while he and Buck made their way down inside the dam and drained the oil from those twenty seven circuit breakers.

Waiting. He knew that would the hardest thing of all for her because it opened the door to emotion. Waiting for the anticipated instruction to come from him via radio to push the button. An instruction that might not even come if something were to go wrong. And if that instruction didn't come, then she was still bound to make an additional nerve racking, worrisome wait because of the agreement to follow through with her part of the mission regardless of what might have happened to the rest of them. And in that case, it would mean yet another hour of wondering for her. Had they simply gotten behind schedule or had they gotten injured, found out or captured.

But she had promised. Wait another hour, then do it anyway. Hit the detonation switch before trying to find her way back to the safety of the car in the dark by herself. Could she do it, if it came to that? And how would she do in a real crisis? Would she be resolute enough, strong enough, sure enough or was she too soft, too fragile, too misguided in her own belief system to follow through? There was no way to tell.

And what about Buck, that crazy son-of-a-bitch. Had he taken his music with him in spite of Kohl's instructions? Was he just wandering around with his stereo headset on, half oblivious to the rest of the world, humming away, tapping out a rhythm on whatever was close and handy? How were things going on his side of the dam? Had he planted the charges which were to take out the separate, internal power generator which supplied just the needs of the dam as yet? And how was he doing on the draining of the other twelve breakers over there? Were these two assholes out here trying to impress each other holding him up, too? You could see across the river.

He and Buck had waved at each other earlier. So, was he still over there or had he finished and moved back inside to complete the balance of his assignment? Or had he not been paying attention, screwed up and gotten caught? Was it all too late anyway? Kohl wondered. Should he call it off? Should they all just try and get the hell out of here while they still had a chance? It wasn't completely too late yet. But it soon would be. Putting a little old, privately owned cement plant out of business was one thing Rendering a mighty, power producing, super hydroelectric generating station, property of the United States government, totally useless was something else. What was the penalty for that, three hundred and fifty years? Or more? Questions, questions, questions. Nerve destroying questions. Kohl shivered. He had to be out of here and back on top in less than forty minutes. What the hell was he going to do? He fondled the oversized crescent wrench he was holding, swung it lightly back and forth in the shadows, getting the heft of it, half seriously considering wrapping it around a pair of skulls when finally the P.A. system came booming on, echoing off the canyon walls.

"Bill Hawser, line two. Bill Hawser, line two," the bored to death voice of the security guard repeated.

"Shit," one of the two men standing not far enough away from Kohl's hiding place said as he flipped his cigarette out into the river. "There's the old lady checking up on me again. Wonder what her excuse is this time?"

His companion made a comment. They laughed and moved

84

back towards the interior. Kohl sighed and went back to work.

Against his own personal desires Buck had complied and had left his stereo headset back in the car, even though he had selected Verdi's Rigoletto for the evening's work. Appropriate enough, he thought, for such a grand performance as this promised to be. The tale of a buffoon who unwittingly participates in the abduction and murder of his own daughter. Why not? He always performed better with the sound of an orchestra in the background. But perhaps Kohl was right. He wasn't used to working in such crowded conditions. There were too many people around, few as they were, and too much chance of getting caught. And worse, things were not going very well. Not very well at all, goddammit.

First of all he didn't like electricity, not one damned little bit. He didn't even like having to jump start his old truck once in a while and always got someone else to put the cables on for him if he could finagle it. And here he was having to work on these brutish things called circuit breakers with all them megawatts or kilovolts or whatever they were, humming through them. Sure as hell they were going to arc over and singe all the hair off his head, crinkle up his beard and his pubics too. Hell, at the least they would probably make him sterile, standing right next to them like he had to do. Especially in the middle of the night.

Then, to add to his distress, he couldn't get the valve open on the first breaker he attempted to drain. The handle broke off the damned thing and he had no way to turn it. But he went on. Kohl said that if worse came to worse they didn't have to get them all drained. One out of three would probably do the trick, two out of three was better yet and all of them made it guaranteed. That's what he liked, however. Guarantees. If he was going to destroy something he wanted guarantees, not odds and probabilities. Now if they could have used dynamite on the breakers also, then he would have had more confidence in the outcome. That would have been the best guarantee of all to his way of thinking.

But, even though he didn't completely understand what purpose draining the oil out of these bastardly things was going to accomplish, he still trusted Kohl and Mike. Implicitly, now that they had taken on a real project. They were some smart dudes, those two. Anybody who could build a device that would burn through six inches of concrete and knock down a cement plant from half a mile away was all right in his book any day. Damned right. Those were the kind of guys to stay friends with.

They were imaginative too and he had to admit that this night really promised to be a lot of fun before it was over. If nothing else got fucked up, that was. Such as his third breaker. Rusty old shit. What was the matter with these assholes anyway. Didn't they understand about periodic maintenance. The second had gone easy enough but the third valve wouldn't shut off once he got it opened and in the process of trying to force it, the drain hose came off and he couldn't get it back on. Oil was gushing out all over the deck. Panic time, what to do now? Be resourceful, he told himself. Improvise. With that he removed his jacket, took off his thick flannel shirt and managed to stuff one sleeve of the heavy fabric into the hole and stop the flow.

Unfortunately, in the process, his boots, socks and pants legs became thoroughly soaked. Then he slipped in the super slick goop and drenched the rear of his jeans and everywhere he walked he left big, oily footprints. Squish, squish, squish. Well shit. Can't have that. Might as well paint arrows on the walkway, dumb fuck.

So, to solve that problem, he walked as far back towards the main building as the oil on his boots held out, leaving traces so that if anyone did come out here they would at least think he had gone back inside. At this point he returned to the wire cage surrounding his next electro-mechanical victim and reached for the bolt cutters to break the lock so he could enter. Of course his leather gloves were also oil soaked, as were most of the tools hanging from his belt. As a result the cutters slipped from his grasp and clanged and banged to the ground while he quickly retreated to the shadows. He waited, peeked around, waited, looked across the river to where Kohl was working to see if he had heard the noise. Apparently not. No Kohl in sight. Buck emerged from hiding once again.

This time he was more careful and obtained entry inside the cage without further incident. Inside, while waiting for the breaker to drain, he took off his boots and socks, then removed his jacket again, slipped out of the T-shirt he had been wearing under his shirt and used it to wipe off his feet and the inside of the boots. Carefully though, he left a little between his toes. Ought to help clear up that nasty bout of athlete's foot he had picked up on his last trip to California and couldn't get rid of. Damned right. Should work, you frigging fungus you. Good thinking Buck.

He almost stashed the socks and shirt behind the breaker but then wondered if perhaps those FBI guys with all their super analyzers couldn't determine his blood type or something from the sweat on his clothes so he ended up tossing them in the river, somehow forgetting about the shirt he had left behind stuffed in the drain of the previous breaker. Fortunately for all concerned, however, the remainder of his outside task proceeded in an orderly fashion and because he had three fewer breakers to drain than Kohl and the first one he couldn't get open, he was already done and had been inside when the two maintenance men came out for their break. Too bad for them. They missed a good laugh when Buck slipped and fell, pawing the air on the way down, then found it almost impossible to stand up again on the slick surface and fell twice more.

But Buck was spared the indignity of his mishap as well as being discovered in a covert act and managed to get back inside before the lack of his shirt, undershirt and socks in the cold air caused him serious discomfort. First he found the men's locker room. Fortunately, there was no one in there. He looked in the mirror. Holy shit. There was oil on his clothes, his face, his beard and in his hair and still more making an occasional drip off some of his tools and pant legs onto the floor. The oil also covered a goodly part of a battery powered, radio signal relay he carried and the single stick of dynamite with its radio controlled detonator that it had to activate in the wee hours of the night.

Taking a chance, he quickly washed his face as best he could with paper towels and liquid soap from the dispenser. Then he started searching through the workmen's lockers that were open, and finally found a pair of jeans that might fit. Too filthy, he decided at last, and put them back. Ain't wearing somebody else's raunchy damned clothes, he told himself, not even at a time like this. Instead he pulled a couple dozen more paper towels from the wall cabinet, went to the farthest toilet stall and shut himself in just in time to avoid the roving night watchman.

"Jesus Christ," the watchmen said after he had finished his little ordeal at the urinal and had decided to wash his hands at the same sink Buck had used earlier. "What a miserable mess," he said, commenting on the oil stained porcelain fixture, and moved to the next sink.

Buck, knowing that the man, whoever he was, knew that he was in there decided correctly that there was no point in trying to pretend differently. Buck didn't know he was the watchmen however, because, even though he tried peaking through the crack around the door of his stall he couldn't see him from there. But he played it out anyway. He flushed the toilet, sending the first handful of towels that he had used to soak up some of the oil from his shorts and jeans down the tube. But then, apparently because he hadn't come out of the stall by the time the watchman had washed and dried his hands, combed his hair and re-stuffed in his shirt tail, (he too was going to stop at the casino on the way home) the man spoke again.

"You all right?" he wanted to know.

"Yeah," Buck grumbled.

"Gonna be a cold one out there tonight," the watchman continued, friendly enough, for he was a friendly enough fellow, he thought. Besides, what was the hurry. A little conversation here and there along the way of his rounds helped break up the monotony. It wasn't the first time he had ever had a few words with someone sitting on a stool behind a closed door, either. It all helped pass the time and he was convinced that he had the world's most boring job. Maybe he did. The only thing of significance that had ever happened at night in all the hundreds and hundreds of nights he had worked there had been a car with a flat tire that had swerved up onto the sidewalk and crumpled the door on the visitors ticket booth topside. And he hadn't even been up there to witness it.

Buck however, was not interested, not at all. "Yeah," he grumbled back again, even more grumbly than before and flushed another wad of towels down the toilet. Then he made what sounded like a moan or a groan.

"You sure you're all right?" came the question again.

"Leave me alone, goddammit," Buck muttered. "I got the goddamned flu, goddammit. Don't need no goddamned conversation."

"Billy?" the man questioned, thinking he recognized the voice.

"No, goddammit. Get the fuck out of here. Person can't even take a crap in peace anymore," Buck said, wishing he were capable of making some disgusting sound effects while he was at it to go along with his harsh words. Instead he flushed the toilet for the third time.

The watchmen mumbled something that sounded derogatory and left. Once Buck heard the doorway close behind him he hurriedly used up the remaining paper towels, wiping down his tools, gloves and clothes. Then he took a full roll of toilet paper, wrapped it round and round his feet in the form of makeshift socks, put his boots back on and cautiously left the locker room. From there on things went somewhat easier for him.

Sue parted the dark curtains leading to the back of the van, crawled through and set another cup of black coffee down beside Mike where he was peering through the telescopic sight, watching the oozing concrete seep from the growing wound he was making around the top of the Nevada penstock nearest the dam as he gently guided the beam of intense, invisible radiation along, the only indication of its presence being the thin slots it had burned through the thick concrete of the tower, carving the slightly dome shaped roof up into pie shaped segments. "How you doing, you handsome thug you?" she asked and put her hand on the shoulder of the stained coveralls he was wearing.

Mike leaned back from the eyepiece, threw back his shoulders, stretched, rotated his head in a large circle to loosen up his neck muscles and grinned at her through all the extra hair on his face. Even after all these many months of having known each other, Sue still went completely weak whenever Mike smiled, something he did constantly, it seemed. Here was the kindest, warmest, smoothest tempered, grinningest man she had ever met in her whole life. And that was just a small portion of his attributes and what she thought of him, even though she knew this particular smile was for a different reason. Did she look that awful?

"Another twenty minutes ought to do it," he said as he scratched the beard he was not used to wearing and flipped a switch on the panel before him that placed the machine in the auto mode for the moment. "Only two more to go," he said cheerfully. The van was parked on the Arizona side of the river in the lot on the bluff overlooking the area, backed up to the edge so as to give Mike a clear line of sight to the penstock towers rising from the placid waters of Lake Mead adjacent to the dam.

Although they seemed to have their foundations on the floor of the lake, the penstocks were actually hung on the sides of the steeply angled canyon walls. There were four total, two on each side. The huge, hollow concrete towers were connected to thirty foot diameter pipes far below the water's crest that served to route the many millions of gallons of necessary water downward to the inlets of the mammoth hydro turbines. The turbines then converted the tremendous momentum of the water into rotary motion, spinning the electrical generators deep inside the dam. Water power became electrical power. Hydo-electric.

The plan was for Mike, with the help of the laser, of course, to almost slice the domed roofs of the penstocks into a number of comparatively smaller segments. Almost meant that he couldn't totally cut any of them completely out. He had to leave just enough support so they wouldn't collapse before the precisely proper moment later in the night. Again, timing was critical. And since they all had to go at once, he could only weaken them. The final precision would still have to be accomplished with nothing more sophisticated than Buck's favorite medium of expression, plain old dynamite.

Those charges had already been placed by their most adventuresome member somewhere around dusk and were neatly centered on top of each tower where Mike could see them through his sighting and aiming telescope, something he had to carefully avoid letting his energy beam drift too close to. How Buck had actually managed to place those charges out there in the full light of late afternoon was still a complete mystery to Mike, but it would have to wait. They could talk about it later.

And speaking of timing, Kohl and Mike had worked out the details for the multitude of events down to the very last second. Some of it was that critical. Most of it in fact. Especially the part that would begin once Buck and Kohl had emerged from below.

"We have company again," Sue stated before Mike had a chance to touch his coffee or to touch Sue, which is what he and she both wanted to do the most. She moved back to the front of the van, slid in behind the driver's seat and waited to see who was pulling into the parking area this time.

"Who is it?" Mike asked over the sound of the idling engine.

"Just another car," Sue said as she watched the vehicle stop three spaces away. A man and a woman got out, left the vehicle running, and went to the edge where they could look down on the site below. They huddled together for a moment, staring at the dam, brightly illuminated by dozens of spotlights and street lights on the structure and along the roadway, then quickly returned to the car. Inside, in the dim glow from the stars and the lights below Sue watched the man put his arm around the woman and pull her nearer. He kissed her. A long kiss. Another. They seemed oblivious of the van. Movement, repositioning, straying arms and hands. "I want to go home," Sue said.

"What's the matter?" Mike asked.

"They're making out and I'm getting excited," She stated.

Oh shit, Mike said to himself, knowing how Sue could be when she got turned on. He loved it, but this was hardly the place or the time, not even for a quickie. Dammit. "Hit the horn," he said. "Let them know we're here."

"They know we're here. They probably think we're in the back doing the same thing."

"Hit the horn Sue. Please? I won't be able to burn a straight line if you keep jumping around."

"You're no fun at... Oh well, so much for that. Here comes another car. Oh, oh. Mike, it's a cop."

Car nine hundred twenty six. It was brave Arizona Highway Patrol officer Smitzen, rolling in to check things out before turning around and heading back towards Kingman. One of his favorite spots, this one. Especially in warmer weather when you could occasionally catch someone in the back seat of their car going to it. The real thing, man. Better than those glossy old porno magazines any day. Had to be careful though and not get too overwhelmed. One time he almost made the mistake of asking if he couldn't be second.

Better to just do as much looking as you can in the dark, (full moon nights were the best), or, if it was too dark, then in that brief instant when you first shined the flashlight in the window. Then back off and wait till they sat up and asked what the problem was. And, if they weren't married, check the girl out, look at their licenses and see if she's the kind that might invite you over some time after you reminded her of the circumstances under which you met. When you were off duty, that was.

As his headlights swung in an arc across the parking lot, hitting first the van and then the car, the couple in the car sat up. Then, when they noticed the red and blue light bar on the roof of Smitzen's patrol vehicle, the man turned on his lights, put the car in gear and backed out of the parking space.

Still unnoticed by Smitzen, Sue pulled the bill of her baseball hat down further and slid down in the seat, pretending she was taking a nap. Smitzen parked his car opposite, reached for his flashlight, turned off the lights and got out. It was then that it dawned on him that there were no windows in the back of the van. They could be doing any damned thing they pleased back there and he wouldn't be able to get a look at it Shit, he said, embarrassed at his own stupidity. He almost turned around and went back to his car but then noticed Sue's outline in the driver's seat. He had to save face and follow through now. He pointed his flashlight in the window.

Look at that long haired asshole pretending to be asleep, he said to himself. The person didn't even move. He rapped on the door with his free hand. The person blinked and stared back. God, it looked like a girl, or was it. Dirty hat, dirty coveralls, frazzled, uncombed hair, smudged face. Christ, no wonder she was sitting here alone. He watched as she rolled down the window. "What'sa matter chief?" she asked in an assumed voice.

"What you doing here?" he asked with new found authority, thinking this one might be kind of fun. Probably had some outstanding tickets, maybe even a record for something petty. Losers like this were always fair game. And the nice part was that this kind never fought back. Maybe he ought to have her get out and spread em. He considered it but her clothes looked awfully filthy. Still, she looked like she had a great set of lungs on her.

"It's a long story," Sue started to say before he interrupted.

"Would you get out of the vehicle please," he said, having made his decision.

Sue shrugged. "Whatever you want chief," she said and

opened the door.

"Face the vehicle, place your hands on the hood and spread," Smitzen instructed her.

"But sir, what's the idea?"

"Just do it."

Sue shut the door and moved forward not quite sure how to oblige. "Just be very careful where you put your hands," she warned him.

"Don't worry about me honey. I got great hands."

"So has my attorney," she stated.

"What attorney is that, honey? The public defender?" he said derisively, keeping her in the light, noticing how well she filled out her dirty clothes. Wow, he said to himself, poor man that he was, married to a woman he couldn't stand to be around anymore. No wonder he had to read dirty magazines and sneak up on parked cars. He wasn't getting any at home. Nor would he have wanted any if she had offered. Not anymore. But her old daddy was filthy rich and the thread that was keeping him alive was stretching pretty thin. He'd be a fool to leave her now.

Sue moved reluctantly forward. Let him frisk me, or whatever they call it, she had decided, but if his hands stray, I swear to god I'll slug the son-of-a-bitch.

Smitzen watched her every step of the way, playing his light up and down her body. He was too busy to notice the sound of the rear door of the van opening above the idling motor and to see Mike coming around the side. It surprised the hell out of him when Mike said, "Howdy officer," with a thick southern drawl. Startled, Smitzen automatically stepped back as his right hand found the snap on his holster and undid it.

Mike, equally and purposely as scrungy as Sue, put out his gloved hand as if he fully expected Smitzen to shake it. Smitzen looked at the once white, now brown stained cloth glove and stood where he was as he played his light over Mike. What a pair of scuzz buckets, he told himself. And what a dumb fuck he was, Christ, what if this guy had a gun? He had never even thought of looking in the back before ordering her out. Thinking about the possibilities, he began first to sweat, and then to get angry. His middle aged face turned bright red in the dark. He could feel it. I'll fix these fuck heads, he told himself, sure that they were secretly laughing at him by now. "Anybody else back there?" he demanded to know.

"No sir," Mike said. "Not a soul."

"What are you two doing out here," Smitzen asked, staying on his guard. He loosened his revolver in its holster and felt a little braver.

"Working," Mike stated.

"Working?" It was then that Smitzen noticed the smeared emblem on Mike's coveralls. Porta-John. At first it didn't register. He swung his light to the sign on the door of the truck that he had failed to take note of before. Porta-John, it said again in big letters. Toilets? Oh god, he cried to himself and cringed.

"Yeah," Mike said and pointed across the parking lot at a row of portable toilets that stood there. "Damned pump got clogged up. I was trying to fix it and we got into a little disagreement because she wouldn't help. Know anything about machinery officer? I could sure use a hand."

Holy shit, Smitzen said to himself. Then he shuddered. He had almost touched the woman. Good grief. He removed his hand from the butt of his pistol and subconsciously rubbed it on his pants leg as if to clean it. "Can't," he said. "I'm on duty."

Mike made an understanding gesture.

"How much longer you going to be here?" Smitzen asked.

"Don't know for sure," Mike said, motioning back to the row of blue fiberglass enclosures. "Have to pump those overflowin things out before we can leave or the boss will kill us both, that's for sure"

"All right, get to it then," Smitzen said. "I'll be back in an hour. Try and be gone when I get here," he warned them. With that he swaggered back to his car and roared off to the south from whence he had come as Mike and Sue hugged each other and used up another three minutes of precious time laughing.

"Hi babe," Buck said in a low voice to Jackie where she stood bent over, with her head under the hood of one of the police vehicles.

"Eek," she replied and dropped the heavy cutters she was using. "Dammit Buck. Don't do that."

"Sorry honey. Had to let you know I was here."

"Okay, but be quiet. That one S O B is still in there," she said, nodding towards the office. Buck grunted softly as Jackie retrieved her cutters, whacked off another section of battery cable, rolled it up and let it drop down out of sight between the radiator and the grill. Then she gently lowered the hood. They slipped around behind the car.

"How many left?" Buck asked.

"Just the one parked in front of the door. Don't dare touch it, though. He can see it from where he's sitting."

"Hmm," Buck said, contemplating the situation.

"Can you crawl under it and drain the tank?" Jackie asked.

"No good. Have to kill the battery or smash the radio so he can't call out."

"What are we going to do?"

"Don't know. Let me think."

Buck thought.

"Why don't you go inside, tell him your car broke down, ask to use the phone or something. Get him turned around, keep him busy for about sixty seconds," he suggested.

"What? Like this?"

Buck looked at her, seeing her this time. Baggy surplus camouflage fatigues and hat, gloved hands, smudged face. "Guess not," he said.

It was then that she smelled the acrid smell of old oil. She looked at his clothes. "What happened to you?" she asked.

"Slipped," he said and that was all he would say. Then he asked, "Can you make a coyote sound?"

"No, what for?"

"Diversion maybe, get him to come to the side window so he can't see out front."

"Can you?'

"What?"

"Make a coyote sound?"

"No dammit. Probably wouldn't work anyway."

"What do we do?"

"I'm thinking Jackie," he said and sat down on the pavement behind the car. She sat beside him. He put his arm around her. A minute later he was reaching for her breast, trying to get his now ungloved hand inside the top of her fatigues.

"Buck. For god's sake. Not now."

"I need to feel some warmth. It helps me think, honey."

Jackie laughed and backhanded him gently across the face with her gloved hand. "What a shit head," she said fondly as he exposed a row of smiling teeth to her and withdrew. After a moment he asked, "Where's the phone in there?"

"I don't know."

"Which way is the desk facing?"

"That way." She pointed.

Buck got to his knees and crawled over to the window. He rose slowly and peeked in, then came back. "Do we know what the phone number is in there?" he asked.

"I'm sure it's on the sheet," she said and pulled the list of numbers Kohl had given her from her pocket. "Here it is," she said, finding it.

"Come on," Buck told her and they crawled away.

Two minutes later Buck had the phone headset, which he had also been forced to carry, clipped into one of the pairs of terminals on the big panel around behind the closed cafeteria across from the station. "It should work," he said. He switched on the set and listened. There was a dial tone. He shut it off and handed it to her. "Should work," he said again. "When you hear me hoot, dial the number."

"Hoot?"

"Yeah. Like an owl. That's the signal."

"I didn't know you could hoot."

"I didn't either but I'm going to learn by the time I get there."

"Hello Bluebird," came the familiar voice on the radio. "Are you awake." It was Kohl's voice calling Jennie to let her know that she should stand by because they were heading into the final phases. There was no answer.

"Bluebird, bluebird, are you there."

"I'm here Ko..ah..." she said at last. She hadn't been able to find the button on her two way in the dark at first and now she had forgotten the code name they had given Kohl. Not that it mattered that much out here, but just in case. "Architect," she said after a moment and added the sounds of "Brrrr."

"I know," came the return. "Hang tight. Hope to talk again

soon. How about you, Hotshot? What's you're status?"

"The pies are cut, waiting to be served. Standing by on the high point ready to go looking for some wheels," Mike came in.

"Sounds good. If the Bushman and Fluffball (Buck and Jackie) are ready we can start the party."

"Bushman ready. The beasts have been bled, guard dog is grounded and the squealer is down. Fluffy took a walk and I'm looking to hear from you again so I can sever my connections with mother."

"Tell your mother good-bye right away," Kohl told Buck.

"Will do."

"Are you on the line Fluffy?"

"Standing by," Jackie said from her new location half way up the road that wound up out of the dam on the Nevada side. She had two 'Road Closed' signs leaning against the wall, both with battery powered red lamps that could be made to flash in warning.

"Fine and decent, party lovers. Put the stopper in, Hotshot. Posters out now Fluffy. Do the big one after Hotshot heads for the cave. And Bushman, don't forget to put the rest of the candles on the cake."

"I would still like to light my own," Buck replied.

"Patience, my friend. Not until it's time to sing Happy Birthday. Architect out."

The dialogue at this point was primarily a status check. Mike had neatly sliced and weakened the roofs of the four penstock towers while Buck had drained the breakers of oil on his side of the river and then helped Jackie disable the police cars and knock out the emergency two way radio that could be operated from inside the security station. Buck, with reference to Ma, as in Bell, was instructed to now cut the phone lines leading from the dam complex to the outside world. Mike, in turn, had been told to move the van down the road a bit to the south and use the laser to try and stop semi trucks in both lanes, not only to confuse the issue but to prevent any vehicles from entering the dam area while the fireworks were under way.

Surely, if there were cars there when this happened, someone might panic and leave their car, putting themselves in serious jeopardy from electrocution. Additionally, the road block would serve to provide an addition safeguard for their escape into Nevada where there were far more roads and highways and towns and cities than adjacent Arizona where the single choice remained Highway Ninety Three.

Kohl, now dressed in the uniform of a security guard, had taken the elevator to the top to make the call and let them know he had completed his work with the breakers and was about to start the final and most crucial phase. Signing off, he went back inside the elevator, inserted his stolen magnetic identity card into the key slot and started back down into the bowels of the dam. At the bottom he unscrewed the elevator control panel, put a jumper wire across the emergency switch to make sure the elevator would be there when he returned and reinstalled the panel. Then he went directly to the telephone service room. Here he opened a terminal box, clipped a headset across the circuit for the public address system and proceeded to make an announcement.

"Attention. Attention. All dam personnel. We have received a bomb threat for somewhere inside the dam. I repeat, we have received a bomb threat. All personnel proceed immediately to the stairway for evacuation. DO NOT attempt to take the elevator in case of power failure. DO NOT take the elevator. Immediately stop what you are doing and proceed to the stairway." With that he proceeded to the stairwell door and waited. Here they came, some laughing, making jokes, others sober, some scared, some bitching badly.

"Fucking ridiculous," one man said. "There are four hundred steps to the top."

"Five hundred," someone else said.

"Six hundred and twenty."

No one seemed to know exactly and none had ever climbed them all before. All they knew was that the dam was at least the equivalent of a forty story building and that was a long damned ways. None of them seemed to question Kohl's presence in the crisp uniform, however, and one of them even motioned for him to go ahead. "Have to wait and see that everyone is out," he said.

"Good luck. Better go check the shit house. I don't think the P.A. works in there."

Damn, Kohl said to himself. Hadn't thought of that. He continued to count. Nineteen, twenty, twenty one. One more to go.

Where the hell was he?

He looked at his watch, following the motion of the sweep second hand around. Thirty five seconds, forty, how long should he wait? Fifty five, sixty, then at last, footsteps. "Come on, get the lead out," he hollered at the man.

"Is this for real?" he was asked.

"Can't take any chances," Kohl told him as the man went through the door.

"Ain't you coming?"

"Not yet. Have to make sure everybody is out."

"Better hurry. Your ass may be grass."

"Thanks," Kohl told him and waited until he was out of sight around the first landing above. Then he shut the door behind him and barred it with a length of pipe he had placed there earlier. Back at the elevator he quickly undid the jumper wire and again rose to the top. Those twenty two men would be there too, perhaps, in another hour or so. Those who didn't just give up and sit down to wait it out. Of course the power would go out in about five more minutes and it would be total darkness until the battery powered emergency lights came on, hopefully, if someone had checked them lately. Regardless, once they reached the top, they would still be trapped because that door was barred too. However, until such time as they were rescued, they were in absolutely the safest place they could for what was yet to come, if they didn't somehow knock the door down and stayed there. And who wouldn't when there was a big sign on the back of it explaining what was about to happen.

Sue was still behind the wheel of the van, driving south on 93. "Here," Mike said when they were a mile down the road.

Sue slowed, pulled out onto the shoulder and stopped.

"Make a U," Mike said, noticing a pair of approaching headlights some distance away and the horizontal row of amber lamps higher up over the cab of what had to be a semi. "And park on the other side."

Adeptly she swung it around, letting the wheels spin a touch in the gravel, just for flare. A bit of squeal when the rubber hit the asphalt and she was there. Fun machine, she thought, the feeling of so much power right there a the tip of your toe. It was twice as fast as the Mercedes, and almost as agile.

"Engage the generator," he told her and climbed in the back.

Bleary eyed and weary, a log book on the dash full of lies about his rest stops and off time, James Perez, a fifty-fifty blend of duel heritage, hummed northbound down one of the most boring highways in the west. Lazing along in top gear in his old, eighteen wheeler Peterbuilt in the middle of the night, he sucked at his teeth, still trying to dislodge a few stubborn jalapena pepper seeds that got caught in there back in Kingman. The radio was silent, as he preferred it. He had no taste for that moaning, begroaning, whining, sniveling country shit about some self destructive fuckbrain having to drink alone because the old lady threw him out of the house because the self destructive cry baby didn't have enough sense to see what a good thing he had going in the first place. What crap. But it was the standard radio fare in this part of the world. God, he hated cowboys.

Didn't they know that cowboys never die, nor do they fade away. They rot away instead, starting with the brain, although that seldom takes long for there isn't much there to start with, especially after it's been well saturated with beer and cheap whiskey. And after the brain rots out and the body collapses, not even the lowest member in a pack of coyotes would touch it, or even a half sensible wild pig half worth his lard for that matter. Fuck them cowboys. Didn't they know about truck drivers? About not dying or fading away, just getting a new peter built. Ha, ha. It was an old joke, but he liked it. Maybe it even had something to do with the fact that he could have bought a Kenworth for the same money but took the Peterbuilt instead.

Well, there wasn't anything wrong with his peter, no sir. And he didn't take no shit from drunken cowboys either. He didn't have to. He had inherited the best of both worlds. He was tall and strong and knew a few tricks for the ladies. Damned right, nothing wrong with his peter, hell no. Recently over hauled, he had dumped a load of ashes into Bevis three days ago, had it tended to by Margareit at the motel in Flagstaff last night and dipped it into some more maidenly juices back there at the truck stop on Interstate Forty just a few hours ago. And what's more, after he had traded the pile of Kaibab stone chained to the flatbed behind him for a load of sheet rock in Vegas and was Frisco bound he would stop at that drive-in whore house up the road and do it again. Yes sir. Life was good, even when you sold your ass for a net, net, net of six dollars an hour to hang onto a steering wheel. What the hell. Old truckers never die, they just get a new peter built. Hmm de dum. Must be about time to pop another pill. Oh, oh, what was that? What the hell, sounds like the radiator blew a seam. Dammit. Look at all that steam. Son-of-a-bitch.

Perez's foot automatically found the brake pedal. He slowed, downshifted, skipped four gears, swearing the whole time, only to be greeted by the shattering sound of metal parts clanging together and then total silence from the engine. At the same time he saw the reflection of tail light lenses from his steadily dimming headlights. A van was parked along side the road not too far away. Help, hopefully. A ride into town that he obviously was going to need. He was down to thirty five now, only the sound of tires on the pavement, but still in control, still slowing. Then another noise hit him, equally, if not more distressing. He had lost his air. There was no pressure. The trailer brakes came on automatically. Hard. Dammit, he was still going way too fast. The damned thing was beginning to fishtail. Oh shit. Time for some Hail Marys.

"Hot damn," Mike said. "Look at that. Perfect."

And so it was, as verified by Sue who had watched the entire scene in the oversized rear view mirror from the drivers seat. Headlights had been coming down the road in the distance, then she saw the glow in the front where first the grill had melted away, then the core of the radiator, followed by a cloud of steam. Finally the entire rig, chromed wheels, chromed bumpers, chromed exhaust stacks, chromed silhouettes of super bunnies on the mudflats, was all zig zagging down the highway, fishtailing around, finally coming to rest neatly across the road, the trailer with its wheels in the ditch, the tractor on the asphalt heading in the wrong direction, almost entirely blocking any possible flow of traffic. Mike reached for some flares. He lit two, opened the rear door and tossed them out onto the road. Then, seeing that Perez was obviously all right, for he had gotten down from the cab and had lit a flare of his own, he told Sue to pull a bit further up the road away from the scene.

101

Perez was at a loss. What the hell were they leaving for? Why hadn't they come back to help instead of just putting out some flares. Now they were driving off. He went around behind the truck and placed his own flare, along with two more down road a bit then looked up to see another set of approaching headlights. It was a car.

Since they were parked on the shoulder and the tractor left some space between it and the ditch, Mike was able to see past it, through the telescope. "Stop," he yelled to Sue.

She stopped the van. "Holy shit," Mike said excitedly when he realized what he was looking at.

Sue crawled back to join him. "What's so funny," she asked.

"It's that hero of a cop from before, right on schedule."

"What are you going to do?"

"First I have to find his radio antenna, then we'll see what he likes most."

Sue found the binoculars and focused in on the scene as good old Officer Smitzen did yet another stupid thing. Instead of stopping on the shoulder back some distance, as all good sense would dictate, his self importance forced him to drive up close as he could, thereby completely preventing anyone from getting by.

And, since the truck driver was already out of the vehicle and clearly unhurt and there were no other vehicles involved, he suppressed the urge to call in right away. Might as well get out and see what happened first. Probably just another one of those hop headed drivers all strung out in limbo land, not able to pay attention. Dumb assed trucks. Shouldn't be any trucks, damned things. Noisy, dangerous, smelly, oversized highway hoggers, playing bumper tag and chicken with the rest of society. Nothing but assholes behind the wheel with all their Smokey the Bear signals on the CB so they could make a mockery of the speed limits. Serves them right when they end up in the ditch. Wonder what the hell this guy's problem is?

Smitzen opened the door, got out, found his night stick and stuck it in his belt, (never know what kind of a mood this asshole might be in after this screw up), adjusted his belt and swaggered towards the truck only to see the driver ignore him and go around to the front and look at the grill. "Holy shit," Perez said in a befuddled voice. "Look at that. What the mother slamming hell happened?"

Smitzen came and looked and he too was equally perplexed. He pointed his flashlight into the ragged hole. Not only was there a hole in the radiator, it extended into the block of the engine itself. The bleary pair of eyes of the driver turned to stare into a baffled pair of the cop.

Smitzen recovered first. Better get a tow truck out here, he told himself, and headed back to the patrol car, not knowing he had already missed the opportunity to talk to headquarters. By now the radio antenna was nothing but a puddle of metal lying on the top of the car.

And then, when Smitzen was still ten feet away the left front tire suddenly exploded and went flat. Smitzen jumped at the sound, his hand reaching for the butt of his gun. He stopped, embarrassed at the action, and looked at the car. Must have been a bad spot on the damned thing. What kind of benevolent luck was this? He could have been chasing somebody at ninety when it blew instead. Hope the spare is good, he thought as he started towards the car again. Pow, there went the right front tire. Now wait a minute. He looked at the truck driver. He was standing there innocently enough, nothing in his hands, no way he could have done it. But, was that a smile on his face? Better not be.

It was the beginning of a smile all right, because the driver, like most drivers, hated cops. Why not? There was a time when the cops were supposed to "Protect and Serve" and the good ones tried. Anymore, however, the motto seemed to be, "Harass and Intimidate". Especially when it came to truckers, bikers, long hairs, kids and poor folks in old cars. Fair game all, for the bullies. Screw the cops. Who wants to live in a police state? That was how Perez felt, and it showed, even now. And correctly enough, Smitzen was subconsciously reacting to it.

But then he made a giant mental leap. Wait a minute, he said to himself. This whole thing was getting much too bizarre. Smitzen looked up in the sky. There were no flying saucers in sight, only that van still parked up the road a ways. That van looked kinda familiar, now didn't it? But even if it was the same one he had seen earlier, how could an old shit pumper and two dirt bags like that have anything to do with something as weird as this? Then he thought he heard another sound. A popping one.

Damn, there was a red hot hole in his grill, and steam was emanating from the radiator. Then there was a small explosion as the oil in the engine caught fire with a flash. Lastly, although he couldn't see it happening, the penetration of the hole continued eating its way through the car from front to back, heading for the gas tank. Fortunately by now, they had both instinctively moved back behind the truck, seeking its protection at the first explosive sounds. They hadn't long to wait for the rest of it.

Ten seconds later the big one came, sending the rear seat, the trunk lid and the spare tire somersaulting fifty feet down the road as a tower of living flame and dense black smoke rose high into the night sky. My God, it occurred to them at this point. What if the truck should catch on fire too? Holy shit!

They ran for the ditch, threw themselves in it and watched with fascination as the flames consumed the rest of the car. The interior, the tires and the paint were already long gone as the flames melted out the remains of the fractured windows, caused the springs to sag and turned the carcass into a bright, cherry red specter that first caused the paint on the truck to blister and the tires to stink and then turned the cab into an oversized oven which soon brought the upholstery to the kindling point.

Once that happened, the rest was history. Perez chuckled happily in the dancing light of the flames and almost slapped Smitzen on the back when the fuel tanks blew and his last seventy five gallons of diesel went up in smoke, such was his new found joy. He now had reason to sue the Highway Department, by god, and get himself a brand truck. Peterbuilt, of course. Stupid fucking cop, parking so close. Who the hell did he think he was?

Half an hour later, when the fury had diminished somewhat, they came out of hiding to find half a dozen cars backed up down the road to the south. There were none on the north, coming from the dam, Officer Smitzen noted, looking back up the road behind him. Nothing. The van was no longer there either.

At the top of the shaft Kohl waited until the elevator door opened, cut as many wires inside the control panel as he could reach, then went outside and spoke into his radio. "Bushman. Have you finished with your mother?"

"Done comrade," Buck said. "Did my rock climbing too."

"Good man," Kohl acknowledged gratefully. Poor substitute for a mountain goat that he was, Buck had somehow still managed to hang charges on all four of the cantilevered towers which hung out over the canyon wall on the Arizona side while Kohl was down below. They were the first towers in the chain, the ones which served to bring the heavy conductors up from six hundred and fifty feet below and began the rats nest of dense wires that criss-crossed the canyon and found their way up the ragged cliffs and boulder strewn hills to where they ultimately fanned out and chased their way across the barren topography towards metropolis land. It had to have been an arduous and trying task, even for Buck. Something not done earlier because of their high visibility. Like the two still remaining right next to the roadway on the Nevada side.

But Buck thought little of his accomplishment. His only complaint was the fact that, thermally, his oil soaked jeans did little to protect him from the cold. Especially since he was also lacking his shirt and undershirt. Let's get the show on the road, was all he could think about. We still have work to do.

"Hotshot?" Kohl queried next.

Mike chuckled into the mike. "We should have brought the camcorder along," he said. "You would have loved that one."

"Any problem?"

"None, all secure on the south," Mike said, looking forward to story telling time later.

"Check. Ready Blue bird?"

"Yes. I think so." There was some hesitation there, quickly noted by all.

"Don't fail us Bluebird. We need you," Kohl told her.

"I'll be okay. I'm just so cold."

"We'll be smelling corks quickly enough," Mike put in.

"Liver and onions for me," Buck said.

"Caviar or nothing," Jackie stated.

"Get your thumb out Bluebird, we'll be by in about ten minutes to..."

"Oh, oh. I have a problem," Jackie interrupted from her hiding place.

"What is it."

"A bubble gum machine (cop car with lights on top) slipped the noose (went around the Road Closed signs) and is heading towards the hive (dam)."

"Roger. Where you parked Hotshot?"

"Waiting on the west side."

"Everybody cool. If he doesn't see anything here he'll probably go on through the slot. Once he's over the hill, follow him and put him too bed."

"That's a copy. We won't let him cry either."

Kohl stood ready to duck back inside the open elevator while Buck stayed put behind the rocks on the west side where he waited to add the final charges to the two remaining cantilevered towers once the lights went out. Sue, meantime, turned the van around and backed it into ready position. They waited.

Buck saw the reflection of headlights on the guard rail first. "He's here," he radioed.

"Noted," Sue said as the patrol car came down the hill. "He's quiet for now." They still had the police scanner on inside the van. As yet, to the best of their knowledge, since the mountainous surroundings partially blocked some transmissions, the disruption on the south highway hadn't hit the official channels yet.

"He's one of our country cousins," Buck informed them as soon as he was able to make out the Sheriffs shield on the front door of the black and white.

Then the winking, side stepping red lights on the police scanner in the van stopped near the middle as a voice came over the air. "Got the coffee pot on Hank?" a male voice said. No answer. "Hank? This is Charley. Do you read?" No answer.

Sue had killed the engine of the van so no exhaust vapors would be visible in the cool air and now she ducked down in the seat as the car came around the last turn. Mike was already in the back, waiting to go to work once they were rolling. "Oh shi..darn," she said into the radio. "I think we have a problem." Two seconds later she came back again. "We have a problem."

Good old Charley in the patrol car wasn't interested in seeing where or why the road was closed. Not his job. It was the Highway patrol's problem. And since it evidently wasn't on the Nevada side to begin with, there was even less reason to care. Let them Arizonians fend for themselves. No, he was just out cruising. Came to see his buddy Hank at the dam, have some coffee, tease him about his third wife, kid him about his cushy job, kill a little time. Anything to break up the late shift monotony. And, while he was there, what the hell, he might just as well use the phone and call Caroline up at the casino instead of dropping in on the way back. Best not to make a habit of going in there too often while he was on duty So, like a good trooper, Charley put his turn signal on even though there wasn't a moving vehicle in sight out there in the middle of the night, slowed at the last curve and made a left turn into the short service road leading to the security building. He stopped directly along side the now last disabled security vehicle, got out and went to the entrance.

From his location down along the dam Kohl quickly realized what had happened. "Darn and damn," he said over the air. At this point Mike judiciously had Sue start the van and ease around to where he had a line of sight on the patrol car and the front entrance. They waited, but not for long. Charley, finding Hank in a position of having to make a fresh pot of coffee, decided to call Caroline in the meantime. How could he help it? He never thought of her as the girl with the fetching eyes as did the rest of the boys from around there. Hell no, he never got past her bust line. To him she was the girl with the fetching boobs.

But of course the phone line was dead so he thought he would go outside and use the police radio to call in the problem. Fortunately or unfortunately as the case may be, had he seen the US West Telephone Company sign Mike and Sue had replaced the Porta-John sign with on the van, he might have been tempted to walk down there and ask them what the problem was. But as always, thoughts of Caroline had blurred his vision a trifle.

Anticipating his move, Mike waited until he closed the car door and then scorched the antenna off the roof, without Charley's knowledge of course, since melting metal makes little or no sound. Then Sue eased the van very slowly back a bit, still allowing a good line of sight to the hood and front tires of the car but just a touch more removed from view. A good game of cat and mouse was underway. Had Charley started the engine, he would have also quickly experienced a flat tire. Or two.

But he didn't. Instead, he chalked his lack of radio reception up to being down in the canyon out of range and went back inside without looking at the roof of his car and got Hank. They were going to walk over to the dam while the coffee was brewing, go below and try a phone there.

There was no time for cutesy slang amongst the others now. "He's coming your way Architect," Sue said briskly.

"Can't wait any longer. We have to go now. Stand by Bluebird, everybody ready. Here go the lights," Kohl said and walked out of the open elevator onto the sidewalk where he could be seen. He had the remote control in his hand with his finger on the first button and went to the edge of the concrete railing and leaned over, something necessary to make sure the relay Buck had planted down below earlier would pick up the signal. He was seen by both Hank and Charley. Before Kohl could hit the button Hank had realized that he was the only security guard still on duty so who was this other guy dressed up like one? "Hey, you," he hollered in a loud voice as both his and Charley's hands sought their weapons.

Kohl's response was to push the button. Charley and Hank were answered by a dull thud deep within the dam and an almost immediate blackout. Shocked for a moment, they recovered quickly, reached for their flashlights and caught Kohl running east along the dam trying to reach safety behind the elevator house. Charley let go with a round. It was too high. The second thumped into the wall waist level two feet behind Kohl while the third came a microsecond too late. He was around the corner.

Kohl was on the radio. "Bluebird. Do it Bluebird, do it now," Kohl shouted into the device, but there was no response at all. "Bluebird, do you read me? Do it now Bluebird, they're shooting at me." Still no response. "Hotshot, do you hear me? Bushman? Fluffy? ...Goddammit." What the hell was wrong. Had his radio gone dead? Or was he out of reach here behind the structure? Had they put that much steel in the damned building, so much so that the signals couldn't get through? Surely the rest of team had their sets turned on, or did they? Jesus Christ! Kohl couldn't see a damned thing except the two flashlights playing over the edge of the building, making it obvious that they were rapidly approaching.

"Come out of there with your hands up, you son-of-a-bitch,"

Charley shouted. "Or you're a dead man."

Oh hell, Kohl said to himself. There was no place to go except over the edge. But it was seven hundred and twenty six point four feet to the bottom. No fucking way, he decided. Let the bastards shoot me. Then it occurred to him to detonate the charges on top of the penstocks as one last diversion. Even though it was not the optimum thing to do, he might as well take as much of it with him before he went as possible. He fumbled for the detonator control and was trying very hard to find the safety and arm that circuit when a burst of lights came on.

Sue had pulled the van up to within thirty yards of the two officers, flooding them with the high beams, the driving lights and two high intensity spot lights. The men froze in their tracks and were greeted by a very serious female voice coming over the PA system in the van. "Stay put gentlemen and drop your weapons."

Half blinded by the lights, they looked back at the van. Charley swung slowly around towards it while Hank kept his weapon pointing in Kohl's direction. "Don't do it," Sue warned.

Charley hesitated.

"If you don't think I'm serious," Sue continued. "Take a look at that bronze plaque on the wall there in front of you."

Surprised at such an unusual order, they turned and looked. Almost instantly the plaque turned glowing red as it began melting and flowed down to the sidewalk, forming a bright orange puddle on the concrete. "Holy goddamn, Jesus shit," they said and very slowly stooped down and laid their weapons on the street in front of them.

"Good thinking," Sue congratulated. "Now, very slowly and very carefully return to the security building. Lock yourselves in and stay there and nothing else will happen to you."

The men didn't move. The van backed up twenty feet so that Mike could turn the laser beam down lower to the ground. Charley misjudged the action and began thinking of picking his pistol back up. Mike however, had already focused on it. He gave it a short burst. Charley reached down and grabbed it firmly, severely burning his bare hand in the process. He screamed and dropped it instantly. The gun went off when it hit the ground and the bullet ricocheted off the wall, nearly hitting Hank. This time they were thoroughly convinced and retreated meekly to the security building. Just to let them know how serious he really was, Mike swung the beam onto the sheriffs car and set it afire.

Kohl came running back to the now darkened van as Sue rolled down the window. "Quick, give me your radio."

She handed it to him. "Where are you Bushman?" Kohl asked rapidly, his heart pumping, his body drenched with sweat.

"Back in hiding. But I did my other little errand. What the hell happened down there?"

"Will explain later. Stand by. We'll pick you up on the way out."

"You mean I don't have to walk home?"

"Not this time. You either Fluffy."

"But I haven't had any fun yet," Jackie said.

"Sorry. Later. Be ready, we have to hurry..."Bluebird, Bluebird, do you read me? Come in"

"This is Bluebird," came the weak voice.

"Do it now Bluebird."

"I...I'm afraid Kohl."

"Do it Jennie, before somebody starts shooting again. Do it now, please," Kohl pleaded.

"Oh my god. Are you all right?"

"Yes, yes, I'm all right. Hit the button," he said loudly, demanding action.

"I will. There."

Nothing happened.

"Did you turn off the safety switch? Is the red light on?"

"There it is. Now I'm ready. Are you sure you're all right?"

"I'm fine sweetheart. Just do it."

"Here goes..."

Unless you've ever heard the sound of high tension wires coming together or being shorted out you have no idea how awesome such a noise is and what a terrifying spectacle it makes. It's bad enough to have a short in a lamp or a household appliance and watch the sparks fly and smell the smoke but multiple that by over a million times and what have you got? Something that would make you think it was the end of the world. Then take that and do it twenty seven more times, for there were twenty seven, one hundred and thirty thousand volt wires in all, all coming to ground almost simultaneously.

The landscape roared and boomed, and thundered and rolled so loudly that it could be heard clear down to the Gold Nugget in downtown Las Vegas more than twenty miles away. The night sky became day, became brighter than day, as balls of lightning bolts rolled up and down the wires and arced over in shattering traces longer than two men were high. Wires were melted, the steel legs of towers burned through. What little vegetation that was in the way vanished with a puff, rocks were turned to glass and even the earth seemed to tremble.

That's what Jennie saw and felt. And no matter that Kohl had done to prepare her for it, it was still beyond her comprehension. She wet her pants and dropped the detonator. She got sick, she tried to run, fell down crying and dazed, got up and ran some more, and some more and some more, hitting things in the dark, falling, inflicting cuts and bruises and welts, too shocked to feel the pain, getting up, running, running, screaming hysterically over and over in the night.

At the dam they heard the thunder and felt the rumble and saw the sky turn into a giant Aurora Borealias, not five thousand miles away but directly overhead, and then that horrible trembling hum and growl as seventeen monstrous generators strained to handle the growing electrical load that now far exceeded the normal four hundred and fifty million watt output. They began to heat. Insulation melted and caught fire, steel armatures began to warp. Twenty seven mammoth circuit breakers began to open, attempting to forestall the process and protect the generators from destruction.

Without their arc suppressing oil, however, it was impossible to break the flow of current. They drew increasing volatile internal arcs that generated enough heat to melt diamonds, the toughest of all substances. Breakers shattered, some at the seams, some disintegrated entirely. There was fire and flame everywhere and enough smoke down in the canyon and inside the power house to leave a layer of scum and smell that would last for years.

And they weren't even done yet. Kohl hit the third detonator switch. The charges on top of the penstocks went off, compressing the pie shaped slices of the roof downward into the penstock tubes where they were picked up and carried along by the rushing internal rivers and slammed with tremendous force up against the turbine blades of the generators, bending them, breaking them, jamming them, bringing the mighty powerhouse completely and totally to its knees.

Then, as if all that were not enough, there was an encore. One more button to push. One more ripping explosion as the legs of the cantilevered towers were torn off and they went crashing, down, down into the bottom of the gorge so far away, pulling a further tangle of hundreds and hundreds of feet of oversized wires and cables with them, rendering one last blow to the breakers, the transformers, the building structure, the decks, the huge working cranes and all the other apparatus below, creating vast echoes that rumbled and roared, rattled and ricocheted back and forth, then found their way down the canyon and gradually dissipated into the night, leaving nothing but an awesome silence and a dark, black, seemingly endless and bottomless canyon standing alone out in the cold desert night under a star filled sky.

Now you could really make out the stars, for the whole southwest was in darkness. There were no house lights or street lights, no sky glow from towns and cities to smudge the sky, dim the view or detract from the beauty. One could see stars and constellations of stars. The Milky Way shimmered in all its glory.

By then Buck had walked down the hill to join them and the foursome stood looking upward and said a silent prayer. Maybe someday they would be back. There was still more to do. A lot more to do. The river needed to be reclaimed for one thing. Fortunately, Mother Nature was already working on it.

There was no doubt that she would be the ultimate victor, either. There was already ninety feet of silt backed up behind the dam and the concrete was past its point of maximum strength and still aging. Metal was rusting, the earth was shifting. And regardless of all of man's grand illusions about his self importance and his indomitable accomplishments, what man has built, Mother Nature can tear asunder, erase and reclaim, sooner or later, one way or another. And although she is very patient, misleadingly patient in fact, in seeking her victory, she is always the ultimate

112

victor. That, however, didn't mean that she didn't appreciate a helping hand now and then.

"Well, we'd better leave," Mike reminded them quietly after some moments of muted veneration. "There are two more ladies waiting for us."

"Yes," Kohl said. "Just one last thing. I need to let those men out of the stairwell before we go."

ELEVEN

It was more than national news, it was international, both in scope and in implication. The work of an army of terrorists, possibly of Libyan, or Iranian origin, maybe North Korean. No, it was the Japanese. They weren't happy with simply having all of their American dollars and buying up the place. That takes too long. There was no sense in attacking Pearl Harbor again either. They had made that mistake. Hit the mainland instead.

Fidel Castro! Yes, by God, that son-of-a-bitch. He had finally figured out a way to get back at us after all these years of boycotting hand rolled Cuban cigars. Who else could it be. No, he said, it was the CIA, instead. They were just trying to make it look like he did it so they'd have another excuse to invade his country. In turn, Libby, Iraq and Iran all came up with their own versions of this story.

For sure, however, it was not the Chinese. The United States was by far the largest importer of Chinese goods and they certainly didn't want to jeopardize that market. How would they ever keep all their minor children busy if they had to close down all the sweat shops. They would never be able to bring their country up to second world status so they could pollute the environment as much as the Western World did. No, it was not the Chinese. But then, maybe it was the United States Army doing one of those secret exercises again and it had gotten out of hand. That wouldn't be too surprising, based on past history.

The gaming landlords in Vegas, however, were convinced that some of their competitors in Atlantic City had done it just to put them out of business. The residents of Los Angeles, however, thought it was a conspiracy perpetrated upon them by those northern Californians who wanted to split off and start their own state. On and on it went. There were more proposed explanations for what had happened than there were people running for congress. The debate raged on in the public sector for weeks and weeks, gaining even more momentum once the utility companies were able to dead end the lines near Boulder and re-route power into the network from other sources so that Las Vegas, Los Angeles and other metropolitan areas could turn their television sets back on.

Then the voices of mass condemnation of the act began, especially among the middle and upper classes. They were more than indignant. How dare anyone infringe on their right to certain levels of comfort and convenience by trying to deprive them of the use of electricity? No microwave, no television, no refrigerator, no electric can open, no electric shoe buffer, read by candle light, are you out of your mind, the whole thing was most unspeakable. It was too base and inhuman to even think in such terms. Hang the bastards, whoever they were.

The churches however, loved it. Secretly, of course, because it put new life back into their sermons. Attendance was up, collection plates were full and more people were shaking the minister's hand after the service. The sheep were returning to the flock. Fear, the subjugators most useful weapon, next to guilt, that is, was on the rise. What a God sent opportunity. Why not capitalize on it?

No clergyman should be driving a car more than two years old. God helps those who help themselves. Renew your pledges folks. Don't forget to put something in there for inflation. Make that down payment on your ticket to heaven. It is later than you think. Such a thing may happen again (we hope). Doomsday is approaching (that's for damned sure). This wasn't some inconsequential little thing way over there in Vietnam or in the Middle Eastern desert. No sir, this is right in our own back yard. Beware! And while you're at it, Repent!

After considering all the ramifications, the President himself, doubled the number of Secret Service personnel guarding the White House and ordered the design of a special, battery powered limousine made of high temperature alloy with solid rubber tires, infrared sensors up top, sides, front and rear and an armor plated rumble seat with a missile operator and a stock of Sidewinder missiles. He also started wearing a flack jacket.

Similarly, the Pentagon asked for and got an increase in defense spending as did half the, behind-the scenes, top secret, Advanced Research and Development boys at Wright Patterson Air Base. The Army Special Services formed an even newer Anti Guerrilla Warfare unit and went to White Sands for an extended bivouac. The Los Angeles Swat team was locked up in Parker Center for two full weeks to undergo advanced training. The bullies who posed for the ludicrous and ignoble Nevada State Police poster that said, Have a drink, We'll provide the chaser, however, all resigned from duty, effective immediately, as did a number of others, along with Smitzen and Sheriff Hank, while everyone who used to work at the dam vowed they would never set foot on the damned dam again, ever. So be it.

Regardless of the number of plausible explanations that had been offered, though, none were as far fetched as to even suggest that the accomplishment could have been pulled off by a would-be, over thirty writer, a former, small company executive and some bushy faced bum who thought he was the personification of some semi folk-hero out of a novel, along with their three girl friends, of course, who lent a most vital and indispensable contribution to the effort. Faw, har, har, har, what have you been smoking, tell me another one, I love your sense of humor you leg pulling, tall tale telling old pirate you, whoever you are. Ridiculous, take a hike, space case.

Even Digand Pry, college graduate, fifteenth degree Mason working on the sixteenth, father of two, balancer of the family checkbook and super FBI sleuth, wouldn't have believed it at first. Nor did he even consider such a possibility. Why should he? This crime had some very, very serious ramifications and, as a result, there had to be some very serious contenders for the title role. Such was the attitude that pervaded the thinking throughout all the upper echelons of decision making. And because they believed that, no one in any position of authority in the ranks above Pry was about to leave such an important case in the hands of one man alone.

Fortunately, however, before things had gotten totally out of control, Pry did manage to get Professor Witley out to the dam site where it was verified that the weapon which had carved up the roofs of the penstock towers and burned holes in all the vehicles was probably the same device that had helped decimate that little old cement plant way down by Clarkdale in Arizona.

"Could such a device be fitted into an ordinary sized van?" Pry asked him.

Witley's eyebrows climbed half way up his forehead. What was wrong with this man? Didn't he listen? He had effectively answered this question the last time. "I'm serious," Pry said. "I want you to think about it some more."

"You mean of a size like the ones the hippies used to ride around in?" Witley asked.

"Yes. Like that. Only one of the longer and newer ones."

Witley coughed and scoffed and reached inside his jacket for his pipe so he would have something physical to do that might help keep him from laughing in the man's face. That was the trouble with these ordinary people, he thought. The ones with the undisciplined minds. Now if everyone had eight years of higher education like he had, then they would understand what was possible and what was not and he wouldn't have to keep answering these ridiculous questions all the time.

There was still tobacco in the pipe so he simple relit it and sucked on it a bit to compose himself. After all, one must be kind, especially to someone who worked for the government. You just never knew where the money for the next research grant might come from. So once again he explained that a laser with sufficient power to do the damage he had examined had to be at least yeah big around and at least so many meters long and had to have thus and such and this and that to go along with it to make it possible to function, even in the lowest of energy output modes and therefore... It was all perfectly logical.

Pry shrugged. Who was he to argue with the voice of authority? But then, if the laser wasn't inside that van, where the hell had it been? There was nothing else around for miles according to the truck driver and Officer Smitzen. The only thing left was an invisible flying saucer, but he never did believe in those things.

Son-of-a-bitch anyway. Now what? Where did he go from here? He didn't know, but what he needed most was to be left alone so he could sit down and think. Thinking was tough. In fact, thinking was one of the most difficult things he had ever been asked to do in the line of duty. Sometimes it became necessary, however, especially when none of the theories fit the facts and there were no hidden cameras around to catch the culprits. He hoped it didn't make him break out in a rash again. If only they would just leave him alone. That was not about to happen, however, because the pressure was on.

"But I don't need ten more men, sir," Pry had told his boss. "I don't even need four. Two would do nicely for now, until I know where we're going with this thing."

"I must insist." his boss said. "We have to man the program. Even the White House is looking over our shoulder on this one. They suggested the whole investigate branch be put on special assignment. My neck is out a mile and a half because I wanted to hold it down to just ten men, plus yourself, of course. And since you have the seniority and since it seems as though it may be tied to that cement plant thing in that little burg out there in Arizona, Sparkdale, or wherever it was, I'm going to let you run with it for the time being. But I want to personally hear from you daily on this, is that clear?"

"Clear enough, sir," Pry stated reluctantly.

"Good. And don't worry about overtime or the budget. Whatever you need. They won't believe we are applying ourselves if we don't start spending some money."

Oh shit, Pry said to himself, even as he nodded in acceptance and understanding of his superiors plight. How was he going to look out for ten other wonder boys besides himself and still be able to get anything done when he was wiping all these extra noses? Ridiculous. And worse, he'd have to set up camp way down in that dumpy damned little Kingman until they got the lights turned back on in Vegas. But Las Vegas was a bright spot to look forward to, however, wasn't it. He loved those topless dancers in the reviews out on the Strip. So, with that in mind, he packed a bigger bag, dutifully kissed the wife on the cheek, patted the boys on the head and got on the early flight out of Dulles, along with most of his new underlings. He had to admit though, they made a fine looking brigade getting into the people mover on the way to the airplane. All them shiny new shoes and over stuffed briefcases. By god, maybe they'd show them yet.

But what did he have to go on, he asked himself, once he had set up shop in his motel room. The description of a well built but scuzzy looking woman and her shaggy looking, equally scuzzy boyfriend driving an old van with a shit-pumper sign on the door that the owners of the portable potty company disclaimed as being any of theirs. What else? A grumbly voice from inside a toilet stall. Another shaggy looking individual playing security guard, bronze plaques melting off the wall in the middle of the night, tires exploding for no reason at all and police cars going up in smoke. An old oil soaked shirt found floating in the river, microscopic traces of dynamite, batteries and transistors, none of which were traceable to anything. Some type O-positive blood, worlds most popular brand, on the rocks up above and some chewing gum wrappers along the highway where there was reported to have been Road Closed signs that night. What the hell was that?

But Pry was patient. He knew very well that good police work was not accomplished by brilliance. Nor with computers, nor with dogged logic. No, most crimes were solved with the aid of the good and loyal citizenry seeking justice. Or revenge. They were all motivated by the best of intentions such as jealousy, fear, greed and self righteousness. Or because their own lives were colorless, odorless, dull and lacking and they volunteered to gain attention and break up the monotony of their nothing existences. What did it matter as long as they came forward? That was the important thing and that was the essence of good police work, waiting, listening, trying to sort out the crackpots from the credible. Motive was secondary.

"Have a seat, Mr. Trulock. But please don't sit on the bed. I have to sleep there tonight," Pry said as authoritatively as possible under the circumstances to the bespectacled, bland looking man standing in the doorway of his motel room and waved him towards the coffee table. He certainly wished there was room for a desk in there so he had something to put a little separation between himself and the public. And another chair, for darned sake. The whole thing was embarrassing. So much so, in fact that the last potential witness, or whatever he was, had up and turned around

118

and left without a word, then called the local sheriff and reported Pry as some kind of pervert. If only the lights would come back on in Vegas where a real office awaited. But who knew when that would be. Darn it, he said to himself, maybe he could commandeer the motel manager's office in the meantime. Right after he got rid of this lout, in fact.

Trulock gave Pry an indecent look, then saw the gun in Pry's shoulder holster and moved to comply.

"Now, you say you are an accountant, Mr. Trulock.

"That is correct."

"And how can I help you?"

"I'm not looking for help. I think I have information which might be related to the Hoover Dam incident."

"Oh really?" Pry said, remaining skeptical. This was the twenty seventh person who had made that claim so far that day, none of whom had a plausible story thus far. "Want to tell me about it?" What a stupid question. Of course he did or he wouldn't be there.

Trulock outlined his theory. One Sue Alexander, his former employer, had essentially given a blank check to these two men. One was named Kohl and the other one Mike. They were untrustworthy fellows, both of them, playing on her sympathy and loneliness. These single women are targets for every conniving so and so that comes along. Such suckers for a handsome face.

"Well yes, I used to work for her," he told Pry. "That's how I happen to know what I'm talking about. Anyway... What? Yes, I suppose you could say I was fired. What has that got to do with it?"

"Nothing. Just like to know all the facts. Sorry to interrupt. Please continue Mr. Trulock."

"Well, you see...And, etc, etc, etc,...And then I called her niece and I just got the feeling that..."

"Would you recognize these men again if you saw them?"

"Most certainly."

"Could these be them?" Pry asked, showing Trulock artists conceptions of the two bearded individuals and the rendition of the female accomplice as put together from the joint memories of Smitzen and the night crew of the dam.

Trulock studied them in earnest. Yes, no, maybe, how could he tell? None of them looked like anybody he knew. And that woman, dear lord, he never would have worked for someone who looked like that. That sophisticated, Mercedes driving, rich bitch doing that to herself? He really didn't think so, much as he would have liked to see her swing. But then, where did all that money go? They were working on some highly technical thing. He knew that, dammit.

Could he prove it?

"Not any more. They took all the records back before I got a chance to copy them."

"But they were her records. Is that correct?"

"Of course. But any good accountant keeps copies of all his clients records. In case there is ever a dispute later on."

"Of course. Well Mr. Trulock you have done the right thing. The FBI thanks you, and I personally thank you for coming in and talking with us. I assure you that we will look into this possibility and we will contact you if we need any further information," Pry said as he rose and extended his hand.

Trulock took the hand gratefully. Never having replaced Sue as a client, he hadn't felt this good in months, damn her. But she wouldn't feel so damned high and mighty once these folks got done with her, he told himself. Served her right.

Pry almost tore the two sheets of notes he had made off his legal pad and threw them away. Just another disgruntled civilian with an ax to grind. But then, wait a minute. He still had those ten men out there stumbling over each other. If nothing else, this would at least give a couple of them something to do. Keep them out of his hair for a little while anyway, and give him something to report back to Washington about. Not only was the heat on high but it was rising. Who should he pick? Smith, or Jones? Hansen? Parsons? Yes Parsons, the pushy prick, vying to take his job away all the time. And who else? Spinnet maybe. The guy with the garlic on his breath. That would serve Parsons right, all right, to have to work closely with Spinnet. Good thinking Pry. Parsons and Spinet it was. He sent for them.

TWELVE

Should it ever have come to that, however, a minimum of investigative work would show that all of the creators of this havoc were away at the time, officially out of the country according to any records the immigration service computer's might contain. They had all left two days before the incident had occurred and re-entered the country a week and a half later. If necessary, canceled airline tickets would back up their claim.

Their return flights were real. Making their departure dates appear three days earlier than they had actually happened, however, had required a bit of computer hacking trickery, but there it was. No one would be able to tell. One other strange occurrence had also happened. Before they returned home, Buck, for reasons unknown, had sworn to be faithful to Jackie for the rest of his life. He had his beard trimmed by a professional and started wearing bright colored sport shirts instead of his usual somber black. He even bought her a friendship ring with a blue sapphire in it and started calling her Honey. Jackie lost another ten pounds in the process and did her calisthenics faithfully for an hour every morning and by the time they were ready to leave, she looked so overwhelming that Buck lapped religiously at her toes and at her contours and her confluences and at anything else she would hold still for.

Mike and Sue, however, didn't need friendship rings to express their feeling for each other. They were already bonded together tighter than the epoxied seams on a fishing boat where time would only serve to strengthen the joint, making the weld stronger even than the base material of the two component parts that were brought together.

But as for Jennie...Poor Jennie. The mind, the person, the human being. Sometimes so full of strength, eager determination and will power. Supple, imaginative, persevering, creating laughter and joy, moving mountains, surviving impossible extremes and impossible odds. And yet, sometimes...Who knows why. Such a delicate balance, thin lines drawn, shadowy figures hiding in the corners out of sight; an ephemeral, spun glass web, delicate as a fresh cut flower, more fragile than the finest of crystal.

Kohl held her and talked to her and soothed her and prayed for her but she hardly seemed to realize he was there. Nor did she seem to care. She cried in the day and screamed in the dark. Over and over and over again for nearly a week, gaining some ground during the day but never less haunted during the night.

He forced her out on long walks, had her spend hours in the warm sun, read her soft poetry and told her how he loved her and how sorry he was, but none of it seemed to help. When they returned to Sedona she quit her job and sent Kohl away and refused to leave her small apartment for days on end. Finally she wrote him a letter and by the time it was delivered, she was gone. Back to Ohio, or to somewhere, she wouldn't say and he was never able to find out. "I love you Kohl," she had written. "I always will. And I'm sorry I wasn't stronger for you."

There were tear stains on the stationary and the envelope but not a trace or a clue as to where she might have gone and every attempt to find her ended in failure. Not knowing what else to do, he went off into the Sonoran desert and made his camp far beyond the nearest road where the only other footprints belonged to the coyote and the jackrabbit. There he found a grove of mesquite trees in a low valley amongst what was otherwise a plain of Saguaro, Cholla and other varieties of spiny plant life. A very small but live spring bubbled from the ground.

Totally alone, there was no place to escape to and no choice but to deal with his own thoughts and feelings. Ultimately, there was only one conclusion. He loved her enough to try and leave her alone, knowing that if she were ever able to resolve things for herself, she would have to do it in her own way and her own time. Someday, maybe, when she was ready, he would see her again. For the moment, however, there seemed no other alternative. And as immense as was the pain, he reminded himself constantly that, given the choice, he would have still fallen in love with her all over again and still counted himself as being very lucky for having done so.

So when he returned to town, he seemed the same, but he was different. Mike knew it, so did Sue. Buck and Jackie sensed it. Untouched, the rest of the world went on about its business. Kohl tried not to look at other people's reflections in windows when he passed, or to listen to voices in the crowd or pick up on lingering traces of perfume in shops and restaurants. He did not dare, otherwise her wistful song would surround him and echo down through the empty corridor that was now his life.

"What the hell are you laughing at?" Mike wanted to know.

"You two," Kohl said, looking at them standing there on the deck of their new home against a backdrop of red, sculptured mountains. "I keep seeing you in those awful clothes." He laughed again in an astonished way.

"Didn't you love those artists conceptions that were in the paper?" Sue asked, smoothing her hair in subconscious reaction. "Did I really look that bad?"

"Worse," Kohl said. But looking at her now, so fresh and beautiful, it was inconceivable that she could have done that to herself. Mike either, for that matter. He had kept the bushy mustache but was otherwise clean shaven and looked his usual elegant self, disarming grin and all.

"Come on Kohl. Sit down," Mike said, waving to the wooden patio chairs on the redwood deck. Kohl sat and Sue brought him a cold drink. He picked up the glass, leaned back and took in the view. In addition to all the rock formations in the distance one could also see the meanderings of Oak Creek Canyon from there, as well as Steamboat Mountain with the old part of town lying at its feet. It seemed to fit them well. They both looked radiant and happy; he had missed them more than he realized. Kohl shook his head in approval and smiled.

Then they began to talk in earnest. Had he heard from Jennie? How did they feel about what they had done? What had it accomplished? Where did they go from here, especially under the circumstances. Not one article in either a newspaper or a periodical or one TV commentator or one evening special seemed to understand the reasons behind what they had done. Blatant terrorism, was all they could say. "Well," Mike said. "Sue has an idea."

"What if we start a propaganda machine of our own. If oil companies, timber merchants and the government can do it, so can we."

"But how, without giving ourselves away?"

"Sue started a non-profit organization and buried it behind half a dozen other companies to hide our identity. We'll hire a couple of staff writers and a stenographer. In addition to swamping editors with bits and pieces of opinion for editorial pages we also take out full page, paid Sunday supplements in all the major newspapers across the country. No doomsday ranting and raving, just facts, statistics and trends about how we are committing national and planetary suicide, all low key, all politely done. We want people to read it and talk about it, not threaten them with eternal damnation if they don't. Today's simple truth alone should be enough to make a believer out of most everyone."

"Probably," Kohl said.

"You sound a little skeptical."

"Sorry. Maybe I am. Or at least I'm getting to be."

"How come?"

"I'm beginning to think that the only lessons people seem to learn is to repeat the mistakes they made before. And to do it on an even bigger scale."

"Then why are you doing all this?" Mike wanted to know. Now he was a bit puzzled. Maybe he didn't understand Kohl as well as he thought he did.

"The same as you," he said and received two quizzical looks.

"Which is?"

"For ourselves."

"Are we doing it for ourselves?" Sue wondered.

"I wouldn't sacrifice myself for anything else," Kohl stated.

"I don't want to sacrifice myself at all," Mike said. "What's the point? Then you're out of the game."

"Exactly."

"So what's the bottom line?" Sue asked.

"We can't save the human race. Not if it doesn't want to be saved, so there is no reason to be idealistic about that. What we do, we do because simply we believe in it, even if no one else does. And democracy has nothing to do with it. Our only reward will be in honoring our own ideals. Nothing else. Otherwise, we don't do it. If worse comes to worse, we take the consequences and when any one of us runs out of reasons, we quit."

"Point made," said Mike.

"Point made," Sue seconded. "But I think we also believe there are far more people out there than we realize who feel the same way we do. People who know we need change and want it. They just don't know how to bring it about. They don't need waking up as much as they need moral support. If we can provide that maybe we can get them to take some action of their own. Hopefully political."

There were no grounds on which Kohl could disagree.

"I'm willing to risk it," he said.

"And we already have, so let's drink to that," Mike said in salute. "Here's to pragmatists."

They drank. Sue called out for pizza. "So, do you think we can find a way to use what happened to the dam as a point in our favor?" Kohl said after they had eaten.

"We can try. And in spite of how the media handled it, we can point out that for the first time in years some of the people in the cities talked to their neighbors, shared their candles and their food supplies, worried about someone else besides themselves and survived with a better appreciation for what they have."

"The written word, punctuated with infrared bursts of high technology and basic old dynamite. Words and music," Kohl said with an enthusiasm that now matched Mike's and Sue's. "I love it. And I love you for thinking of it. You too, Mike. May the ink win in the end, however."

"Bravo. Sounds like we're ready to roll again."

"As soon as I hear from Buck. Which reminds me, have you had this place swept for bugs?"

"We just moved in," Sue pointed out.

"I know but maybe it's time to tighten up. Have Buck or Jackie been here yet?"

"Not yet."

"Good. Nor will I come back. No offense. I love the house but we need to establish a new meeting place. No more public gatherings, either."

"What would you suggest?"

"I'll find a place. Give me a couple of days," Kohl said. And then he asked, "Do you know where we might find some scramblers for our telephones, Mike?"

"No, but it shouldn't be hard," Mike said with a smile on his face, then got up and went inside. A moment later he was back. "You mean like this?" he asked and handed Kohl a small, round cell of an object.

Kohl examined it. It looked very similar to a telephone mouthpiece and would obviously slip right over most of them.

"And here's the receiver," Mike said and handed Kohl a second and somewhat similar looking item he had brought out with him. "That set's yours. I made a pair for Buck too."

Kohl looked at the two devices, one in each hand.

"Talk over it all you want and don't worry," Mike assured him. "It has some cute multiplexing tricks inside of it that they'll never decode."

"You made these?" Kohl wanted to know.

"What else?" Mike shrugged nonchalantly. Who else was better qualified to put something like this together than he.

Kohl's emotions were thoroughly touched. Sue had, at her own time and expense, created another weapon for them to use, perhaps even more lethal than the laser itself. And Mike, helping her and helping Kohl, was constantly leaping ahead with his ever surprising intellect. What would he come up with next? What could Kohl say? Nothing. He hugged them both instead. And then Sue hit him with it.

"There is one small problem that has come up," she warned Kohl, however, before he left.

"Oh?"

"Linda!" Sue said.

"Linda?"

"My niece."

"I know. What has she done?"

"Nothing yet. But she's convinced that we are somehow involved with this. Now I'm glad we didn't include her. I'm not so sure we could have trusted her after some of the questions she's asked and some of the things she's hinted at."

"Like what?"

"Buck is hanging around all the time and that can't be good because she's convinced he's a terrorist. And what about all the money my old accountant told her I was giving to you. If we were breaking the law, I could lose all of it. And then, what happened to Jenny? Every since the dam was destroyed, Jenny did nothing but cry and seemed unable to function. And now she's gone. Where? All of that."

"That's too bad. I thought she might turn out to be one of our biggest fans? If we ever decided to confide in her."

"I know. She's always been like a sister to me. Better, even. We've never had an argument or even harsh words until now. But this was more than just an argument. Would you believe she threatened me?"

"With what?"

Exposure, if it doesn't stop."

"But she has no proof of anything."

"I know. Thank god. And to think how close we came to letting her in on it."

"Maybe she's just concerned for your safety," Kohl said kindly enough.

"Then she should have left it at that but she also went into a tirade. She called us a bunch of misguided anarchists, destructive revolutionaries and... What else, Mike?"

"Over the hill idealists..."

"So what the hell. That's what we are."

"And, un-American," Mike concluded.

Kohl laughed out loud. "She said that? Good grief. What happened to her?"

"Seriously? Bottom line, I think it's mostly about the money. I should have bought her a new car in the beginning."

"I suppose you still could if you wanted to."

"No, it's too late. Now it would be a bribe and she would know it. Then we would really be vulnerable."

"I think you're right. So far she doesn't have anything specific to go on. She hasn't even seen the van. Of course we can still change our minds. Just restrict ourselves to the written word, which is one great idea. Maybe even the most effective. There is nothing Linda would be able to say about that."

Mike said nothing. Whatever Sue wanted, that was what he wanted. Sue was no fool and, blood relative or no blood relative, she was not about to let Linda interfere with her plans, whatever they might turn out to be.

Kohl left it alone, also. Ans even if he had been there, Buck didn't have a voice in it at all. Whatever Sue decided, that would be it, one way or the other.

THIRTEEN

Most of Chicago had been plunged into complete darkness and remained that way for nearly a week. High voltage transmission lines leading into the city had been toppled in half a dozen different places and two coal burning, power generating stations had been put out of service, one on the Wisconsin River in southern Wisconsin and the other in northern Illinois.

The tower lines, however, were soon rebuilt in spite of heavy rains during the earlier part of the week and power was obtained from other locations in the interstate network to bring the lights back on in this major city at five thirty in the afternoon of the sixth day. It was a Friday. The power plants themselves, unfortunately, would be a matter of much longer duration, depleting a large portion of the reserve capacity in the Midwest for at least six months. As long as there weren't any severe thunder storms in the surrounding area or an unseasonable cold snap which would unduly burden the line, however, or those gangsters didn't destroy something else, it was not a problem.

A large gathering and a ceremony had been arranged for the following day in the park along Lake Shore Drive to commemorate the executives of the utility companies for their quick response and cooperation in the matter. Both the Mayor and the Governor were there, along with the Chief of Police, a dozen aldermen and two state senators. It was election year. What did it matter what the excuse was. It was an opportunity to do some back slapping, their own if possible, as well as those of some of their heaviest contributors. After all, good politicians always know where the peanut butter comes from.

A stage had been quickly assembled, bleachers erected and a public address system installed that had sufficient wattage to reach almost to South Milwaukee, approximately sixty miles away. Four different High School bands were bussed in. A giant American flag had been hung on a cable between two large elm trees in the background and banners flew from the streetlight poles.

Then the bands began to play the Star Spangled Banner to get everyone's attention and to let them know that the proud occasion was about to begin. A retired, one star general who smoked a corn cob pipe in emulation of old Doug MacArthur stood up and came to center stage. He was a brave General who had tried to cash in on the glory of the Atari massacre in the middle east war by threatening to dust the ass of an ordinary citizen who couldn't see the necessity of killing innocent people or setting the clean air campaign back fifty years from all the jet fuel burned in thousands of sorties, multi tons of expended explosives and many dozens of oil well fires burning out of control. He coughed loudly, came to attention and led the pledge of Allegiance.

Next, one of the local aldermen got up and introduced the Chief of Police who introduced the mayor. The mayor then spent nearly fifty nine minutes in circumlocution and self aggrandizement and before finally introducing his old friend and good pal, the governor. The Governor extolled on all the virtues of his fellow party members who were present and ended up by lauding the executives of the utility companies and some of his other heavy campaign contributors.

The workers who had waded around in the muck and the mud and hung upside down off hundred foot high steel towers in the rain and the darkness in a non-stop effort to put things back together went entirely unnoticed, however, because the Governor had been told that they were a rowdy bunch of non-voting no-goods who spent all their off time in the barroom anyway. But did they care? Hell no, they weren't stupid. All that additional overtime they had received in the process was worth far more than the Governor's compliments any day.

At this point the State Attorney General showed up and preempted the Chief of Police who was going to speak out about the sabotage. The Chief became miffed, told the Mayor to forget about tearing up any more of his relatives traffic tickets and stormed off. The Attorney General walked to center stage and roundly condemned the perpetrators of the barbaric crime and summarily assured the audience that they would be promptly apprehended and locked away for the remainder of their natural lifetimes since the law prevented the authorities from hanging them from certain private parts of their male anatomies.

Unfortunately, however, since the start of the noble occasion had been seriously delayed because the Governor's wife had refused to ride up Lake Shore Drive in a closed limo and it took two hours to find a suitable convertible, it was now dusk. Fortunately the Mayor's campaign manager had covered all bases and had a lighting crew standing by in case the formalities should run over time, which they usually did whenever the Mayor was allowed to speak.

The lights came on and being unable to resist the spotlight, the Mayor again rose to make some concluding remarks but was beat to the microphone by the Governor. The Governor thumped on the mike to get everyone's attention just as the beer truck driver pulled up behind the stage and began unloading. Not to be outdone, the Governor stood tall and proud with his arms outstretched in a magnificent gesture and began to speak. In the middle of the third sentence, however, something very unusual happened.

Once again the lights went out as the entire city of Chicago was thrown into darkness for the second time in a week. Fortunately for the Governor the public address system also went dead at the same moment because the Mayor distinctly heard him say, "What the fuck?" into the lifeless microphone. Had he also known that this time it would take much longer before the power came on again, however, he might well have added son-of-a-bitch, or some other choice set of explicatives to his words.

In the orange yellow glow of the roadway lights along the Indiana Turnpike, Buck reached between his knees and separated a can of Old Horse Lager from the plastic binder on a half gone six pack and popped the top. He took a swallow and looked across the front seat of their rental car at Kohl in the dim light and said, "Wished we could have arranged it so that we could have been at that celebration in the park back there. I would have loved to see the look on the Governor's face when the power went off again."

"How could you see his face if the lights were out?" Jackie wanted to know from the back seat.

"I always carry a flashlight honey. You know that," Buck chided her.

"Smart ass."

"Anyway, can't you and Mike make a stronger powered detonator relay or something so we could be in the company of some of our more esteemed countrymen at times like that?"

"We'll have to see what we can do."

"I'd appreciate it," Buck said.

"Thanks," Kohl told him and readjusted the driver's seat for more comfort.

"Where are we off to now?" Buck then asked.

"Philadelphia," Kohl replied.

"What's in Philadelphia?" Jackie asked lazily. She had now stretched out in the ear seat, about to sneak in a nap.

"A lot of people sitting up late to watch the second episode of that new mini-series," Kohl said.

"That'd be a great time to put them in the dark, all right. What's it called?" Jackie asked with a slight bit of interest.

"What?"

"The mini-series."

"The Hairdresser's Drawers," Buck said, taunting her again.

"Want a bet?" she said.

"What then?" he asked.

"The Tiger's Revenge by Claude Balls, Buck, and that's what you're going to have if you don't stop teasing me."

Kohl laughed as Buck handed his beer back to Jackie as a sign of goodwill. Jackie sat up enough to take a sip and then set it on the floor. Buck, seeing it wasn't going to be returned, helped himself to another.

"Actually I believe it's called, The Trials and Tribulations of a Wall Street Magot," Kohl said.

This time Jackie chuckled only slightly as Buck said, "Gee, I wouldn't mind seeing that myself. Can we get a motel room so we can watch it?"

The humor continued about possible titles to the series and ranged from, The President who Barfed on the Premier to, Love in the Oval office to, Hanky Panky Under the Pool Table to who knows what and, stupid though it was, it helped to eat up another fifty miles or so even though everyone still knew that they had a long ways to go and a lot of work to do before the third and final episode of the series came on the following evening. Since a portion of the story had been filmed in Philadelphia and almost the entire population of the area would be watching it, it would be a marvelous opportunity to demonstrate to these folks just how uncertain life in the big city can be.

Jackie fell asleep shortly thereafter while Buck and Kohl talked a while longer. "Is Mike going to join us?" Buck asked.

"No, strictly dynamite here, too. We'll try and keep them confused as long as possible. Let them think that the movement has expanded into different elements. It will keep the authorities busy farther from home."

"And the next one?"

"He'll be there. After that and one more, we'll start taking turns again. One faction of the group will always stay home and make them selves highly visible so they have an air tight alibi. That way the authorities will have a more difficult time connecting us all together."

Buck grunted his approval, leaned back in the seat and shut his eyes. What he really wanted to do, however, was to get in the back seat with Jackie. He wondered what Kohl would think if he got back there and removed her jeans. Probably nothing. But Jackie would object, so he might as well forget it. But then, if they had a blanket to hide under. But they didn't so what the hell, might as well get some sleep. It would be his turn to drive soon.

Kohl, driving onward through the night, all alone at last with his thoughts, tried hard not to think of Jennie. It was a lonely business, this, made lonelier still by her absence. God, how he missed her. God how he wished he hadn't left her alone out there in the cold in the middle of that night, back then. But then, no matter what her weaknesses, Jennie was not Linda. She would never betray their secrets.

So too, as in Chicago, did the lights of Philadelphia dim and die two days later as shouts of fear and anger thundered even further across the land. At first everyone was quick to assert that it was the same wild bunch of bandits that had crippled Hoover Dam. Upon detailed examination, however, no traces of a laser being used were found and that was bad news. Just as they had hoped, the media believed that a second band of heathens must have come ashore and were now roaming the land. Protect us from this evil, everyone cried and went out and hoarded candles and kerosene and filled their freezers with chunks of ice so that their porterhouses wouldn't spoil if it were to happen again.

In further response, there was an emergency meeting of the Joint Chiefs of Staff and both the Armed Services and the National Guard were put on standby. The FBI was promptly and properly informed that if something significant wasn't uncovered very shortly, they would have a new Director. They might anyway because one of the President's fraternity brothers from way back at Harvard had left the private sector and was in search of bigger opportunity.

Inspector Pry's immediate superior had already been given the ax, however, and Pry, who knew the present presiding Director's brother-in-law who had once painted his house, was promptly promoted. Unfortunately, however, Inspectors Parsons' and Spinet's revealing report on Sue had gone unread, although Parsons and Spinet had worked very hard and diligently on their make-work assignment and had uncovered some highly questionable facts about what Sue might have spent her money on. They had also learned the identity of Kohl in the process, along with his technical background and a possible association with one Buckly Hudson, suspected anarchist. The report went unread in the pile on Pry's desk simply because he was far too busy administrating his new, and larger, empire to look at it. So slow, the proceedings of the law.

In the meanwhile, hundreds of mothballed helicopters were stripped of their cosmoline and their plastic cocoons and pressed back into service to fly routine patrol along all the major networks of high tension lines leading to all the major cities of the nation. Simultaneously, the think tank at Rand Corporation was given a three million dollar award to conduct statistical probability studies to try and predict the next target such that the Green Berets might be there in advance to waylay the bastards who had so little respect for the American way of life. And though the pipe smokers and the head scratchers and the beard pullers stayed up late many a night as computers analyzed and integrated, and sorted, and extrapolated while Congressmen bet heavily on a football type of pool and the Pentagon threw darts at a board and the President consulted his favorite psychic, none would have guessed that the team had already assembled itself at Three Mile Island.

133

"Holy frijoles," Buck said the first time he saw the immense, inverted funnel shaped cooling towers rising upward from the surface of the island for what seemed to him to be at least two hundred feet. He had seen all the pictures but first hand and a block away from across the river, he gained a different impression. "I hope you're not going to burn those babies down," he said to Mike and Kohl, however.

Quite surprisingly, Buck seemed to be a minor authority on the workings of a nuclear power plant. He knew immediately which part of the complex was TMI-1 and which part was TMI-2. He seemed also to understand some of the basics about reactors and had researched both the Brown's Ferry, Alabama fiasco in seventy five and the farcical Three Mile Island catastrophe in seventy nine. The Brown's Ferry incident was his favorite because of the fact that a small fire caused by a candle in some building insulation that could have been put out in a matter of seconds (had anyone enough sense to pour water on it) went on for six hours, creating enough damage to shut the plant down for eighteen months and cost the taxpayers more than three hundred million dollars.

Three Mile Island was equally absurd and began with the cleaning of a clogged filter wherein about a cup (one little cup) of ordinary water seeped into an air pipe connected to the generating system. It was all down hill from there, as the public well remembers. Especially for those forty thousand souls who evacuated the surrounding area. Another billion dollars down the drain. But money is one thing, lies are another, and oh how the administrators and the government lied about the escape of radioactivity and the true potential for meltdown as well as the multitude of inadequacies in safety procedures and equipment. Why not? Heads might roll if the public knew the truth and when careers are at stake, the public be damned.

Quite impressed with Buck's knowledge, Mike and Kohl assured him that in no way were they going to tamper with the normal functionings of the reactors and thus create a new hazard for the local population. "Good," said Buck whose comprehensive understanding of the workings of such a plant were due to the fact that he had once been part of a radical group whose original intent had been to destroy the Poco Diablo nuclear station out in California. But, after doing some research on his own, he had withdrawn from the project when he learned of the potential hazards for the neighboring residents when tampering with those kinds of things.

So what exactly were they going to do here to disable this plant without endangering anyone, he wanted to know.

"Like Hoover Dam," Kohl explained. "Only different."

"Okay," Buck said, quickly comprehending what they had in mind. "But what's the different part?"

They had been sitting in a rental car parked along the roadway to the east doing their talking. The van had been left parked deep in a woods out of sight ten miles south of town until it was needed. "Come on," Kohl said, reaching for the binoculars. "We'll show you."

The three of them left the car and walked into the trees alongside the river bank where they could stand and survey the scene. Jackie had been sent home on this one and Sue had purposely stayed behind. Kohl handed the binoculars to Buck.

"See the circuit breakers in the substation to the back?"

"You mean those things with the small insulators on the back and the large ones on the front? They don't look the same as the Hoover dam ones."

"No, those are the transformers. Just behind them are some more large, steel box like things."

"Gotcha," Buck said. Then he looked cautiously from Kohl to Mike. "But you mean we have to crawl in there and let the oil out of them like we did before?" Holy shit. It seemed incredible to even consider such a thing, what with such a jangle and snarl of wires running everywhere and all that electricity bussing around overhead. Hoover had been one thing with its banks of breakers all lined up in a neat row but this was ridiculous.

Mike smiled craftily back at Buck and was silent. Buck looked at Kohl. Kohl shrugged. Buck began to get nervous. He took another peak through the binoculars, put them down, scratched his ass, then his beard, and said, "SHIT".

"Well, we wanted to send you home too," Mike pointed out. "But you wouldn't listen. You had to be here, so guess who gets to swim the river tonight?"

Buck looked downcast. "Didn't we even bring an inflatable dinghy?" he asked, staring across the water.

Mike and Kohl began to laugh. "Okay, you wise asses, what is it?" Buck wanted to know, turning back on them, knowing that he had been had.

They chuckled a little longer and even Buck began to grin. Then Mike put his arm on Buck's broad shoulders and pointed back across and explained. "On the sides of the breakers, see the square metal housings?"

Buck nodded.

"That's where the sensing mechanism for the breakers is. One on each breaker. We're going to try burning holes through them. Hopefully it will disable them so the breakers won't open when we short things out."

Buck nodded again. Good idea.

"And then, on the front of the breakers," Mike continued. "See the big wires coming out?"

Buck nodded for the third time.

"Follow them out to that cage like structure where they hook up to those long bus bars. They're live too. After we disable the breakers we simply burn them down and let them short out. That should wipe out all the generators inside the plant without interfering with the reactors."

"That easy, huh?" Buck said.

"Strictly a job for the laser." Kohl asked him.

Buck shrugged. "You're right. It's too easy. I should have stayed home."

"Well, you had your chance," Mike said, staring at him.

"Oh shit," Buck said. "What is it now?"

"The two end breakers down there," Mike said, motioning to the east. "We don't have a direct line of sight to them so we have to use the relay mirror. Somebody still has to swim the river."

"Right," Buck said. "Meaning me. Because I was too stupid to stay home."

"Actually," Kohl said. "We did bring a dinghy. And since it was going to be my job anyway, you can stay with Mike and drive the van in case he has to make a quick exit.

Feeling much better, Buck rapped them both on the arm and they headed back to the car.

"How come," he wanted to know, however. "If it's that simply, how come we didn't do that back at Hoover?"

"We could have," Kohl agreed. "But then they would have been back up and running in a lot less time. Besides that was special. Not only was it our coming out party, which called for lots of fireworks, but it gave us a chance to get a good look at each other and to see what our various talents were."

"Probationary period, huh?" Buck said, giving Kohl a shrewd look. Kohl shrugged as if to say, why not.

Driving through a city without lights had a spooky feeling to it, even at three o'clock in the morning. What were the people feeling, Kohl wondered, those who had been up and about when it had happened? Were they frightened and angry, or were they just irritated at the inconvenience of it? What would they say tomorrow when they found out it might be another three or four days before power came back on. Would they be beginning to lose confidence in the ability of the system to isolate and protect them from such annoyances? What if it happened twice in a row, as it had in Chicago? What attitudes would that change? Maybe they should hire one of those public opinion firms to do a survey. It might be helpful in telling them how to proceed.

Fortunately for the moment, however, they were headed in the right direction, at least geographically, because by now it was clear to the powers that be that the coterie of gangsters who had done the Hoover job were on the loose again and that was very serious. Those guys didn't screw around. After Hoover Dam and Three Mile Island, surely Niagara Falls was meant to be their next target. As a result, the Green Berets were promptly rousted out of their bunks in the middle of the night and put aboard a military transport with barely enough time to grab their socks and their assault rifles. Their thoughtful commander, however, having been already dressed when the word came down, since he had just gotten home from a cocktail party, had enough time to run by the all night donut shop on the way to the airfield and pick up six dozen assorted varieties. There was nothing too good for "our boys," he always said. By the time the Berets were airborne, however, Mike, Buck and Kohl were rolling along back towards the southwest in the van, totally in the opposite direction from where half a million dollars worth of computer analysis said they should be.

At the moment the van was safely signed, painted and equipped quite properly in keeping with their new specialty. Indiana Gas and Electric as it clearly stated on the sides and rear door. They had even found an aluminum ladder and a rotating amber caution light for the roof.

The three of them sat together in the front. Mike driving, Kohl in the passenger seat and Buck in the jump seat in the middle. Mike and Kohl were talking about old times back when they used to work together as Buck alternated between listening and dozing. Soon they were out of the black out belt and back in the land of the living and an hour and a half later they were wandering through the streets of Indianapolis looking for an all night diner. Suddenly Buck yelled, "Stop Mike."

Mike slammed on the brakes and pulled to the curb. "What's the matter?" Kohl asked him.

"Nothing," Mike laughed. "Just thought I'd break up the monotony for Buck."

Kohl looked out the window to see what Mike was talking about. "No, Mike. Don't do it."

"What the hell, nobodies around," Mike said, grinning as though he were about to knock the teachers hat off with a well aimed snowball.

"I really don't think you should. Tell him Buck. I don't think he should do that."

"Well, if we're being democratic," Buck said. "Then he has my vote. Sorry old man.".

"We're a long ways from home, Mike," Kohl reminded him.

"Yeah, but I sort of promised Buck," Mike explained.

"You promised Buck?"

"He did Kohl. He promised."

"We don't even have a place to hid if something goes wrong."

"He criss-crossed his heart and hoped to die," Buck said. "And I aim to hold him to it."

They sat there for a moment glancing back and forth at each other, Buck quite serious about proceeding, Mike smiling, thinking of the comedy of it and Kohl looking as though he were about to get out and walk.

"Well, what the hell," Buck said. "Let's do it."

With that Mike got out and went around to the back of the van and climbed in as Buck slid over into the driver's seat. "Back up a little so I can get in a better position," Mike hollered at him.

Buck eased the vehicle back until he felt it was about right. Up went the periscope, giving Mike a shot at a long row of city police cars neatly parked side by side in a fenced lot beside the street. Surplus, late model vehicles all in good repair, sitting there for use during periods of more demand such as the Speedway Races, holidays, especially New Year's Eve, and as general backup for the regular patrol vehicles.

"If you have to do this, try not to set any of them on fire. We don't need the attention," Kohl pleaded.

"I'll just run a little slice down through all the dashboards and wipe out the instruments and the wiring," Mike said. "That ought to be as effective as anything."

"It's your party," Kohl said, resigning himself to it at last.

"How's the street?" Mike asked.

"Clear up here," Buck said.

"Clear in the rear," Kohl shrugged and replied, looking in the outside rear view mirror.

Buck slipped the gear shift into neutral and engaged the generator. Fifteen seconds later Mike yelled ready. Kohl looked out the window for the folly to begin while Buck scooted over, trying to see around him. The glass in the first car glowed dull orange down in the front corner as a web of cracks found their way across it. A neat, round hole popped through it and a trace of smoke started to fill the interior of the car, then stopped. Buck and Kohl heard the back door of the van open and close and Mike came back around, opened the front door and motioned for Buck to move over.

"What happened?" Buck wanted to know.

"Kohl's right," Mike said. "We'd better wait."

"But look at all those goddamned cop cars all in a row. Where the hell will we ever get another opportunity like this?"

"So how many cop cars do you think there are in this country, Buck?" Kohl asked him.

"Too fucking many."

"Sure, but make a guess."

"Millions, I suppose."

"So what's the problem? We'll find some more."

"So much for promises. Jesus, shit."

"I promise again," Mike said. "Double criss-cross."

"Screw you," Buck said in a disgusted voice. "You can buy me breakfast."

"The way you eat? Forget it," Mike said.

"Then burn them goddamned cars."

"We can't. As soon as it hit the news, every law enforcement agency in the country would know what direction we were headed in."

"Well, damn," Buck said. "I see your point but god damn, will you stop teasing me like that all the time."

"Okay. Sorry. Breakfast is on me," Mike told him.

"And then on to St. Louis. I think you'll enjoy that one Buck," Kohl assured him. "It's the real thing."

"What are we going to do there?"

"Show you another of technologies little wonders."

Buck looked at Kohl, then turned to Mike. "Well, let's move it Mike. You bastards kept me up all night and I'm hungry."

They drove through the rest of the night and well into the following afternoon, got off Interstate Fifty Five at a small town in southern Illinois, found the nearest motel and crashed, sleeping through until the next morning. Then they began again with Kohl at the wheel. Approximately twenty miles later, he turned south on Two Fifty Five, went to the first exit and got off. He drove a few miles west on Collinsville Road and then turned into the Cahokia Mounds State Historical Site. Even though he didn't know why they had stopped there, Buck, for once, was silent. He got quietly out of the van with Kohl and Mike and looked around. What was this all about? There were no tower lines here. Mike opened the rear door of the van and reached for the binoculars where he had left them last.

Kohl lead off with Mike close behind, heading in the direction of what to Buck was a very large pile of grass covered dirt. He shrugged and followed. The sun was out and though there were some lingering clouds in the south, it was as good a day as any for a walk.

They climbed the two long, steep levels of steps and arrived at

140

the top of the one hundred foot mound, walked out some distance towards the middle and went to the western edge. Buck was impressed. The view was quite astounding. He could see the high rise buildings of downtown St. Louis from there and what looked like the river and the spans of bridges crossing over. The mighty Miss-iss-ip. But what were they doing up here? Some reconnaissance perhaps. But for what? Awe inspiring as the view was, the site seemed a bit remote from anything they might be interested in. "What is this place?" he asked.

"Former site of the Cohokia Indians," Kohl explained. "They lived here from around seven hundred to fifteen hundred AD. The mounds were built for ceremonial purposes apparently, this particular one being used for sacrifices."

"Blood?" Buck asked.

"Yes," Kohl said.

"People?"

"Maidens, I believe, as well as animals," Mike said.

"Never did understand that mentality," Buck stated and shook his head in disgust.

"Obviously you're referring to the maidens."

"Those old priests had to either be queer, castrated or damned awful stupid," Buck said with disapproval and sat down on the grassy edge of the mound.

"Or they had a big surplus of maidens," Mike said, and sat beside him.

"How could there ever be a surplus of maidens? Even if it were a hundred to one."

"Maybe the priests were really priestesses," Kohl offered. "And were doing away with some of the competition."

"And calling it religion. What kind of civilization is that?"

"About the same as ours," Kohl stated.

"How do you figure that one?" Buck asked.

"What would you call Vietnam, if it wasn't a blood sacrifice? The only difference is that it was men instead of women and was done in the name of country to appease the President instead of in the name of religion to appease the priests. The Indians here only killed about five hundred maidens over a period of eight hundred years. The United States sacrificed what, fifty eight thousand in a matter of a few years," Kohl pointed out matter of factly and sat down also, the three of them side by side.

Diverse of background, united in common cause, heroes to be if they ever succeeded, criminals if they were caught, they sat for awhile and contemplated the countryside. Kohl, who had made it there from the humble beginnings of a poor midwestern farm which eventually led him to the inner sanctum of Beverly Hills and back again to a strange minded, small Arizona town where his soul intent had been simply to become a serious writer of stories. Alone now, he missed his Jennie desperately, although he rarely spoke of it.

Buck, wayward misfit in any world, one eighth angry Apache, one eighth hapless Hopi and three fourths who knew what else by blood except maybe his white eyes pappy who wouldn't have shared the truth with anyone except the devil himself. Having to a large extent raised himself out in the backwater regions of the California desert, Buck had his own code of honor that was not to be crossed if you valued your skin. He had turned destructive after he had first traveled to Hopiland in search of his heritage and had learned of all the subversive tricks the federal government was still using to divide the people and steal their lands.

Mike, bless him, by far the most congenial of the bunch, product of a good eastern family and an Ivy League college, a man who could have been CEO of any top ten corporation had he the intent and desire to do so, had put himself through the last two years of school because his father couldn't seem to adjust to his wanting to be an earnest, lowly engineer instead of a super slick, big city attorney and had cut him off. As opposed to buck, Mike wasn't in this adventure because of emotional reasons. He had initially gotten involved because of his friendship for Kohl and had been converted to the cause by his own logic which showed him how clearly and quickly the environment was sliding down the hill towards the dung heap.

So they sat there inside their separate skins, individual in entity but fused together in spirit by the searing heat of an invisible laser beam, cases and cases of dynamite, shared undertaking and seditious action. The morning sun warmed their backs, sparkled in the grass and illuminated the world before them, reflecting off the stone and glass of the distant city and turned St. Louis's modern day claim to fame, the six hundred and thirty foot tall stainless steel arch, to shining gold.

They were privileged to be completely alone on the top of the immense mound of dirt at this time of day, sitting there in unruffled solitude and silence, as feelings of what it might have been like hundreds of years ago in the past permeated the air. It was almost such that if one were to shut ones eyes and listen carefully one could almost hear the distant, hypnotic beating of ancient drums coming from the background accompanied by the low, haunting sound of a reed flute hanging in the air, lulling the mind and seeping into the soul.

Strange, Buck thought as he sat there. Sacrifices or no sacrifices, there was still something very reverent about this place and he actually began to find that he was starting to feel very humble. Even though it was a new feeling for him and a bit frightening at first, it was a good feeling once he became used to it. He leaned back and laid down in the soft grass and shut his eyes while Kohl and Mike began taking turns looking through the binoculars and commenting on how the bridges were constructed. What a dumb thing to talk about. Who gave a damn about bridges at a time like this?

In St. Louis, Kohl rented two full size pickup trucks using a phony Illinois driver's license and he and Buck followed Mike in the van to an old abandoned house far out on the east side. Two hours later he said, "Let's hope it doesn't rain."

"You mean this stuff is water soluble," Buck asked as he surveyed the handiwork which had converted the two brand new and shiny vehicles into State of Illinois, Highway Department trucks. Numbers nine-o-three and nine-o-four. He wet the tip of his finger and wiped it across the tailgate of the one he was standing behind. "Hmm," he said, looking at the orange-yellow. "Sure is."

"Come on Buck. Don't screw it up," Mike told him.

"Like you said, Kohl. I hope to hell it doesn't rain," Buck said, looking at the afternoon sky, which had suddenly turned uncertain.

"Get in," Kohl told him. "We have work to do."

They drove back into town, Kohl and Buck in one vehicle and Mike in the other, crossing the Mississippi over the Poplar Street Bridge. "Is that what we're going to knock down," Buck asked as he looked at the giant, sweeping, catenary arch that climbed gracefully towards the sky on the west bank of the river.

"Sorry," Kohl said.

"Why not?" Buck asked. "Easy as pie."

"Too easy," Kohl assured him.

"What are we doing here in these trucks then?"

"You're riding on it."

"Riding on what? You mean the bridge?"

"Uh huh. Six of them."

"Cut the shit, Kohl. I'm not that stupid," Buck said, looking first at Kohl and then out the rear window at Mike following close behind in the second pickup.

"I never thought you were Buck," Kohl assured him. "We're going to do this one and five more up river to the north."

Buck looked out the window again, trying to see the other bridges but the view was blocked. He looked back at Kohl, calm and composed with his gloved hands on the wheel. Kohl wasn't playing with him. He was serious.

"For Christsake, Kohl. It'd take us half the night just to place charges on one of them. And only then if we had free access to it without all this traffic and streetlights. Even then the best we could hope to do would be a span or two."

"A span or two is all we care about. But we have a better way," Kohl assured him.

Buck laughed. "Sure," he said. "We just rent a dozen cranes and demolition balls, hire three hundred welders with cutting torches, close the fuckers down one by one right in broad daylight and go to work. Are you going to try and draw a weekly pay check from the city too, while you're at it?"

"Maybe," Kohl said, amiably.

"But I don't want to be here for Christmas and Easter both. Besides, it'll rain before that and all the paint will wash of the trucks and then we'll be in deep shit," Buck said, kidding but not kidding.

Kohl laughed. Especially at the thought of trying to draw a check from the city. "Actually," he said. "It shouldn't take us more than two or three hours to set things up, maybe a few hours of whacking away with the laser and then we can take them all down in about fifteen minutes apiece."

"Now I know you're full of shit Kohl. I was at the concrete

plant and at the dam, remember? Not even the laser could do that, even if you could get in the right position for it. We'd still need two days to burn through that much concrete and we'd still be dead before we were half through."

"I agree with you a hundred percent."

"So how you going to do it then?"

"Well, this business is like any other. If you're going to stay ahead of the competition you have to do your homework, and spend a little money on research and development."

Buck was about to tell Kohl he was still full of shit but then he remembered he was talking to one of the two guys who had put that awesome laser together that they fondly referred to as Maggie once in a while. Maybe he'd better shut up about that part of it and see what developed.

"Why bridges?" he asked instead. "Why not power lines? That's more of our specialty anyway."

"But the games the same. Disruption is disruption. With disruption comes dissatisfaction, provided we don't get caught and the disruption continues, of course. Create enough disruption and we may start a revolution. Deprive enough people of their easy way of life and modern conveniences and we may even have a return to something more basic and self reliant, with more freedom and a little less government."

"Dream on, old man. Dream on."

"Why not? It doesn't take any more imagination to dream a big dream than a little one," Kohl said and put on the turn signal.

Followed by Mike, he turned off the main street, drove south a ways, made a few more turns and stopped in front of a mini-storage complex where he produced the keys for unit number ninety one and stopped in front of it. Mike pulled in directly behind. They got out and Kohl unpadlocked the door.

"Jesus," Buck said as he looked at the pile of assorted, brand new signs and barriers with battery powered lights attached to them. Men Working, Bridge Out and, Detour. "Where'd you get these?" he asked.

"Mike and Kohl's custom sign shop," Kohl replied, reminding Buck to keep his gloves on. "Come on, put these in Mike's truck."

They loaded them up and managed to get a light tarp over the top before another tenant pulled up two units down and went looking for something. They retreated inside to be out of sight as much as possible. Mike sat down on one stack of wooden boxes still in the storage unit and took out his cigarettes. He offered one to Buck. Buck accepted, sat down beside him and the two of them lit up. Kohl ducked back out to the truck, brought back a tool box and a six pack of beer and pulled the overhead door down half way. Then he too sat down and passed the beer around. No hurry. It was still a long time to dark. They might even have time for a nap.

When the beer and the cigarettes were gone they went back to work. There were six identical boxes about four feet long which they pried the lids off of. From these they lifted heavy, strange looking mechanisms that Buck could only wonder at. Each had a baseplate made of quarter inch thick channel iron the full four feet long. Bolted to it was a large metal eccentric weight on a shaft mounted in a heavy arbor with bearings so that it could rotate freely. This device was belt driven by what appeared to be the starter motor off a truck, stepped up in ratio by means of different sized pulleys such that the weight would run at much higher speeds than the motor.

A small aluminum chassis mounted to one end of the frame contained what an electronics technician would have recognized as a large power thyristor, some over sized power transistors, a number of integrated circuit chips and an assortment of other electronic components. Protruding from the top was a miniature radio antenna. They loaded the six units into the second truck and opened the remainder of the boxes which contained an assortment of long, sturdy J-hooks, U-bolts, standard machine bolts, over sized clamps, washers and other odds and ends. These they sorted out and placed in the back of the same truck in neat piles. There were also metal enclosures, an assortment of multi conductor cables and a number of tubes of quick cure epoxy which were also loaded.

The last items in the storage space were a dozen, brand new, twelve volt, heavy duty truck batteries and a pile of battery cables. To save time later, they attached one cable to each battery so that they could quickly be connected in series out on the bridges. Once these were on the truck, Kohl pulled down the storage unit door, locked it again and proceeded to throw the key over the building into the empty lot behind. Then they got in their trucks and went to find some dinner.

Full bellies and a few burps later they returned to the van, converted it back into a septic tank pumper with a new name on the doors and set out, one man in each vehicle. They found there way to Front Street which paralleled the river on the east side and stopped along the road where they had a clear line of sight to the large stone piers rising from the water. These supported the ends of the spans of the immense structure locally known as Eads Bridge, first opened to traffic on May twenty third, eighteen hundred and seventy four. Mike locked the fronts doors of the van from the inside and climbed into the back while Kohl and Buck took the two pickups and drove out onto the bridge itself, put out Men Working signs to block one lane of the west bound traffic and also went to work. What goes up must come down. History was once again in the making.

Elsewhere, sitting comfortably behind his oversized, oiled mahogany desk, now Section Head, Digand Pry was finally doing something to justify his new title, carpeted office and exorbitant salary increase. He had finally and inadvertently read the report that Inspectors Parsons and Spinet had prepared some time back. Surprising, from out of nowhere, some hound dog sense of something came alive in him and he quickly decided he needed to know a lot more about one Sue Alexander and the rest of the cast of characters in the script. But who to put on that task this time?

Having looked at the date on the report and seeing that he had been sitting on it for nearly three months he could hardly give it back to Parsons and Spinet. What if it really amounted to something and the word got out that he had done nothing with it in all this time? A span of time in which the lights had gone out in Chicago on two separate occasions and Three Mile Island had also gotten its generators smoked. That might be rather embarrassing. Surely, the only sensible thing to do would be to transfer Parsons and Spinet to that civil rights affair down in southern Alabama, put some fresh talent on the case and act as if he had been doing some of the leg work himself in the interim.

Which is exactly what he did.

From that point on things proceeded in rapid order. Five days later he had a new and thicker document on his desk top. This time he read it promptly, not knowing, however, that he already had competition on the case, coming from an entirely different quarter.

Behind another mahogany desk in another district of the capitol city, not all that many streets away from Pry, sat another man who had been given his own set of orders. One Mr. Rapier. A man who was a much sharper, more extreme version of Pry. A man without a need for a sign on his door or a listing in the confidential government directory. Another puppet whose strings were pulled from on high. Quite high, in fact. But an unemotional, uncaring puppet, however, whose greatest thrill was the sense of power he felt when stalking the unsuspecting quarry, knowing what easy targets they all made.

His new assignment? Find out who was behind those subversive newspaper supplements that are appearing in all the major papers across the country, he was told. They're not really illegal, however, he pointed out, just in case the folks in the big house on Pennsylvania Avenue failed to realize it. "All the more reason why they have to be silenced," he was told.

Ah, ha, he thought. Those articles had been hammering away for three months now, pointing the finger, naming names. The President's former connection with CIA drug traffic, arms deals, mass assassinations abroad and other covert and clandestine activity. Under the table sellouts to the Japanese, the Chinese and anyone else able to pay the price. Senators, congressmen, governors, judges, the police, all on the take, an insidious and sinister connivery and crookedness that pervaded almost every aspect of life. It did make interesting reading all right, and the people were beginning to take it seriously.

The thought of that pleased him, no less. He loved to see people sweat, whomever they were and for whatever reason, be it his next victim or someone from as aloof and far away as the White House. Didn't matter, there was a certain sense of power in knowing how vulnerable they all were because they cared too much about their status, their money, their positions, or maybe just about their lives, the pathetic things. Better yet, impressed as he had been with the tactics of J. Edgar Hoover, each new case was a fresh opportunity to rake around in the muck they all waded in and use it to add to his growing vault of private files.

As he went to work on his new assignment he soon found that it wasn't all that easy, however. Whoever the principals were, they had taken great pains to hide themselves from view. The ads were paid for by checks written against phony corporations, signed by fictitious persons and mailed from several different locations in the country. He couldn't seem to pierce the veil.

But think a moment, he told himself. Obviously the perpetrator had to be a person or an organization with a considerable amount of resources at their disposal. And why? Why do such a thing? Had they been treated badly by someone in power or by some function of government. That seemed unlikely. The rich were seldom abused. To the contrary, they were the biggest beneficiaries of the system, immune and isolated from the strife, seldom paying taxes, rarely getting more than a handslap when they erred. No, it was the middle class who paid dearly for their American way of life.

But still, this was no middle class thing. The middle class was far too busy working trying to feed the family, pay the mortgage, make the car payment, boat payment, furniture payment, insurance payment, health club dues, credit card installments, property taxes, income taxes as well as paying for all their kids designer clothes to even begin to get involved in such a thing. No, contrary as it seemed, it still had to be some wealthy individual or a very small group of wealthy persons. But why? If he knew why...

Not knowing where else to turn, he sent his secretary down to the computer room for a complete compilation of every related article from every newspaper in the country and read or reread every one looking for trends, traces, or tones of other messages that might provide a clue.

At last. How interesting. And how potentially dangerous.

It was one thing to bitch about corruption. That was all part of the game. Let the corrupt take their chances along with everyone else, the assholes. But this. My god. Didn't these people realize that all the American economy really had going for it anymore was the manufacture and marketing of frivolous, semi-useless, shoddy goods and over stated services.

Things that filled up kitchen cupboards, hall closets, attics and garages. Things that were used once or twice and put away to be forgotten, or used three times and broke and had to be thrown away because they were either made to be unrepairable or they cost more to fix than they cost new in the first place. Things that any sensible person would have realized they could easily have done without in the first place and would have been better off not to have bought to begin with. No way. We certainly couldn't have that kind of talk going around. The country would really fall apart if people woke up and began listening to that. It would be a recession to end all recessions. Another depression. Totally disallowed. It was downright heretical.

But... Could it be possible? What about the underlying undertones of environmental messages running through it all? Could it be that this person, or persons, were somehow associated with those anarchists who were blowing up dams and power plants? They seemed to be giving them a sympathetic plug every now and then. Sneakily, of course, but there if you looked for it. Hmmm... Wonder how those wizards over at the FBI were doing on that one? Even though they weren't half as competent as his own veiled little operation, it still seemed like they should have made some progress by now. Maybe it was time to insist on a look at it.

FOURTEEN

Thus it was that Rapier became privileged to look at Pry's latest file, without having to ask Pry, however. And what was this odd electronic sounding phenomenon that showed up in the bug on Alexander woman's phone, he asked himself. All the experts could make of it was that it acted like two fax machines talking to each other but which, when analyzed, was not fax machine language at all. Or any other kind that made any sense. Even the Pentagon's cryptographers had failed to decipher it.

What was that all about? What would a woman living in a small Arizona town have need of such a contrivance for, whatever it was? And look at this. She was also rumored to be independently wealthy. Well, well. Time for more leg work. But should he put his own people on it, do it himself, or could this man Pry be trusted to do it properly? There was only one way to find

150

out.

After Pry had been clearly informed by his branch chief that he was to cooperate fully with Rapier and to consider any order given by him just as bonafide and binding as if it came down from the Director himself, Rapier summoned him to his office.

"You'd look inconspicuous enough," Rapier told him after critically looking him over, "without that department store suit and tie. Buy yourself some jeans and a cowboy hat and go to Sedona, personally. Nose around, listen, observe, put a stake out on this woman's house. I want to know where she goes, what she does, who she sees, what she thinks and I want you to call me every day before the sun goes down. Clear?"

"Clear enough," Pry said, almost adding, yes sir, to it as he tried to conceal the defiance in his voice, not fully appreciating as yet who this man was that was treating him more like Pry was his personal man-servant than a fellow member of the intelligence community. He stared at Rapier, trying to fathom the man, to see what was lurking behind that hollow eyed mask of a face. But he couldn't categorize him except to note that he obviously wasn't one to screw around with, so he shifted in his seat, made some comment about mingling with cowboys, got up and left without benefit of well wishes or even a handshake.

Back at home just in time to interrupt his spouse's Monday afternoon bridge game, he dug out the luggage from under the pile in the front closet, kissed his wife for the second time that week, right in front of all her friends, got her to promise that she would pat the boys on the head for him when they got home from school, and was off. Meanwhile, behind him, back in Washington, Rapier had already started his own best men digging into Sue Alexander's true financial status.

"Well, that should do it," Kohl said to Buck as he examined the installation of the heavy device in the beam of his flashlight where it had been firmly attached to one of the main supporting steel trusses underneath the Eads Bridge with the oversized clamps and husky J-bolts from the truck.

"Looks good to me," Buck said from where he was standing on a cross beam, hanging on like a baby gorilla to a tree branch.

"But how the hell do I know. I still don't believe that little thing can do all that."

"I don't know for sure either," Kohl admitted as he looked down into the muddy water some fifty feet below. The steel was damp and cold and a bit slick and the wind had come up. He'd already dropped his oversized crescent wrench into the river. "But we'll soon find out," he told Buck. "Why don't you hook up the batteries while I crawl out and glue the accelerometer onto the bottom of the roadway."

"No problem," Buck said as he turned on his own light and made his way closer to where the batteries were already hanging from the steel in an oversized sling of plastic mesh that swung back and forth in the breeze.

Kohl worked his way along in the near dark, trailing the small, multi conductor cable behind him. When he found a spot he liked he pulled himself upward and sat on a beam where he could reach the reinforced concrete above his head. Here he squirted two long beads of epoxy out on the steel, mixed it with his screwdriver and applied it to the back of the accelerometer case. He then placed it against the underside of the roadway and held it in place until the mixture had set.

"What does an accelerometer do again?" Buck asked him for the second time, after Kohl had returned and taken one last look at everything to make sure it was all in order.

"It senses motion and sends a signal back to the main unit here proportional to the amount it moves. The main unit then keeps changing the speed of the motor, driving it to the point of maximum motion of the accelerometer, then it locks in on that and keeps it there. It's called a closed loop system if you want the technical term."

"Fantastic, but that doesn't tell me shit about how something that small is going to make this big fucking bridge fall down."

"It's the same phenomenon as a tuning fork or the reason a piece of crystal will sometimes shatter way across the room when certain musical notes are hit. Most everything has a natural frequency, which is the frequency it will vibrate at with the least amount of energy. Find that frequency and provide a small amount of extra energy and the amplitude of the vibration will continue to grow. If the material is rigid enough it will literally self destruct.

That's what we are attempting to do here."

"I don't know," Buck said, once again expressing his doubts about the whole scheme, looking at the bridge pier ahead of them as it glowed slightly in the dark where Mike was cutting vertical slots in it. "This is a damned big bridge."

"Maybe your not aware of it but there was a very famous case of a bridge about this size up in the State of Washington many years ago which the wind destroyed just exactly the same way by getting it to sway at its natural frequency. Remember too, that the guy who invented it, one Nikola Tesla, also almost destroyed a New York City police station with the same kind of toy way back in the early part of the century. And a far smaller one at that, without benefit of a closed loop system and modern electronics."

"God damn. A police station huh?" Buck said as Kohl caught the glint off his teeth in the dark.

"How about that?" Kohl said. "Would have pulverized it too, if he hadn't stopped the thing so soon."

"If this sucker works, do you think we could try it on the Los Angeles County Jail?"

Kohl chuckled and they began their climb back to the top. "Oh shit," Buck said when he peeked over the edge.

"What's wrong?" Kohl asked as he caught up.

"There's a car parked behind the truck with a couple of guys in it. What do we do?"

"Go and talk to them might be best," Kohl said and kept climbing.

"What if they're cops? Want me to sneak around behind?"

"No, just stay here. They don't need to see us both."

"What are you going to do?"

"I'll think of something," Kohl said and pulled himself up onto the roadway. Instead of heading towards the car to see what they wanted, however, he merely glanced briefly in their direction and went directly to the truck where he casually took off his tool belt and began rummaging around in the back as if looking for something while his mind raced for a plausible story.

The driver got out of the car, a big man with an air of authority about him, and came Kohl's way. Kohl waited for him to speak. The man looked him over. "What are you doing under the bridge this time of night?" he asked with importance.

Ignoring the question, Kohl looked at his car then back at the big face and said, "You shouldn't park there like that, blocking my signs. Might be dangerous."

"What office are you out of?" came the next question.

"Why do you ask?" Kohl said, refusing to back down.

"Because I happen to run the East Saint Louis office and this here structure is part of my domain and I don't recall seeing any work order come through or my people would be doing it."

"Well," Kohl said in a kinder tone now that he knew what he was dealing with. "Didn't mean to step on your toes. We came down from Chicago to put some special kind of strain gauges on the structure. Apparently they are doing some big, new research project in conjunction with M.I.T.. They want to compare some of the statistics on all the bridges in the area."

The man pondered Kohl's comment while he scanned what he could see of his hairy face. "Why this time of night?"

"What better time?"

What better time for sure. Couldn't argue about that. "Can I look at your yellow copy while I'm here?" he wanted to know, not willing to give up just yet.

Kohl looked at him. What yellow copy? Was this a test? If there was some multicolored document, would the workmen get the yellow copy or some other color?

"Don't know about a yellow copy," Kohl said, going all the way. "We get the white." With that he started feeling through his coat pockets. "Guess it's in the other truck. Or maybe I left it in the motel," he said and stopped looking. The man didn't reply.

"Tell you what," Kohl said. "We'll come by your office tomorrow and I'll show you all the documentation. It's a pretty interesting study. How's that?"

"Know how to find the place?" the man said at last, giving Kohl the benefit of the doubt. Might as well. The trucks looked legit, they didn't seem to be doing anything overt and besides, there was no way to check his story until morning anyway. Just like those bastards in the main office to go around the local boys whenever they could. But it wasn't this guys fault so why take it out on him.

"I think I remember. But don't expect us till at least noon. We'll probably be sleeping late."

That appeared to be acceptable. "What's your name?" came the last question.

"Barnes. Tim Barnes. And yours?"

"Matheson."

"Okay, Mr. Matheson. See you tomorrow. And, oh, by the way. Have to do the same thing to all six of these along here so if you see our other trucks out, that's what it's all about. We'll try not to hold things up too badly."

"All right Barnes," the man said, easing up. "Don't fall in the river," he said in jest to let Kohl know he had accepted his story.

"Have a good night," Kohl said and started rattling things around in the back of the truck again.

"How you doing Little Brother?" Kohl asked over the radio some two hours later. There was still a sliver of moon hanging in the sky. But not for long. Only three more hours until sunrise.

"Tidying up on number five," came Mike's voice after a moment. "How about you?"

"Crawling under number six but the wind is getting heavy."

"Do you think there's a problem?"

"Not unless we get five or six semis on the same span at once."

"How is the traffic? I can't see it from here."

"Light, fortunately. Give us another hour and lets do it."

"Not enough time."

"Let number six go. Let's see what happens without your help."

"Might be interesting," Mike agreed. "See you on the west side."

Milton Towser, recently retired from forty one years of drudgery in the bottle factory back in West, by god, Virginia, was heading westbound down Interstate Forty in his fifteen year old, undersized, over burdened pickup truck with a third hand camper shell hanging on the back end. So what if it leaned a little in the wind and swayed on the corners. So what if the tires might be a size too small for all the shit in the back. All that shit was good and necessary for where they were going.

Discounted canned goods, a weeks supply of day old bread and muffins that had left the store more than ten days ago, old clothes stuffed in ancient suitcases, two cane poles, two fly rods, a cardboard box full of fishing gear, a chain saw, never know when you might need a good chain saw, blankets, pots and pans, pappy's old squirrel rifle, camp stove, toolbox, spare tire, grease gun, ten cartons of cigarettes, a two months supply of chewing tobacco, five bottles of prescription pills, a jar full of stale oatmeal cookies, extra batteries for the hearing aids. What the hell, they needed it all, they did. They were touring the country by motor vehicle, by god.

Mable and Milton, it said on the rear of the camper below all the decals of fish jumping and deer standing in the woods. Mable and Milton were on their way west. With everything under control Milton gripped the wheel with both hands, stared out into the night through his trifocals and pitted windshield and cussed at the drivers roaring by him at frightening speeds.

Stop honking at me all you city slicker bastards in your shiny cars, he said to himself, not wanting to wake Mable who was dozing in the seat beside him. So what if I'm only going forty five in a sixty five. I helped pay for this road too, by god, and by god I'm going to drive on it whether you like it or not.

Pullin into East Saint Louie now, speed limits down to fifty five, better slow down to forty. Lots of crazy people in these here cities. Oh, gee. What's that up ahead? One damned big bridge. Must be the Mississippi, by golly. Better wake Mable up for this. As soon as we cross it we'll be out west. What do ya think of that? Wish the sun were up. Ought to stop and get some of them picture postcards for the folks back home.

Now what in tarnation is all them cars stopped there for? Bridge Closed for Repairs? Detour? Like hell I will. I didn't pay all them taxes all those years to have to come this far and then take a detour off this here United States Governmental highway. Damned if I will. Get out of the way you crazy bearded fool and stop waving at me like that or I'll be likely to run over you.

"Kohl, Kohl," Buck shouted into his radio. "Shut it off. Some old fool in a camper just ran the blockade."

"I see him but I can't shut it off. It doesn't work that way."

"Oh shit," Buck said as he watched the rear end of the old camper move out onto the bridge, two dim bulbed, broken tail lights rising up towards the crest of the bridge. "Oooh shiiit," he said again as he saw the bridge shudder slightly and begin to sway gently back and forth.

Mable woke up with a start. "What's wrong?" she asked Milton as she reached for her glasses on the dashboard.

"Don't know, lambykin. Wind must be blowin again."

"It's not the wind Milton," Mable said, having found her glasses. "Something's wrong with the truck. Maybe you'd better stop and find out what it is."

"In a minute Mable. I'll just slow down a little and ease it across if I can."

"OH DEAR," Mable said loudly as the concrete guard rail alongside began to crumble. "Look at that, the plaster's cracking off the bridge."

"By god, must be one of them earthquake things they have out here in the west. Hang on Mable, I'm gonna speed er up and see if we can't out race this thing."

Down went the gas pedal but the old eight cylinder engine, working on just six and a half, responded slowly. "Come on Bessy," Milton said, encouraging it and rocking back and forth to help things along. They were up to twenty six miles per hour now and gaining. After what seemed like an eternity to those looking on, however, the old vehicle made it across the expansion joint that separated one span of the bridge from the next. Better, but not good enough yet. Keep moving you dumb son-of-a-bitch.

Milton was too busy gripping the wheel and rocking back and forth, however, to notice what was happening behind him. Mable noticed though and went into a swoon as the span they just passed over began to twist, as well as to sway, while the guard rails turned completely into powder, the motion beginning to carry over onto the span they were on.

"Pray," Mike said to Kohl, "and hope to hell that pier holds just a little longer."

Surprisingly enough, it did. Barely. No sooner had Milton crossed the next expansion joint onto the last span, however, than the supporting pier under the junction of the previous two spans collapsed where Mike had weakened it with the laser. Then, both spans shuddered one last time and plunged into the cold, muddy water below. Milton, now looking in the rear view mirror and feeling the portion of the bridge he was now on stop shaking, put on the brakes and stopped in the middle of what was left of the bridge. Then he got out and walked back to the edge and peered over. "By golly, look at that," he said. "That was some earth shaker all right. Maybe we ought to go back to West Virginy where it's safe."

"Looks like he made it," Kohl told Buck. "You okay?"
"Are we going to do the rest?" Buck asked.
"Are you up to it?"
"Hell yes. Any more cocksuckers try that and I'll put my fist through their window."

FIFTEEN
Digand Pry, now back in his off brown, cotton polyester blended suit and soup stained tie, scowled at dark eyed Linda in the small interrogation room in the back of the Sedona Police Station that they had taken over for the occasion.

"You have a moral obligation to help," he stated as he and Rapier played their little game of, he the good guy, Rapier the bad.

Was it working? It seemed to be. This girl was as nervous as a third grade kid in the principal's office after getting caught throwing paper wads in class at school.

"You could go to jail," Rapier said coldly, his icy look boring through her. Far more sinister looking in his sharply creased, black English woolens, crisp, stark white shirt and dark gray tie with angled blood red stripes, he bored down on her. "Prison, actually," he said heavily. "Maybe twenty years. Have you ever seen the inside of a woman's federal penitentiary, Miss Yates?" he asked with lurking threat and eyebrows raised.

"I...I...Haven't done anything," Linda stammered, afraid that she might begin to cry.

"Conspiracy," Rapier said. "Withholding evidence. Interfering with federal officers. And treason, Miss Yates. These are all treasonous acts being committed against the people of the United States; and you, with your silence, are as much of an accomplice as if you were actively engaged."

"But I don't know for sure. I never actually saw them do anything. I never saw that thing they used either or any of it. It was only on one occasion that I overheard something about the cement plant. But it was a long time ago and I don't even remeber exacty what it was anymore."

"But your aunt, Sue Alexander, she knows, doesn't she? And she's a part of it too, isn't she?"

At this Linda remained silent. "You must tell us," Rapier warned her again. "Or there is no way we can help you."

"But I don't need help. I haven't done anything, and I don't know for sure if they have."

"But you admit your aunt is very wealthy and that she may have given a lot of money to that boyfriend of hers and that other fellow, Kohl, and that they have spent a good deal of it on some technical venture and that they were all friends of one Buck Hudson who has a rap sheet. Did you know that he had a rap sheet, Miss Yates?"

"No I didn't. What did he do?"

"Unfortunately nothing we can prove as yet, but he has been a suspect in this environmental disruption business that goes way, way back. The man has no respect for authority, Miss Yates. He was thrown out of high school for drinking on campus and refused to register for the draft. Once he broke a bank president's nose. He also spent six months in the Los Angeles jail for assaulting a police officer. I assure you that you would be best not to associate with him under any conditions."

"But I've never associated with him. I don't even like him."

"That's very wise, Linda," Pry came in gently. He looked at her compassionately from across the small table, reached in his pocket and brought out a packet of chewing gum.

She took a stick, put it in her mouth and looked down at her hands in her lap.

"How can we help you?" Pry said sincerely.

"Help me?" she asked in a puzzled voice.

"Yes, help you. I know you are a good person Linda, and a sincere one and I know you would like to help your aunt, and your country, and yourself. But it seems there must be some problem in the way. Something holding you back from doing the right thing," Pry said and waited quietly.

"If it's your aunt you're worried about," he said after a few moments. "Please remember, it's not her we're after. It's those other hoodlums we want. They are the ones who have led her astray and caused all these problems."

Linda looked up into his eyes. "You don't want her about the newspaper stuff either? Of course I don't know that she did that, either. I think it was Mike's idea too."

Rapier and Pry looked at each other in silent understanding. "We promise you," Pry said, "that no harm will come to her in that regard. After all, she was only expressing her opinion as a concerned citizen."

But then, surprisingly, Linda withdrew. "There's nothing I can do to help," she said.

"Have you been threatened by anyone?" Pry asked wisely enough.

"Not...No...," she said.

"What then? What happened?"

"I..." she started, then stopped.

Rapier coughed and she made the mistake of looking at him. A sign of fear came over her face again.

"Tell us," Pry soothed her. "I'm sure we can find a way to help, whatever it is. If you need protection, all you have to do is say so. We can even give you a new life somewhere at government expense."

"It's...It's not that. Nobody can make her change her will."

"Her will?"

"Yes, I think she cut me out of it and I can't do anything or she will find out and I'll never be put back in."

"I see," Pry said with understanding. "Not a serious problem I wouldn't think," he said and looked again at Rapier as if seeking approval. Rapier nodded to him.

"What can you do?" Linda asked as if still in doubt.

"Any probate would go before a judge. And as you know Miss Yates, judges are people to, subject to all the whims and pressures of life."

Linda's face reflected a clear understanding of the implications. "You can do that?" she asked.

"Even that," Rapier assured her.

"But I really don't know anything except what I've already told you."

"Yes, and we believe you. That's not what we want."

160

"What then?"

"Go to her. Apologize for whatever it is between you. Make friends with her again. Try and find out as much as you can about these friends of hers and what they might be up to next. We need to know what their next target is so we can catch them in the act and put an end to all this disruption and chaos that is tearing the country apart. Once that is done, you and your aunt can go your own way without interference. In the end you will be doing her, and you, and your country a big service. There will probably even be a sizable reward in it for you. Now what do you think of that, Linda?"

"I guess I really don't have any choice, do I?"

"Goddammit," the fleshy faced man bellowed out to his captive audience of appointed underlings as he whipped off his frameless glasses, "doesn't anyone in this room understand that there's an election coming in eight and a half more weeks, goddammit?"

The half dozen men around the extra large conference table first checked to make sure the President's zipper wasn't undone again and then turned their eyes downward onto their notes, or their neighbors notes, or looked at their hands or studied their fingernails. Anything so as not to look him in the eye. Who knows how he would take it in his present state of mind.

"Don't you realize that the popularity poll shows this administration down to twenty one percent?" he continued in his irate harangue, badgering them into humble embarrassment. "Do you realize that's the lowest rating any administration has ever had in the history of poll taking? Do you realize what that means? It means that we will all be without a job come January. All of us, gentlemen, unless something is done quickly," he said and glared around the room. What the hell was he going to do? What could he do unless someone did something for him, for them all. But who, and how, and when? Where was the answer?

"Goddammit," he said again in total frustration. "Hoover Dam and Chicago and Three Mile Island and three Mississippi River bridges in Saint Louis and two in New Orleans and all the TV towers in Los Angeles and San Francisco and Cleveland and Atlanta and all the microwave relay stations in Colorado and thirty one police cars belonging to the District of Columbia. Police cars, gentlemen. Police cars. Right here in our own backyard, goddammit. That's worse than lying under oath any day. And not a clue, dammit, not a goddamned clue. They are just as invisible as that laser beam they're carving everything up with. Goddammit, the next thing they'll do is destroy the Supreme Court Building or the Lincoln Memorial or the Washington Monument and then what the hell will we do? Tell me, by God. What the hell will we do then? There won't even have to be an election at this rate. We might as well give the keys to the White House to the Democrats right now."

At this point the Attorney General looked over at the President's shoes and bravely let his eyes drift upward, clear up to silk tie knotted about the neck. Might not be a bad idea, he felt secretly, as he surveyed the puffy body standing at the head of the table next to where he sat. A now pathetic caricature of a man no longer jaunty and vital, who pretended to have eternal youth at his side but who, instead, had aged ten years in the last two. Let them hang him. Even that would be too good for him.

But then he reconsidered. Perhaps some god fearing Baptist Congregation would feel sorry for him and give him a job polishing the pulpit some where in the dark, narrow minded halls of southern bigotry instead, when the voters were done with him. What better end to this administration than going down in the worst defeat in the nation's history.

But would the next one be any better? Effete elephant or demented donkey, what did it matter? The real string pullers were all behind the scenes anyway. Maybe, if the people were lucky enough, this whole episode might do something to help change that. There was a stirring going on, way down in the dim consciousness of the country all right, and it seemed to be gaining momentum. Was the over drugged giant actually beginning to wake up? If not the next election after this one, maybe the one after that. And if not in my own lifetime, he told himself, then at least in that of my children or of my grandchildren.

The President waited vainly for some kind of response, but no one ventured to speak. He removed his stained handkerchief from his hip pocket, wiped his sweating brow and put his glasses back on. "Well, has anyone got any progress to report on this matter at all?" he asked at last as his eyes skipped around the table. He went past the Attorney General, five star General Ballsey, the Director of the FBI and the Head of the CIA and his campaign manager and... And who was this man? Where had he come from? How come he hadn't noticed him before, this man whose eyes seemed to refuse to waver?

"Mr. Rapier," came the answer. "From..." and Rapier mentioned a code name he was sure the President would recognize.

"Ah yes," the President said and waited, since it seemed evident that at least Rapier had something to say.

"We are quite certain we know who the individuals are," Rapier said, taking his time. What did he care. Officials come, officials go. But as for himself, well, he dealt in things that made for permanency. "Both the perpetrators of the sabotage and the originators of the newspaper articles," he stated.

"Hmmm," said the President, studying Rapier's face. "You're sure?"

"Quite sure," Rapier said, without adding the customary, Sir, or Mr. President. Fuck him, he said to himself. I'm as good as he is any day and he knows it, too. Maybe better, because inside I'm not half as frightened as he is, or ten percent as frightened of the world as that insecure little boy hiding inside blustering old Ballsey's bloated frame, or half as psychotic as the head of the CIA, or half as self deceiving as the head of the FBI. Fuck them all. At least he knew where he stood with his own conscience.

"Where did you find them?" the Head of the CIA asked, leaning forward with great interest He hadn't been informed yet, nor had anyone else in the room because Rapier had just gotten back in town the night before.

"In Sedona," Rapier answered. And for those who didn't know where that was, he added, "Arizona."

"You mean that place where those goddamned new aged hippies keep moving the stones around on government land to make medicine circles?" the President asked knowledgeably, surprising his audience because for some strange reason he suddenly remembered reading something about it in Newsweek not too long ago and the gall of those people out there had angered him. In fact it had seemed almost as sacrilegious as burning the flag at the time, the way they kept at it in spite of Forest Service warnings. For sure they needed another amendment to the Constitution to cover such issues.

"Wheels. Medicine wheels," Rapier said, correcting him about the word circles. "That's the place."

"Well if that's the case, why don't we just initiate our operation Subtle Strike," General Ballsey said, throwing out his chest and looking to the President. "That would resolve the whole matter in a hurry."

"What is Subtle Strike, if I might ask?" said the Attorney General, who was rarely included in such covert matters.

The President shrugged, but nodded his approval.

"We have been anticipating certain foreign terrorist activity for years," said the General. "And so has the public to a large extent, especially after what's been happening lately, which many of our citizens still believe is the work of outsiders. And since the public is already mentally prepared for this kind of activity and somewhat used to it, Subtle Strike is a means that would allow us to capitalize on that situation for our own benefit. This case would seem to be as good as any other to try it out on."

"What does that mean?"

"Simply that we would take a low yield thermo-nuclear device to this Sedona place and level the whole damned area. Then we blame it on the Libyans or the Iraqis or the Iranians or the North Koreans. Simple. It would eliminate our detractors and that would be the end of that. It would also give us the justification we need for keeping the defense budget alive, which as you gentlemen all know, is in deep shit now, thanks to that peace loving, chicken ass Gorbachev."

"Makes a lot of sense to me," the Head of the CIA said. Why wouldn't it. He loved it. Wholesale assassination was a good part of his business. So what if they were American citizens. It wouldn't be the first time.

"I object," the Attorney General said. "We can't do that in our own country. It's immoral."

"Immoral or not, that's beside the point," the President's campaign manager said, speaking for the first time thus far.

164

"And what's immoral about it?" Ballsey asked, trying to intimidate the man into silence.

"Because it's very bad politics," the campaign manager said, since that was his whole concern. He had been promised an appointeeship somewhere, if by chance they were to succeed in getting the president re-elected. Slim chance now, but if wiping out a mere ten thousand people or so would save the day, what the hell. Carpe deim, right? There were nothing but a bunch of second rate anti-progress environmentalists in that town anyway, if he remembered correctly.

"Now how do you figure that one?" the FBI Director asked.

"It's damned good politics if you ask me. So maybe you'd better explain yourself." Ballsey said, rubbing his gold stars with the back of his hand while he spoke.

"We need to do more than just exterminate people," the campaign manager pointed out. "There's no mileage in that. The public would never believe they just happened to be in the same place where a Libyan bomb went off. None of those factions would wipe out a bunch of American dissidents for Christ's sake. Hell no. They'd give them a reward. And if the power didn't go off somewhere for awhile the public would think that they had simply gone on vacation and would reappear again later, once the bridges were back up and the lights stayed on for a while. No sir, Mr. President, we need to catch them in the act, then convict them on network TV and have a public hanging on the White House lawn. Drag them through the streets in cages on the way to the gallows, too."

"You have a good point," the President admitted, feeling considerably better now that there was something to go on.

"Yes, and it's a pity that the guillotine is outlawed. It would be the perfect way to end it, watching heads role live on CNN. But, regardless. However it's done, that's the only way we will ever get our credibility back. After all, there must be quite a big gang of them. It should be quite a sight."

To gain maximum effect, Rapier waited to let the room quiet down again before speaking. "There are only three," he said. "And two women. And they don't all participate all the time. They take turns."

"What!"

"I don't believe it."

"Impossible, totally impossible."

"You are fucking crazy."

"That's completely ludicrous. There has to be a small army of them to have created all that havoc."

Thus went the comments around the table as the attendees jumped up and down and shouted back and forth. And then there was silence again. They all finally stopped talking and again stared at Rapier. Rapier sat quietly and smoothed his thin pencil of a mustache. When he was sure all eyes were on him, he simply shrugged in an affirmative manner and said nothing.

"Who are these people then, who can do all that?" the CIA Director asked. He certainly needed to study this case in more detail. There was obviously much to be learned here that might be put to good use later.

"A couple of ex aerospace engineers. One claims to be a writer and the other is a small company executive. The third is a low life bum and the other two are their girl friends."

"Come, come, Mr. Rapier this is no time for joking," the Director said as he squinted at Rapier.

Rapier looked him coldly in the eye. "My good man, I never joke."

There was no doubt about that, they all decided at last, staring at him. Finally the President leaned on the glossy table top and spoke. "What would you suggest?" he asked of Rapier, not knowing where else to turn, flabbergasted as he was.

"Just as this gentleman said," Rapier replied, indicating the campaign manager. "We catch them in the act and hang them high. Except for the one woman. She seems to be the power behind the news supplements and is certainly the source of funding for all this illicit activity."

"What do we do with her?"

"Terminate her, of course."

"Yes, of course" said the President, nodding thoughtfully. "What else can we do."

"Great. Wonderful," said the General. "But how do we catch them in the act? Nothing has worked so far. They're totally unpredictable."

"I believe I have a reliable informant," Rapier shared with

them. "I'm waiting for a phone call."

SIXTEEN

The five of them met secretly back in one of the many canyons amongst the red rocks where they were well off any trail and out of sight. They sat on small slabs of sandstone and in the red dirt and shared what they had carried in. Sandwiches, apples, some cheese, beer, nuts and chocolate bars topped off with the ripe fruit of the prickly pear, now in season. A balmy day, warm and desert dry.

Buck teased Jackie and Jackie teased him back. Mike went for a short walk and Sue sat beside Kohl and tried to cheer him for, as a woman, she knew he was feeling alone. Then Mike returned and it was time to discuss the reason for their being there. What did they want to go after next?

The list of potential targets was long. There was always, "The Dam," still sitting there waiting for the noble day when the backed up waters of Lake Powell would be freed. A most symbolic thing, that would be. One that would probably unite die hard environmentalists from around the world. But not yet, they decided, although that day was coming. In the meantime their campaign of disruption was working even better than they had originally hoped for.

"I'm glad to hear that," Buck said, "because I have news."

"Good, or bad?" Kohl asked.

"I'm branching out," Buck said. "Me and Jackie are going into business for ourselves."

"Doing what?" Mike asked.

"Now that I know a few more tricks, thanks to you guys, I thought we might push a little further afield."

"I see," Kohl said, not too sure he liked the idea.

"Yeah. A couple friends of mine from back in L.A. came by. What with all the stuff in the papers, they thought it was a good idea to start up the old gang again and wanted to know if I wanted in. Of course I didn't tell them about already being in but after thinking about it, it seemed like it might be a way to expand our campaign. We could do all the outlying stuff while you and Mike do that high tech shit. You don't need me for that anyway."

"We couldn't have done it alone Buck, don't ever forget that,"

Kohl stated.

"Well, thank you," Buck acknowledged. "But just think, when I get these guys trained, I'll split off and do it again with someone else. Can you imagine what it would be like with four or five different groups wandering around the country by themselves? Hell man, we'd have the whole country shut down by Christmas."

"Actually it's not a bad idea," Mike had to admit, although he had grown very fond of Buck.

Kohl sat without speaking at first. Not a bad idea at all. A spreading offensive certainly had its appeal, as long as the same ground rules applied and no-one was injured in the process. But, in his own mind, as he saw the targets he had mentally laid out for the near future. Buck would be important. On the other hand, with a little different planning, they could probably manage. With that he assented and gave Buck his blessing.

"I'd like to place an order for about a gross of those radio activated detonators too," Buck said. "If you guys can find the time."

"Jesus," Mike said. "Here he wants to leave the nest and he hasn't even learned how to use a soldering iron yet. God, Buck. How do you ever expect to amount to anything?"

"I'm a specialist," he said, sticking out his bearded chin. "However, I just happen to know someone who is very good with their hands. Has that nice gentle but firm touch, if you know what I mean. Maybe you could show her...Ahh," Buck said, as Jackie made a lunge for his crotch.

"I'll show you what I can do with my hands," she said maliciously and rolled on top of him, sending him on his back in the sand.

He wrestled her to a standstill, pinning her to the ground with his bulk and then started up her leg with his callused paw, stopping just sort of total embarrassment for her. At this point he kissed her quickly and let her up, point made. Bulk wins over beauty. They grinned at each other, knowing what they would be doing for the rest of the evening, once they were by themselves.

When the laughter died down Mike and Kohl agreed to give Buck the parts list and wiring diagrams for the latest version of the device which was considerably smaller and more powerful, and to show him how to put it together, with Jackie standing by to pick up anything he might have missed. Thus always, there is change. Winds blow, lakes run dry, rivers over flow their banks, earthquakes alter the landscape, lovers come together and part, friends say good-bye.

Everyone hugged everyone else. Feminine hugs, burly hugs, caring hugs all. Then Buck and Jackie left.

"Where do we go from here?" Sue asked after they were gone. "What's next?"

"I was thinking of Navajo," Kohl said, "but I'm not sure we can manage it alone."

"Sooner or later we need to do it," Mike said. "That and Four Corners. We have to start working on those coal fired plants."

"No doubt about it," Kohl agreed. "They are still the nations greatest physical obscenity, other than the politicians."

"Well, polluted skies and polluted thinking kind of go together," Sue pointed out.

They opened more beer, carved up the cheese and thought about one of the largest generating stations in the southwest.

"It would be a tough one," Kohl said. "Even with Buck."

"Why would it be so hard?" Sue asked because she had never been there and didn't even know where it was.

"Because it sits out there six or seven miles east of Page in the desert all alone. Smoke stacks rising so high they make the tower lines look like toys, visible for miles and miles with but only one road running past the place and not a damned thing to hide behind in any direction except maybe for a rabbit and only then if he's a small one."

"It's that bad?"

"Worse, said Mike.

"Then let's think of something else," Kohl said. "Maybe run up to Seattle."

"Or New York City. They haven't had a brown out in a long time."

"Why not spread the discomfort," Sue said. "Pass some of it on to the rich? Do some of the Palm Beaches, Beverly Hills and Belaires of the country."

"It's on the agenda," Kohl said. "Just thought it might do them good to worry a little longer. Give them a chance to redeem themselves a bit first."

Sue cut up an apple, handed them each a slice and sat down again facing them.

"But Navajo intrigues you doesn't it?" she said, coming back to it as she watched the two men's faces.

Kohl got up from the rock he was sitting on, put his hands in his pockets and looked out at the tree tops below. Mike sipped at his beer and nodded his head.

"Me too," Sue said with enthusiasm, her eyes sparkling at the thought of such a challenge.

"But you can't come," Mike told her firmly.

"Yes I can," she said. "You'll need me."

"Tell her Kohl."

"Listen to Mike, Sue."

"But I want to go," she assured them, patting Mike and looking at Kohl.

"It's too dangerous, honey."

"I like a little danger."

Mike stood up and put his arms around her. "Sometimes I wish we had this all to do over again," he said. "I think I would have done it a lot differently."

"No you wouldn't," she said, looking up at him, "because I wouldn't have let you."

"Oh damn," Mike said wondering why she had to be so exuberant about everything.

"Stop worrying dear heart," she said. "And just remember that no matter what happens, no regrets. Even if I die tomorrow."

"Easy said," Kohl replied, not liking the subject. "But what about Mike?"

"What about Mike?" Sue asked in a perplexed way as if it had never occurred to her how Mike might feel if something happened to her. Something she had never given credence to in her own zesty way of living. She stared into his eyes for a minute, then said, "Oh god," and hugged him tighter, yet still came back with, "But if you're going to do Navajo, I'm going, and that's the end of it."

How could anyone argue with such a women? Especially one like this equal rights advocate demonstrator, horse lover, gun lover, college trouble maker, tax evader, occasional cusser and brandy drinker who got married once, went on a honeymoon cruise and filed for an annulment as soon as she landed. What were they to do?

The two men resigned themselves to it for the time being. They would try and settle it later, if they could. But if the Navajo Power Station was going to be the target, how were they going to go about it?

"We could leave the van at home, just use explosives and come by water down Navajo Canyon and hike in from there," Mike suggested.

"Long hike, but we could come by sea and leave by land, or come by land and leave by sea," Kohl said, drawing a weak analogy to other historical times. "That would help to confuse the issue."

"Or..." Mike said, and made a suggestion.

"Well, why not...too?" Sue added to it.

Rapier's phone buzzed. He picked it up. "Yes," he said because that's the only way he ever answered the phone.

"There's a Miss Yates on the line," his secretary informed him.

Without acknowledgment, Rapier hit the button for the other line. "What is it Miss Yates? Do you have something for me?"

"I'm not sure. Maybe."

"What is it?"

Hearing the unappreciative coldness in his voice, she hesitated and almost hung up. But it was too late. He would only call her back. He might even come back to Sedona, heaven forbid. Seeing him once was more than enough.

"I'm still waiting," he reminded her.

"Is there something by Page, Arizona?" she asked.

"One moment please," he said as he switched on his computer and called up the list of potential targets that had worked up by a member of his staff. "Glen Canyon Dam," he said. "And the Navajo Generating Station. Is it either one of those?"

"I don't know. All I saw was a road map with a circle on it."

"Where was that circle and what makes you think that might be it?"

"It's to the east of Page a few miles I would guess."

"Navajo land. And?"

"I did what you said. I went to see her and the phone rang. She was busy talking to someone about some business matter and I happened to see the map there, but she took it and folded it up right away. Then I asked her if we could go out to dinner and she said not until next week because she had to go somewhere. There were some airline tickets on the counter too. They always leave the country and come back in somehow when they do something big so they will have an alibi. At least that's what it looks like when I think back about it."

"Thank you Miss Yates," Linda heard him say, "you have done the right thing," and the phone went dead in her ear.

"I think she's full of shit," Pry shouted to Rapier over the noise of the engine and rattle of the craft as they circled the generating station in their helicopter, looking down at the dried and barren terrain. "They would have to be absolutely mad to try and do this one."

"I'd almost have to agree with you," Rapier said, puzzling over it. "But we dare not take the chance, do we?"

"But how will we manage it? We have the same problem they do. There's no place to hide a surveillance team either, except inside."

"So that is what we do," Rapier said and instructed the pilot to land inside the compound and wait. They walked the grounds.

"We will have long wavelength infra-red scanners from the Air force here by this afternoon," Rapier explained. "We can install two on the elevator tower there. With their respective fields of view they will be able to detect the laser from anywhere in a ninety degree sweep from the south to the east. Two more on the southwest corner of the building and two more on the cooling towers over there and we will have the area covered, even if they come across the sand. The helicopter will be on the roof out of sight, engines off. Another will be standing by in Page and one more down there hiding in the canyon."

"Where will we be?"

"You will be up there on the roof with two sharp shooters with night sights on their weapons while I will be out of sight at the front gate, backing up the guard."

"I thought you wanted to take them alive?" Pry said and started picking his teeth with his fingernail.

172

"The men, if at all possible. The military wants to interrogate them rather badly as you might suspect. And the weapon must be taken intact regardless."

"Understandable. But, hell. If I was running things, I'd be the first one to offer them all a job instead. Get them on our side. We could use some talent like that."

"Yes," Rapier said. "Unfortunately it's election year and a second term happens to be more important to the president than a couple of lives." He stopped to lean up against one of the cars in the parking lot, wishing that Pry would sto picking his teeth. It was distracting. Shouldn't have bought him that steak sandwich for lunch.

Pry made one last effort at his front teeth, found the problem and corrected it, then asked another question. "When do you think they will make their play, assuming this is this place, of course."

"How would you plan it, if you were doing such a thing?"

"Come in after dark when there is no moon, cut or burn some holes in the fence, plant the explosive, go back outside, start carving things up with the laser, then set it all off at once."

"Kind of how I visualized it too," Rapier said. "And this is the dark of the moon. The plant manager is going to brief us on normal routine. We will also keep an eye out for delivery trucks, anyone unloading anything from their car in the parking lot, whatever. Anything unusual at all. Then we keep an eye on them and wait for that laser to come on."

That might have been the way Kohl and Mike would have visualized it too. That, or in any one of half a dozen other possible ways also, as far as that goes, had they been given half a chance. But, as yet, they hadn't fully completed their homework and that was something they were very meticulous about. The plan of attack must be very clear and precise.

And how can one formulate a clear and precise plan of attack without first surveying the scene of the impending crime, as any good strategist would ask? You cannot. One must examine the structures one wishes to demolish and the services they wish to disable first hand and in detail in order to determine the most vulnerable portions thereof. Then, after comparing that aspect of it to the weapons one has at their disposal, the most effective and efficient means for rendering them useless can be determined. One would hope that such logic would prevail, especially under such demanding circumstances as these. Additionally and furthermore, one would keep doing their homework until all the pieces fit together and the whole thing, the steps, timing and action made air tight sense.

With this as the final goal, they entered the facility for the second time in two nights running. Not to demolish it, but to complete the plan of action for doing so in a safe and logical manner. They came not with a torch or a battering ram, or with a Trojan horse of their own construction but as might more normally be expected, in cars at the change of shift along with the rest the night crew, with badges, hats and clothing that was consistent with their disguises. The men were clean and beardless as any normal Indian would be, with hair long and dyed solid black. Two cars, too. Just in case.

So there they were and there was still a lot more to check out. They had to be completely sure of certain routines and procedures within the organization to establish safe routes into the various buildings and structures and determine the tools necessary to gain entry and exit and the exact amount of high explosive they would need to do the job. Timing and planning, planning and timing. Do a dry run of sorts too, while they were here. Why not? They had a full eight hour shift to put in

Kohl joined Mike and Sue in their vehicle. "All set?" Mike asked Sue after the majority of the other night staff had left their parked cars and gone to punch in.

"All set," she said, and turned to him.

"Okay, up to the roof tops. Look for a place where we might cache a few extra sticks while you're there too."

"Gotcha, but give me a kiss first," she said.

Mike gave her a quick hug and a kiss both. "Be careful," he cautioned.

"You too," she said, and they got out.

"Later," Kohl said and patted them both with a quick touch and headed towards the entrance lobby from where Kohl would be off towards the coal pulverizers while Sue proceeded to the elevators and Mike made his way into the turbine rooms.

Sue reached her destination first. It was with a feeling of exhilaration that she had gotten on the elevator after having first passed two other workers in the hall where, with her long, dark hair pulled around behind in a braid, dark eyes, lack of makeup and choice of bulky, loose fitting clothing which made her look more chunky than shapely, she seemed to have passed herself off without arousing any serious suspicion.

But what if someone spoke to her in their native Navajo? Even though they had versed themselves in some more basic parts of the language, if she had to say anything more than yes, no or maybe, she would be in trouble. Better be careful.

She got off at the last stop, the sixth level, and started down the catwalk into the maze above the number one generator. Here she would find her way up to the roof to see what additional havoc they might create by lowering charges down from above. Half way along, she happened to look up towards her destination on the roof and caught a glint from something through the open skylight. She stopped. What was it?

Something, or someone, had moved. And what was that she was beginning to make out against the dim sky? Something very long and flat. And there, at a sharp angle to it was another, like...like what? Whatever it was, she was certain it hadn't been there the night before. She stood there looking up into the dark for an abnormal length of time. What did that mean, she wondered? Probably nothing, she finally concluded. She wasn't exactly an expert as to what went on around there. Not yet, anyway. She shrugged it off and continued across the open walkway to the steel stairs.

"What is it?" Pry demanded to know of the rifleman who had drawn back from the edge of the wall but was still looking through his night scope.

"Just some fat, dumb Indian looking up at the sky, I guess."

"Did he see you?"

"Don't know for sure. But it's a woman, I think."

"What do you mean, you think?"

"It's hard to tell from here. These Indian women are just as chunky as the men and half the men still wear their hair long..."

"Let me look," Pry said and peeked over the edge as Sue

proceeded across, purposely keeping her gaze in front of her.

"What's that on her belt?" Pry asked.

"Probably a two way radio. Maybe she's one of the night watchmen, watchlady, watch person? What the fuck ever you call people these days."

"What if she comes up here?" the second rifleman asked.

"Not likely," he was told. "Unless she was goofing off. And if that's the case, we just have a little talk with her," Pry said, knowing that the plant employees themselves had not been briefed about their presence there.

He peeked over the edge to take a second look but he was too late except to see the dark hat with the long pigtail hanging out, disappearing under the structure below. Nothing to be particularly concerned about, he decided and turned to scan the ground below and caught another employee heading off towards the pulverizers. Nothing unusual there, he thought. The parking lot was also quiet. Nobody else around outside either, nor the slightest peep from any of the infra-red scanners. Looked as if it was going to be a long night.

"Oh," Sue gasped almost outloud as she slowly raised her head up to the point where she could make out what was on the rooftop. A helicopter! And men. Three of them. And what was that? She hung on the ladder in total silence, waiting for her eyes to adapt a bit more. It looked as if two of them had rifles. Oh my god, they're waiting for us. God, what do I do now?

She was nearly paralyzed with fright. Careful, she told herself. Be careful. Have to get down from here and warn Mike and Kohl. Easy now. Gently. One rung at a time.

Slowly she forced herself to relax her grip on the cold iron crossmember of the vertical ladder and ease her way downward, trying hard not to tremble. What if there were more of them around? What if they found Mike or Kohl before she had a chance to warn them? What if they resisted and were shot? How were they going to get out of here? She had to hurry. But what if she slipped? Sweating profusely, she finally made it to the bottom. But now what? Did she dare walk back across that open walkway? Could she do it without giving herself away? Surely they had been watching her from above. That was what had attracted her attention in the first place. No, she had better find another ladder and drop down another level or two first.

Since there might be times when even the lowest of tones or the dimmest of flashing lights might give them away, they had rigged their two way radios with small electrodes that could be taped to the skin and made it tingle when someone was trying to reach them. This then allowed them to find a place from which they could reply verbally before attempting to respond.

Kohl, being still out in the open, reached for his unit and pressed the transmit button once, indicating that he could receive. Obviously Mike had done the same thing for Sue's voice came over the air from where she was now hiding in the maze of plumbing and machinery two flights down.

"There's a helicopter on the roof," she said, trying her best to hide her fear. "And I saw three men. Two of them had rifles."

At first all she got for a response was shocked silence. Then Mike spoke. "Where are you at?" he asked from where he had ducked into a vacant office in the main building.

Sue told him.

"Have they seen you?"

"Yes, once. They had to have when I crossed the open walkway on the sixth level but I don't think they suspected anything. Then I went up the ladder in the back to the top to make sure what was there. But no one saw me, I'm sure."

"What do you think, number one?" Mike asked.

"Looks like we're out of a job. Best we find a hole and stay in it until this shift is over."

"I can't," Sue said. "I'm too afraid."

"Stay there," Mike said. "I'll come get you."

Mike found her shaking and cold in her hiding place but feeling stronger. Then they found their way back to the elevator and went down to ground level where they rendezvoused with Kohl in an empty office with the door locked and the lights out.

"How did they find out we were coming here?" she asked in a low voice where they were huddled together.

"We don't know that they did," Mike said. "Maybe they just picked some high profile targets to stake out."

"Yes but why this one?" Sue said. "And why tonight?"

"She has a point, Mike," Kohl said.

"What else could it be?" he asked. "Only the three of us knew we coming here."

"Or we were followed somehow," Sue stated.

"Which seems impossible. They would have had to follow us out of the country and back in again and Kohl and I never went near Sedona. And if they had somehow followed us, they would have caught us right at the gate. All they'd have to do then was to arrest us. No. I don't think they know we are here already. But it certainly looks like they knew this is the place we would be coming to. If not, they wouldn't be waiting here with a helicopter and riflemen because there are a whole lot of other places we could have gone to, like Glen Canyon Dam," Mike said, his voice beginning to sound raspy from trying to talk so quietly.

"But we aren't even set up yet," Kohl said. "There isn't a stick of dynamite in the place."

"True, but they may not know that. They may also have seen us last night and figured tonight was it."

"I just can't believe we were seen," Kohl said. "We were much to careful."

"Maybe they think we're going to use the laser, which would have been the logical choice for this place."

"Or they are waiting for someone else," Sue said, having found Mike's hand by now, which she was holding onto tightly.

"Who? When it comes to a target like this, we're it, aren't we?" Mike asked.

"There's no on else."

"Then we must have gotten careless. Somehow they found out. But how dammit? We've only met out in the canyon, no phone conversations, not even with the scramblers, nothing written down."

"Did you happen to notice anything which looked like an oversized TV camera anywhere on the edge of the roof?" Kohl asked Sue.

"Not that I know of," she said.

"Stay here. I'll be right back," Kohl said. Carefully checking the hallway first, he quietly left the room.

Five minutes later he was back. "There are scanners on the

elevator tower. Infrared, it looks like. Which means they're expecting the laser."

"Which means they are expecting us and no one else," Mike said. "It's not..."

Mike was interrupted by the sound of Sue sucking in her breath. "Goddamn her," she said with a vengeance. "Would she go that far?"

"Who? What?"

"Linda."

"What happened?" Kohl wanted to know.

"She's been coming around a lot lately and being very nice about everything, even with Mike. She saw the airline tickets lying there the last time which told her nothing except that we were going somewhere. But then, I don't know, she might have seen the map too."

"What map?" Kohl asked suspiciously.

"I didn't know where this place was so I got the road map out and asked Mike. Maybe I scribbled on it or something. I don't know but I did burn it just as soon as she left."

"Jesus Christ," Kohl said. "Would she really turn us in?"

"She was pretty upset when I cut her off, the damned little bitch. How could she do that?"

"Holy shit," Mike said. "Now what?"

"I think you're right about the laser. They probably think we'll use it to take down the chimneys. And if that's so, then they don't know we're here yet so we're safe for the time being. All we have to do is wait."

"I don't want to wait Mike," Sue said in total frustration and anger. "All I want to do is get out of here and strangle that... Goddamn her."

"Honey, I don't think we have much choice," Mike said to her, trying to keep her calmed down.

"Couldn't we pretend that I got sick on the job and that you're taking me home?"

"What about Kohl? We can't take both cars out now and it would look pretty suspicious if both of us went with you in one car. The guard may have been instructed to look for anything unusual."

"And since they are here waiting, they may have also counted the number of employees on this shift and counted the number who came in. In which case they already know there are three extras in here somewhere," Kohl theorized.

"Son-of-a-bitch," Mike said, giving admission to the possibility.

"I'd feel a lot better if we could leave now," Sue declared.

"I don't know," Mike said. "What do you think, Kohl?"

"How do we tell? But no matter what, we can't all go at once. It might be best if Sue went alone. Then you wait an hour or so and take the other car."

"But what will you do?" Mike asked.

"Wait until the shift is over and then try and catch a ride with someone going into Page."

"I don't want to leave alone," Sue said. "I want us all to go."

"It's too risky," Kohl emphasized. "But if you feel that strongly, you and Mike go if you want. I'll come later."

"Please Mike," Sue pleaded. "Let's try it."

The young, uniformed Navajo guard left the small island cubicle in the middle of the two gates and looked into the car at Mike and spoke in Navajo.

"She's sick," Mike said and nodded to Sue who was sitting with her face covered by her hands. "I'm taking her home."

The guard spoke again in Navajo, looking hard at Sue. Not knowing it was addressed to her, she remained silent. He repeated himself. Mike nudged her and she looked up with an expression of agony on her face. The guard studied her face for a brief moment then stepped back and waved them through.

"They weren't Indian," Rapier said to the guard when he came back inside the tiny edifice, somehow trying to correlate his impression of Mike and Sue through the window with the photographs he carried. Unfortunately both the windows in the booth and the car were streaked with dirt and half of the time the guard was in the way. The guard gave him a contemptible look and shrugged. So what, his expression said. Do you think I'm stupid.

"So why did you speak to them in Navajo?" Rapier asked.

"How do you know it was Navajo?" the Indian baited him. "Have you been on our reservation before?"

Rapier admitted that he didn't know and that he hadn't been

there before, then asked, "Do you know those two?"

"No."

"Is that the usual procedure if someone is sick?"

"She looked sick to me."

"But that's not the normal procedure?"

"If someone wants to go home, that's their business. My job is not to let anyone in who doesn't belong here and to make sure no company property goes home with them when they leave," he said and shut up. He'd already shared far more than he liked with this man in his big city clothes and smelly cologne.

But Rapier kept after him because he wasn't satisfied. He reached in his jacket and withdrew some photographs, leafed through them and held out two to the guard. The guard looked at them casually at first, then his eyes narrowed. He looked at Rapier and back at the photos. "What is it?" Rapier demanded.

The guard remained silent for a moment, contemplating. White man's business, he finally decided. No concern of his. He nodded in the affirmative and handed the pictures back.

"You're sure?" Rapier asked.

Again the guard merely nodded. Rapier picked up his radio and called Pry on the roof. "Which way did that car go when it got to the highway?" he asked.

"West," Pry said. "What's up?"

"I'll handle it," Rapier said. "You come down here and stay at the gate until I get back. If anyone else tries to leave early, detain them until I get back."

"Where are you going?"

"After that car," Rapier said as he cut Pry off and reached for the phone. He dialed a number in Page which was promptly answered. "Get airborne," he told the second helicopter crew. "A new, gray, Chevy Celebrity just left the plant coming your way. Set down in the road and stop it before it gets to town."

"Yes sir," came the reply which he didn't hear because he had already put down the phone and was heading towards the government car that had been issued to him.

It was a Huey, no less, rotor blades thumping away in the night, shaking the brush alongside the deserted road and stirring up the dust, spotlights on with side door open and a man with a fully automatic weapon standing in it. Not much point in trying to outrun them, Mike quickly decided, looking at the fearsome craft blocking his way. "Stay calm," he told Sue. "All they can do is get us for illegal entry."

"I'm okay," she assured him, even though she thought her chest was about to explode.

Mike left the car running and the lights on, rolled down the window and waited. Glancing in the rear view mirror he noticed headlights coming up behind him. The car stopped some twenty feet away and a man in a suit got out. He motioned to the helicopter. The man with the weapon jumped to the ground and came forward. Another armed man opened the cockpit door and got out also.

Pistol drawn, Rapier came along Mike's side of the car. "Tell your passenger to stay in the car," he instructed, shouting above the noise of the helicopter, squinting the while to keep the dust from his eyes. "And you get out slowly and raise your hands."

What kind of choice was that? Mike did as he was told and got slowly out of the car.

"Put your hands on top of the car and spread," Rapier said loudly. Again Mike obliged.

Rapier motioned to the closest man. "Handcuff him," he said. "Feet too."

It was soon done. "Now put him on board and stick him in the Page jail. I'll meet you there," Rapier ordered him loudly.

"What about the other one?" he was asked.

"I want to question her first. By myself."

"Just a goddamned minute," Mike shouted angrily. "We go together."

"Who the hell asked you," the man who had handcuffed him yelled maliciously as he grabbed him by the shoulders and jerked him around, then pushed him hard towards the waiting helicopter. Unable to move his feet very far with the handcuffs around his ankles, Mike stumbled and fell. Sue was out of the car in a flash, coming around to the side. Almost as if in anticipation of such a move, Rapier had already moved forward, giving him a clean line of sight over the hood of the car out into the desert away from the helicopter. It was exactly the opportunity he had been hoping for.

Sue's voice started to shout out Mike's name but was harshly cut short and drowned out by the thunder of Rapier's big forty five shattering the night over the sound of the big blades of the helicopter, shattering Sue's chest also, piercing her heart, tossing her down on the cold, black asphalt in a small, helpless, broken slump where she lay, while Mike, screaming and kicking, was bodily hauled and tossed savagely onto the bare metal floor of the machine where he was chained to a bulkhead. It had taken the pilot, and the two men and Rapier too. Between them it had cost them a broken nose, some broken fingers and dozens of bruises but they had done it while Sue was left to lie in her own blood, no one caring enough to even see if she was still alive.

Kohl, having gone outside to where he could see the main gate, watched the guard talk to Mike and then wave him on through. But then another man in a suit that hadn't been there earlier left the guard shack and quickly drove out the gate. Who was he? Kohl wondered. He went to the parking lot, got in the second car and headed back towards the gate just in time to see Pry enter the shack and talk to the guard. Car lights still out, he stopped. They hadn't seen him yet. He could still go back and wait it out. But the still open gate beckoned and he drove through without stopping. Pry, not having been told exactly what Rapier was up to, let the incident pass. The guard had purposely failed to tell him the whole story also.

Kohl was still half a mile away when the helicopter lifted off, turned and headed towards Page. By now there were three stopped cars. Two on his side of the road, another on the other side waiting to pass. Closer now, he saw the man who had left the booth step out and wave the one car through. Then he could saw Mike and Sue's car in front of the one the man had driven out the gate in. Kohl unclipped the power station identity badge he was wearing from his jacket and dropped it under the seat, pulled the bill of his hat down lower and eased ahead. Everything looked okay thus far, except that Mike and Sue weren't there. The truth hit him. They must been captured. Where would the helicopter be taking them.

"What happened?" he asked when he alongside. "Need any help?"

"Just keep moving," he was told.

183

Kohl moved ahead, came abreast of Mike's car with its lights still on and saw Sue's body lying in the road. Badly shaken, he pulled up and got out of the car, walked back a ways and stared, unable to speak.

"I said to keep moving," Rapier ordered him coldly.

Kohl found his voice. "But don't you need help? Is she still alive?"

Rapier had his weapon out by now, pointing it at Kohl.

"Stay away from her. She's dead," he said without emotion. "Now get out of here."

Kohl stared at the big automatic and slowly retreated back to his car, trying to control himself. It was Sue lying there. Sue, goddammit. And where was Mike? Where were they taking him?

SEVENTEEN

"There is nothing you can do," Arron Barister, silver haired, heavy jowled, five hundred dollar an hour attorney, told Mike and Kohl in a hard voice, stating the facts as he saw them. "Doesn't matter what you know or what I know. That's the way it is. And if you're smart, that's exactly what you will do. Nothing. For the record she was resisting arrest and interfering with a government officer. There are three other witnesses."

"It was murder. Cold blooded murder. He set her up, the son-of-a-bitch, and somehow he'll pay," Mike said, his eyes hard and bitter, as were Kohl's.

"I wouldn't recommend it," Barister said. "You're dealing with some one who has some pretty high connections. So high in fact that even I'm not privileged to know exactly who he seems to be working for."

"Well, we'll see," Mike said. There was no smile on his face now, nor would there be for a long, long time to come. He stared out the window of the coffee shop on the main street where they had gone after they had gotten Mike released from jail over Rapier's loud objections just a few hours later, thanks to Kohl's quick movements in getting Barister up to Page before they had a chance to move him elsewhere. Rapier had been doubly angry at the time because it wasn't until they were in the Judge's chambers that he had realized who Kohl was and how badly he had erred out on the highway in not recognizing him.

Mike and Kohl sat, still in shock, still too numb to realize in total what had happened, the feeling of loss displaced by anger and hatred. And what about Linda, goddamn her? What were they going to do about her?

In the meantime Barrister had something else to say. "It's very unusual thing for a woman to do what she did. If I didn't know better I'd have thought you might have had a hand in it."

"Hand in what?" Mike asked. "What are you talking about?"

"It's almost as if she knew this was going to happen. Almost everything she had was put into joint tenancy not over a month ago. You are the surviving party."

"What are you trying to say?" Mike said, staring at him.

"That she left it all to you in the most expeditious way possible."

Mike seemed puzzled for a moment and then he turned sad, biting back the tears. Was it possible? Had she foreseen her own fate? Had she even sought it out? Suddenly he felt very weak and looked as though he would collapse. But then, with an intense effort, he bit back more tears, pulled himself together and looked at Barister. "So," he said. "It looks like you're working for me now, if you want the job, that is."

"I do." Barister said without pause to reflect.

"Good," said Mike, looking at Kohl, including him as part of it. "Here's what we need. First, the best private eye in the country. Put him to work. Find out who that son-of-a-bitch was that shot Sue, who he works for, where, and where he lives."

Barister was about to offer some advice in that respect but Mike put up his hand and cut him off.

"We also want custody of her body and a burial permit."

There was a small funeral home service without benefit of clergy for close friends and immediate family. The press arrived but were not allowed in and the private detective they had hired took a camera away from a man sitting in a plain, government issue automobile across the street photographing the attendees, and smashed it to bits.

Linda came, teary eyed and forlorn, beaten and trapped in her own hell. She viewed the body and retreated like Jennie had, never to be seen again. Buck and Jackie were there alongside Mike and

Kohl and later that evening they wrapped Sue's body in white linen and carried her unseen, back into the depths of Secret Canyon where they buried her high on a talos slope beneath a smoke stained Anasazi alcove that she had loved.

They built a fire and kept it going round the clock for three full days, honoring her, mourning her, offering their prayers. Then at noon the following day, Mike put the fire out.

Two weeks later Rapier was sitting at his desk reading a letter of congratulations for a job well done. Although it was unsigned except for an initial down in the corner it was still an important letter for him none-the-less. No sooner had he finished it than his secretary beeped him, however, and he was forced to put it down. "Yes," he answered.

"There is a man downstairs in the lobby who wants to see you," she told him in her usual voice.

"Who is it?"

"He said it was confidential."

"He'll have to do better than that if he wants to see me. Doesn't he have a name?"

"He wouldn't give me one. Just told me that he would be there until you left the office tonight, if necessary."

"Well," Rapier finally relented. "Escort him up."

"He insists on talking to you down in the lobby."

"That's a bit unusual," Rapier said, his curiosity aroused. "Have him searched and I'll be down in a minute."

He came into the lobby occupied only by the security guard and a man standing with his back to the room looking at a painting on the far wall. A younger man, tall, dark haired. Rapier stopped for a moment. The guard nodded towards the man. Rapier proceeded towards him. The man turned and grinned at him. A handsome man with piercing dark eyes. Out from underneath the dark bushy mustache Rapier could see the flash of white teeth slightly spoiled by one discolored tooth in the front. He caught his breath, unable to speak.

Mike spoke instead. "Good afternoon Mr. Rapier. This is an interesting place. How long have you been at this location?"

Rapier stared but didn't answer.

"Three years, four months and one week today, I believe,"

Mike said. "Since before you moved to your condo over in Silver Springs I believe. How do you like living on the top floor like that? Seems like you have a bit of a view. Not as good as the one from your office window though, I don't think. But certainly much better than that dumpy little place you lived in when you were in the fifth grade." Mike said and stopped to let Rapier grasp the implications of what he was telling him.

Rapier studied him carefully. How had this man found out all this? He was supposed to be literally untraceable. Suddenly he wasn't so sure of himself anymore.

"What exactly do you want?" he asked, finding his voice. Then stronger, "Did you come here to threaten me?"

"Of course not, Mr. Rapier. Why would I do such a senseless thing as that? No, I just came by to drop this newspaper article off and to let you know it will be appearing nationally in most major morning papers. I think you are familiar with the routine," Mike said and handed a folded up page of newsprint to Rapier.

Rapier unfolded it carefully and opened it up. Across the top in bold headlines it said, MURDER IN THE DESERT.

"Why don't you take it back to your office and read it where you'll be more comfortable," Mike said and turned and left the building as Rapier followed him with his eyes.

When the door closed behind him there was a sudden hollow sensation inside Rapier's gut, but he forced it away and turned slowly back in the direction from which he had come, his thin mustache twitching a bit as he went. By the time he reached his office he knew very well what the article was all about. It was his ass, and maybe even his life if it ever went to press. But how could he begin to stop it? There wasn't time.

He opened the door to his office and walked in. Captured in thought, he sat down glumly with his back to the window. Then slowly it began to occur to him that something was burning. He turned around and sniffed then looked up and noticed that a notch was being carved through the outer brick wall of the building and the inside plaster. A notch with molten material oozing from it that was already more than three quarters of the way around the periphery of his room and climbing rapidly towards the ceiling. It was such an unusual sight that he was unable to take his eyes from it and stared at it as it completed the loop across the top. At this point there was a sudden, loud rumble as the whole section of wall, window, pictures and all, fell outward and downward the three full stories to the ground below.

Shocked into action at last, he jumped up and looked out, peering over the edge. Below, standing on the sidewalk not too far away was the man who had just handed him the newspaper article. The man who now gave him a quick wave and turned and walked off, leaving him to think some very woeful thoughts about his own future.

Much to his own surprise, Rapier was not relieved of his duties, however. The administration was clever enough to realize that here was a man completely without conscience who would go to any length to redeem himself. His new assignment, therefore, was to personally assassinate those who had so thoroughly embarrassed him. Great. That made it official. But he didn't need their endorsement, however. One way or the other he was determined to get them, anyway. If he didn't, he feared, they might well roast him alive with that awesome laser. Unfortunately for him at this point, however, both Kohl and Mike seemed to have vanished off the face of the earth. Barister himself never knew where they were, even though he occasionally received little notes slipped under his door outlining specific instructions and power of attorney in regard to certain business and legal matters.

In that regard, most of Sue's property was quickly sold and converted to cash which was dropped at certain out of the way places or converted into bank drafts in the names of aliases, or changed into foreign currencies or placed in overseas accounts. The house they had lived in was given to Buck and Jackie and a foundation was established with enough endowment to keep the news campaign going for at least another decade, no matter what might happen to Mike or Kohl, although they would remain the ruling policy makers for as long as they were alive.

EIGHTEEN

The national elections were now but three weeks away. Although there was a growing distrust and disrespect for the administration, it still was no where near the level it should be at as far as Kohl and Mike were concerned. Americans were truly sheep. Whipped and spineless sheep who laid down like a blanket across the mire for all to walk on. To them, their efforts seemed senseless and hopeless in equal proportions.

Here was a nation of people who were afraid to drink the water that came from the ground, afraid to eat the food grown on the land, afraid to breath the air of the sky around them, afraid to leave their houses at night in their own cities, afraid to speak out or even to have an opinion that differed from the norm, afraid of what their friends or neighbors might think, afraid of their own police, afraid of the IRS, afraid of the law, afraid of the government, afraid of the Chinese and the Japanese and the Libyans and the Iraqis, afraid of their doctors, afraid of disease, afraid of getting old, of being different, of standing up, of speaking out, of making an effort.

Afraid even of their own thoughts, or so it seemed. And as a result they were quite equally guilty of complicity in the very scheme of things against which they secretly cried out against in the emptiness of their own hearts, a cry stifled and suffocated by a pillow of fear. What was life worth under those circumstances? Nothing, as far as Kohl and Mike were concerned.

What they believed was as Einstein himself, once said, "Conscience supersedes the authority of the law of the state, when it comes to moral issues", as well as, "It is the right, or the duty of the individual to abstain from cooperating in activities which he considers to be wrong or pernicious".

They also believed they had the right to take it one step further. The individual had the right to oppose by whatever means, short of physical injury and death, the infringement of the government onto the rights of the people just as the American forefathers had. Not a legally recognized right, to be sure, but with three short weeks remaining before the election, what else was there to do. And who cared. Except for the news ads, nothing else they had done thus far was legal, either.

The news campaign was foremost and it came out strong and clear, even though the Washington Post and the New York Times yielded to pressure and refused to accept the material. Surprisingly, however, from a different quarter the foundation received a sizable contribution from an old rancher in Texas and

189

another from an industrialist in Missouri as well as smaller amounts from individuals here and there across the country. But it was not enough. They went on to something else.

It was Kohl's idea, but Mike, when it was presented to him, laughed as he hadn't laughed in weeks. No explosives this time. All they needed was the van with the laser and a couple of good shovels. Then they would take a long vacation.

The van came out of hiding late on a Sunday afternoon looking like a military vehicle, desert camouflage and all, with fatigues, helmets, rifles, ID tags and special cut orders signed by old General Ballsey himself for the boys. Colonel Mike and Captain Kohl, just arrived in from Camp David Maryland.

Without a moments hesitation, they turned right off of Golf Links Road and drove through the main gate of Davis-Montham Air Force Base, another training ground for Atari warfare cowards, where they proceeded directly to the main runway.

Kohl, of lower rank for the moment, was driving. He pulled up behind a hanger and shut off the engine. His Colonel needed a smoke and he needed a beer. They got out and walked around while they gloated at what lay before them. My god! F-15s and 16's, some 106's, a couple of 104's, T-38's, half dozen UH-1's and, lo and behold, believe it or not, down on the end three monstrous C-141's all shiny looking and too good to be true.

They first checked out the office of the nearest hanger, cut the phone wires, disabled the large motor driven main doors, locked up the van, climbed into a jeep sitting nearby and did a reconnaissance run around the airfield. Since it was Sunday, since the cold war was over and since the budget had been cut there was no flight activity underway. All seemed vacated except for the presence of two lowly Airmen, one on each side of the flight strip, walking guard duty with their carbines slung over their backs.

Kohl pulled up to the first one. He came to immediate attention at the sight of the silver and brass ornaments on their fatigues and saluted. Kohl snapped off a quick salute in return and said, "Get in Airman," and motioned to the back of the jeep. The Airman quickly obliged by hopping over the tailgate and into the rear. Kohl drove on and told the second guard the same thing, then drove back to the hanger office. "Leave your weapons in the jeep

190

and come with me," he told the men and got out of the vehicle. Like good disciplined troops they complied readily with the scowling Colonel directly behind. Inside Kohl sat them down. "When are you scheduled for relief?" he asked.

"Twenty one hundred sir," the Airman First Class told him.

"Me too sir," the second man said, still somewhat surprised to see an unshaven officer. Sort of reminded him of pictures he had seen of Fidel Castro somewhere. But then the service was changing and these guys had some very unusual looking shoulder patches sewn to their blouses. And who was given the liberty to question authority anyway? That was the key element that was driven into the heart of every serviceman, short or tall. Jump, obey, squat, if ordered. Yes sir, Sir. Lick your boots sir, right away sir. Thank you, sir.

Kohl looked at his watch. Twenty one hundred. That was nine PM if he remembered military time correctly. Five more hours. No problem. He stared at them as hard and menacingly as he could and gave them a new set of orders.

"There will be a special contingent of personnel here momentarily for a special services exercise which is to be conducted in secret on the airstrip. For your information it is related to guerrilla warfare tactics which, unfortunately, you are not allowed to participate in, or to witness. Your orders are to stay inside this office until such time as I personally give you permission to leave. Is that clear?" Kohl said as Mike stood back scowling even more heavily at them as though questioning their very lowly competence to comply.

"Yes sir, sir. Yes sir."

"Under no circumstances are you to attempt to leave these premises not matter what you might hear going on out side. Not only is that a direct order but more than likely you may well get yourselves shot if you disobey. Is that also clear?"

"Yes sir, sir. Yes sir."

"At ease then, men. Find some magazines, make yourselves some coffee, play cards if you can find some," Kohl said, easing up a bit. "We shall return," he said in farewell and snapped off another salute, followed by Mike who continued to stare holes through them before they turned smartly and left the building.

Outside they wired the door tightly shut and drove back to the van. Mike chuckled heartily from the rear. It was ridiculous how rapidly a well focused, ten kilowatt, continuous wave, infrared laser could melt its way through thin layers of aluminum when compared to six or eight inches of thick, well seasoned, reinforced concrete. And, wasn't discipline nice? It was all so perfect. All those beautiful and very expensive machines of war so very neatly and precisely lined up side by side in a row. By raising and lowering the periscope various amounts they had been able to line the beam on the centerlines of all the smaller aircraft and neatly melted holes, first through all the cockpits to destroy wiring and controls and then through the side into the engine compartment, through the engine and out the other side on into the next aircraft and the next and the next. Hell, Mike thought. He could just as well have cut them all in half with a little more effort. Not in the plan, however. Even though it was fairly dark out by now, having aircraft fall apart right there on the runway might be pushing their luck just a little too far. Besides, they had even more interesting plans for later on.

Finishing up the smaller aircraft, they drove up next to the huge cargo masters. "That one's for Sue," he said as he bored holes end to end through the engines and whacked up the cockpit. "And that one, and that one, and that one," he continued as he finished the job.

"Ready?" Kohl asked when Mike leaned back in his seat.

"Almost," Mike said. "Stop in front of that large hanger over there on the way out, Captain," Mike said as Kohl put the truck in gear.

"Yes, sir, Colonel sir," Kohl said. "How about right here?"

"Well done, Captain. At ease now. Have a beer while I go back to work."

"What's up," Kohl asked, looking back at Mike.

"Patience, my friend, patience. This will only take a moment," Mike grinned.

Taking him at his word, Kohl reached to find a beer.

With that Mike turned on the generator, adjusted the power level of the laser and quickly engraved the words, UP YOURS, MR. PRESIDENT, in very large letters into the hanger door.

"Well done, Colonel," Kohl told him and stepped on the accelerator. They were now on their way to the Fort Huachuca

Army Intelligence Center seventy miles away to the south east.

Stopping at a deserted ranch house along the way only long enough for a coat of quick drying lacquer on the van and a change of uniform for their bodies, they rolled through the gate of Huachuca at ten thirty sharp, looking like a Military Police vehicle. Clean shaven, Mike was at the wheel this time, now demoted to the petty rank of Corporal while Kohl, as an official looking, smooth faced, bad assed, chicken shit, don't fuck with me, Major, United States, bury the poor bastards alive, Army, sat in the passenger seat.

"Do you suppose we should check the hole first to see if anyone has found it?" Kohl asked Mike after they cleared the gate, thinking his salute was certainly improving.

"It's getting a little late," Mike said. "Let's take a chance. I'd kinda like to get up to Tombstone before the bars close."

Kohl nodded. "Onward then, my good Corporal. Onward please, with all due consideration."

Driving at a modest speed, Mike pulled the van in behind the Base Headquarters Administration Building. With the rear of the van towards the building, he stopped and shut the lights off. "You're turn," he said to Kohl.

"You mean I get to do this one? What's the occasion?"

"Well, since it was your idea in the first place it seems only appropriate that you should be the last one to use this thing before we put her to bed."

"Yeah, why not," Kohl said, accepting the offer. He hit the power switch, waited till the green, status ready light came on, raised the periscope, flipped on the small, red beam of the helium neon, visible laser and pointed it at the slumpstone wall of the building just beneath the windows. He squeezed the switch on the periscope handle and a small area on the wall began to glow.

How long did he have to hold it in one spot in order to burn clear through and into what was beyond? he wondered. The long row of locked metal file cabinets filled with classified documents along the inside of the wall were the real targets. Set them all on fire. Not that they couldn't be replaced. It was the idea of it that counted. He hollered his question up to Mike over the sound of the engine and the generator.

"Turn the horizontal auto scanner on and set it at about ten inches per minute," Mike said. "That ought to do it."

Kohl complied, then relaxed and let the mechanism take care of itself. Fifteen feet down the wall he switched the eyepiece to the wide field of view so he could also see the windows of the building. "Smoke," he said. "But not too heavy. Maybe five more minutes before the smoke detectors go off."

"Whenever you're ready to leave," Mikes said.

"Oh shit," Kohl suddenly said in a loud voice.

"What happened?" asked Mike.

"Some asshole must have left a bottle of booze in one of the cabinets. The damned thing just exploded. There are flames all over hell."

"Best we get rolling," Mike said as Kohl put the big laser in stand-by mode.

They reached the end of the street just in time to be passed by a firetruck coming from the opposite direction. Kohl, who had joined Mike in the front said, "Well, looks like we've made our point there," Kohl stated.

"Fun, huh," Mike said.

"Yeah. Too early to quit yet. Let's do one last thing before we hang it up."

"What did you have in mind?"

"How about that water tower there," Kohl said, pointing at the old fashioned steel tank supported by four erector set legs.

Mike put on the brakes. "Help yourself," he said.

Quickly Kohl was in the back. He burned through the bottom of one leg. Nothing but a tiny settling. He burned through another. A tiny bit more settling. "You're going to have to cut a whole section out of one of them," Mike yelled from where he was watching the procedure out the driver's side window.

"Gotcha," Kohl acknowledged.

"Wait a minute, though. M.P. vehicle going by," Mike said as a white Blazer came down the street, obviously heading towards the fire.

Instead of continuing however, the vehicle stopped alongside and the white helmeted driver rolled down the window. "Seen anybody suspicious come by here Corporal?" the man asked, his

Sergeant stripes showing on his sleeve and on his helmet.

"What kind of suspicious, Sergeant?"

"Cars, kids, unusual vehicles?"

"No Sergeant, not this way."

The Sergeant looked more carefully at the van. He had never seen this style of Military Police Vehicle on the base before. Not that he remembered, at least. "Where you from," he asked.

"Just got in from Fort Benning."

"Well, follow me. We may need some help."

"Sorry Sergeant, I have other orders."

At this the Sergeant got out of the Blazer and came over to the van in his crisp khakis, sparkling brass, coiled gold braid, stark white belt, black holstered forty five and dark, gleaming boots. It was certainly different, he noticed now that he took a good look at it. Big, off road tires, extra lights and antennas hanging on it, a cab full of lights, instruments and radios. Holy shit, it suddenly dawned on him. Maybe it was the vehicle that contained that terrible laser weapon. After all, it was hardly a secret. Almost everyone in the whole country had read about, or heard about it somehow. And apparently it was already on the base. That's what the fire captain had speculated anyway, from the looks of the damage to the building.

He was just about to order Mike out of the vehicle when Kohl emerged from the rear. "What exactly seems to be the problem, Sergeant?" he asked haughtily.

"Ah, well, ah sir," the Sergeant said with a salute, and backed up a step. "Nothing I guess, we were on our way to the Administration Building."

"And you best get down there before that fire gets out of control," Kohl said, eyeing the water tower in the back ground lit by a street light a hundred feet away. The son-of-a-bitch was about to topple. "Move it, Sergeant," he ordered.

"Yes sir," the Sergeant replied as he saluted again and headed back to his own machine, wondering if he was doing the right thing but well reminded with all too clear memories of the last time he had raised a Major's ire. And besides, he thought as he reconsidered even further, both the Corporal and the Major certainly looked authentic enough, even if there might be some question about the vehicle. So stop fantasizing about all this starwars shit, he told himself, and check it out later or you might be back to PFC again.

They watched him go. "Better turn around," Kohl said.

"Shit, that's right," Mike said and backed part ways down in the ditch, then made a sharp turn and came around on the narrow road. "We want to go that way too, don't we?"

"Pull up just a little further and then let me have one last whack at that damned thing," Kohl said. "What the hell's the matter with it anyway?"

No sooner had the words left his mouth, however, than there was a very audible screech of metal, followed all too soon by a tremendous noise and ground shaking thump as tons of heavy steel and water came crashing down, splitting the riveted seams of the big silver painted tank and spewing a vast cloud of spray high into the air.

Up ahead, almost simultaneously, they saw the brake lights of the Blazer come on as the vehicle stopped in the middle of the road, not all that far away. Both doors opened as the Sergeant and his PFC passenger piled out, moved toward the back of the truck and started to draw their weapons.

"Hang on," Mike shouted and put the accelerator down. The big engine, rich with fuel and air, sent a powerful burst of torque to the rear wheels and shot ahead as Mike, bright lights on, overhead spots on and horn blaring, veered left with driver's side wheels on the shoulder to pass the Blazer. The Sergeant, fortunately for his own sake, was intelligent enough to move out of the way as Mike purposely skimmed the side of his vehicle in an attempt to destroy the tires with the big bumper and tore the driver's door from its hinges.

Unfortunately, badly bruised as it was, the tires still held air and the machine was still runable, door or no door. Looking back Kohl could see the Sergeant cuss visibly and shake his fist, then jump into the open driver's seat. The chase was on.

Kohl was already in the back trying to get a sight on the radiator of the pursuing vehicle but was having some difficulty because of the rough condition of the road. He swore.

Mike swore too, as the scanner in the cab stopped at an FM

channel and the Sergeant's voice came over the air, giving a clear description of the van and the direction they were headed in. "Better hurry," Mike yelled to Kohl.

"You too," Kohl said. "Get some distance, then hit the brakes so I can find the radiator."

Mike speeded up, gained a hundred yards easy enough, then screeched to a halt. Rapidly Kohl brought the beam up and over.

At this point the Sergeant said, "Oh fuck," realizing what might be about to happen and began to zig zag.

Kohl triggered the laser and all the Sergeant accomplished was to help Kohl burn a groove almost all the way across the front of the vehicle. The radiator went first, then the right front tire and the left and the Blazer came to an erratic stop. Quickly Kohl raised his line of sight and cut a hole through the roof of the cab where the radio was located. "Go," he shouted to Mike as the Sergeant and his companion exited their disabled machine and pointed their forty fives.

Seeing the muzzle flash, Kohl ducked as the Sergeant let go a round. Missed. Faster Mike, faster dammit. Another flash. Missed again. They were moving rapidly away now.

The PFC, however, perhaps the cooler one of the two, took time to stop, take a proper stance, put both arms out stiff and pulled off a round. Pow. It thudded into the roof of the van. A second shot took out the right rear tail light. Fortunately, the third missed. They were now too far away and out of range of the heavy, but slow and inaccurate, regulation slug slingers carried by the MPs.

Mike slowed, shifted down, crossed the ditch, came up into the athletic field, roared across the baseball diamond through the fence and back up on the street heading towards Pine Canyon Road only to be interrupted by another excited voice on the scanner. "This is Unit Seven. I have him in sight," it said, and gave the location.

"Try and head him off, Unit Seven," came the order over the airwaves.

"Fuck that shit," Seven stated. "The bastard will scorch me."

"Affirmative Seven. Keep your distance but keep them in sight. We're sending out a portable rocket launcher."

"Bull Shit!," Mike said.

"I second that," Kohl said and hung on dearly as Mike once

again spun the big van around and accelerated heavily.

"Ohhh shit," came the voice on the radio again as the van headed towards him with full brights and spot lights on once again, with Military Police, red and blue lights flashing on the roof to supplement the effect. "Now they're coming after me. What the hell do I do?"

"Get your ass out of there and wait for backup," came the reply. With that, the driver came nearly to a stop and did a hard left on the wheel for a U-turn. It was another Military Police unit, a Bronco this time, instead of a Blazer, but fully outfitted with two white helmeted personnel inside. But the turn wasn't quite hard enough and, coming around, the vehicle went out onto the shoulder and down into the ditch where the driver, had he been more skilled, could have still saved it. But he panicked, hit the throttle too hard and upended the machine in the ditch, lights still on and wheels still turning.

"Good show," Kohl complemented Mike, as Mike also slowed and did his own U-turn with Kohl now up front again.

"Yeah, but what are we going to do about a rocket launcher?" Mike asked as he killed all the lights. Too bad they had put all that white paint on the van, however. It was far too visible, even with the lights out.

"We could try hiding and wait. Try to catch them off guard, except..."

"Except the choppers will be up any minute, right, and we'd best not do that."

"Right. Time to head for the hole and hope the hell we get there in time."

They did another turn and were once again headed back in the direction of Pine Canyon Road when it was Mike's turn to say, "Oh shit," for there along side the road half a block away stood a weapons carrier with three soldiers standing in the beam of the headlights. One was armed with a carbine while the other two were in the process of loading a small projectile into the aft end of a portable launcher.

"You take the back," Kohl said. "You're handier with that thing than I am."

Mike locked up the brakes and skidded to a halt. In less than two seconds, Kohl had the van headed back in the opposite direction, moving as slowly and steadily as possible to give Mike every chance of finding his target. Not so easy to do at that distance without severely burning or killing someone.

"Stand still, you son-of-a-bitch," Mike said silently to the soldier who was now hoisting the launcher up to his shoulder.

Mike found his body, the small red dot of the aiming laser on the man's chest. He moved it upward. The launch tube end was coming around to point in the direction of the van. Quickly now, quickly, Mike told himself. Don't fuck up. Good. He had the end of the tube in his cross hairs. Trigger on. A glow on the end of the tube followed immediately by the plume of the rocket exhausting out the rear of the launcher. Too late. "Step on it Kohl," he yelled at the top of his voice.

Precious milliseconds went by before the van responded. The rocket was on its way, armor piercing warhead and all. But what was that? So was the launch tube. Apparently the laser had connected just long enough. There had been just enough molten metal in the launch tube to prevent the missile from traveling clear through. Trapped at the exit, the thrust of the missile tore the entire launcher from the soldiers grip and carried it away on a dizzying flight path that ended about a hundred yards out. Here it came to ground and exploded, throwing a cloud of shrapnel, gravel and debris into the air.

The soldiers were still all face down in the dirt when Kohl brought the van around once again with all four wheels screaming on the asphalt, burning rubber and picking up speed. He passed them going forty miles an hour and still accelerating.

Up the canyon they went, past the picnic area and into the trees. The road had turned to dirt. Rougher, with tighter corners, Kohl was forced to slow somewhat. Then they began to climb as Kohl watched the odometer, checking the distance. Another quarter mile and he slowed even further. Mike had come up front to help him look. Where was that stone marker they had beside the road? It should be there somewhere on the left.

"What's that? Mike asked in an alarmed voice.

"We're in trouble," Kohl said as he saw a person in fatigues and boots, with a rifle over their shoulder, standing beside the two stones they had placed there previously so they would know where to turn off into the woods. "Get in the back. I'm going on by. We'll have to think of something else,' he said to Mike.

"Wait, it's a girl!"

"Well, I'll be damned, " Kohl stated as he confirmed Mike's observation. The person was not wearing a helmet and they could now see long blond hair hanging off her shoulder.

"Is she alone?"

"Looks like it," Kohl said in disbelief. "What the hell do we do now?" he asked as the girl started waving at them with a hurry up motion of her arm.

"Beats me," Mike said, ready to get in the back if he had to. The laser was still powered up and ready to go but he certainly didn't want to have to point at a some girl.

Kohl did the only thing he could do under the circumstances. He ground to a stop beside her with the window already down. She quickly came over to the side of the truck. "Better get moving," she said. "They'll be here soon. Don't worry, I'll sweep out your tracks."

Unable to believe what he was seeing, Kohl continued to stare at her. Then he noticed the large pine bough she carried. "Better hurry," she reminded him.

It took Kohl another moment to recover. He shifted down and eased forward. "Get in the back," he said to Mike, "and see if she's really doing it."

Sure enough, from what Mike could see in the dim night glow, she was brushing away at the dirt with the pine bough. In a leap of faith he shut down the laser, lowered the periscope, sprayed plastic foam over some key exposed areas, made other routine storage preparations and then untied the large roll of black polyethylene sheathing they had brought along and moved it closer to the rear door as Kohl wound his way carefully through the woods in the dark. Then he found the shovels and a bundle of fresh clothing. He was ready.

The van stopped. Mike got out quickly, as did Kohl. Front parking lights on only, so they could see, they began dragging branches off a large, deep hole in the ground hidden amongst the taller trees.

Kohl drove the van down into the hole, climbed out the rear door and out of the excavation. Unrolled in a well practiced motion, the plastic went over the top and down around the sides. Off came the military uniforms and into the hole. More respectably dressed underneath, they threw all the branches in the ramped, rear section of the pit, grabbed the shovels and began throwing the spare dirt they had saved in behind as the sound of helicopters grew louder in the distance.

The hole itself had been very precisely dug with but an inch or two clearance on the sides. It even had holes for the wheels to fall into which brought the frame right down to the ground. It meant less dirt to shovel in during this critical moment, and less settling later on. What they hoped for now was that they had calculated the displacement of the van accurately enough and had hauled away just the right amount of extra dirt. They certainly didn't want to leave any give-away hump or slump in the ground level.

It was then that they realized that the fancy Military Police lights they had added to the roof to make the van look more authentic, stuck up too high. Mike tore them off with a pry of the shovel and dropped them down in front of the windshield, then worked even faster. If it hadn't been for all the anxiety of getting caught, this part of the task would have been a pleasure compared to what they had undergone digging the hole in the first place. There had been rocks down there, for one thing. Hauling all the extra dirt further up the hill and spreading it so it wouldn't be detected, wasn't that easy, either. Finding and cutting enough tree branches to cover it effectively had also been difficult.

By now the sides were full, the hood was covered and the ramp area was over half done. "Who the hell was that girl?" Mike asked, now that they were closer together and he could talk softly.

"I don't know," Kohl said, "but I hope we didn't dig this hole for nothing."

"You and me both," Mike said between breaths, as he labored away.

"Stop. What's that noise?" Kohl said, leaning on his shovel.

"Maybe it's her."

"Let's find a tree just in case."

They were too late again. "Do you have another shovel?" came a sweet and tender voice. They squinted into the dark as she leaned the rifle against a tree and came towards them.

"Yeah," Mike said after he recovered from the shock of seeing her again. He handed her the one he had been using, then found the spare. Without a word she began to help.

There was no time for questions, the ominous thumping sound had changed directions and appeared to be coming closer. Quickly they ran over the loose dirt, packing it down as best they could in the starlight, shoveled in the remainder and buried two of the three shovels so they would have less to carry. Then they spread dried leaves and some of the smaller dead branches they had saved over the dirt. "How does it look?" Kohl asked, having to raise his voice in the growing noise.

"Good enough," Mike stated as they worked their way further into the trees. "Here they come."

They didn't have to wait long. Searchlights on, the helicopters came, one after the other, directly over the road some quarter of a mile away, creating an ear shattering noise, bending the trees and raising the dust. Unbeknown to the military, however, with the wind from the blades and two more police vehicles following shortly behind the choppers, they were doing Kohl and Mike a big favor by helping to wipe out what tracks might have remained along the road.

When it finally seemed safe, they chanced another quick scan of the area with the flashlight, rearranged a few of the leaves and branches and backed away, heading downhill towards the east. Keeping silent and going slowly so as not to create any undo sound of their own, they made their way. Thus far they hadn't even had a chance to ask the girl even one of the hundred or so questions that had already come to mind. Before they felt safe to do so, however, the girl stopped, pushed the button on her watch to illuminate the dial and checked the time.

"I have to leave you," she said. "I'm on duty in forty minutes."

"But, wait. We don't even know your name."

"Daphne," she said. "And don't worry. It's supposed to rain early tomorrow. That should take care of anything we might have missed."

"Yeah, we were sort of counting on it," Kohl said.

"I'm sorry," she said. "I should have known."

"What?" Mike asked.

"That you would have thought of that, too."

"God, I don't believe this," Kohl said. "How did you find us, anyway?"

"You mean tonight?"

"That's a good place to start."

"I've been reading about you guys for over a year now and I always had the dream that one day I would get to meet you. Then tonight, when I heard the reports about Davis-Montham Air Base, I had a strong feeling that this was the night you might be coming this way."

"You mean they already know about Tucson?" Mike said.

"It was that salutation you left on the hanger door that did it," she said with a gentle laugh.

"Can't have any fun at all," Mike said, stopping for a moment. "But what do you mean, this might be the night? How did you know we had picked this place, and how did you just happen to be out there by the road?"

"Yeah," Kohl said. "Explain that, would you please."

"Pure luck. I just happened to be out here in the woods the day you came in that old pickup truck."

"You saw us?" Mike asked, his voice rising.

"Shhh," not so loud, she warned him.

"But what did you see?" Mike insisted.

"I saw you dig the hole and haul the excess dirt away. I thought I recognized your from your descriptions and I had a guess as to what it might be for. I was afraid that you might not come back, however, if I had made myself known at the time."

"You got that right, Kohl stated.

"But what a brilliant idea, to hide that marvelous invention of yours right here on the base under their own aristocratic noses," she said with a giggle, in response.

"Wonderful", Mike said with a groan.

"Jesus," Kohl said. "I wonder how many others know."

"No one," she told him quite positively.

"Well, let's hope not," Kohl said.

"Don't worry," she assured him. "It was my day off that day so I hid in the trees near the road and made certain. And I've kept an eye on the place for you for the last week as best as I could. I haven't seen any people or any tracks at all. I'm sure it's quite safe."

"And so tonight I suppose you just happened to be tuned in on the police band here and knew exactly when we were on our way," Mike said.

"Exactly."

"But..." Kohl started to say.

"But I have to go now," she said, standing there in the dim light of the stars. "And I'm really glad I got to meet you. You're Kohl, right, and you're Mike?" she asked, guessing their identities correctly.

"How come you know our names?" Kohl asked. "That's never been public information."

"I did a little snooping in the Base Commander's files."

It was too much. Even outspoken Mike was silent. Then, with his handkerchief folded double over the flashlight Kohl turned it on to get a close look at her. Oh, God Almighty, he said to himself as he looked into her gray eyes and surveyed her face. "Could you possibly be Athena?" he asked and turned the light off again.

"Who's Athena?" she replied.

"Gray eyed Greek Goddess of wisdom, skills and warfare. Daughter of Zeus," Kohl said, thinking it might even be true.

"Maybe," she said, liking the idea. "But my name really is Daphne."

"Daphne?"

"Yes. The nymph chased by Apollo who escaped by turning into a laurel, my mother once told me. But if I don't get going I'll turn into a court marshall, instead," she said, and with that she was gone, disappeared into the night like a wisp of a dream, without a sound and without a trace.

"Interesting girl," Mike said after some minutes of silence.

"Sure was," Kohl admitted, afraid of the emotion in his voice.

The end.. The sequel to this book is titled,

Out Of The Fire Mist.